Femme Fatale~ish

MISHA BELL

♠ MOZAIKA PUBLICATIONS ♠

Copyright © 2021 Misha Bell
www.mishabell.com

Published by Mozaika Publications, an imprint of Mozaika LLC.
www.mozaikallc.com

Cover by Najla Qamber Designs
www.najlaqamberdesigns.com

Photography by Wander Aguiar
www.wanderbookclub.com

ISBN: 978-1-63142-711-4
Paperback ISBN: 978-1-63142-712-1

Fabio grabs my chin and tilts my face up. "Show me your tongue."

Feeling like I'm five, I stick my tongue all the way out.

He shakes his head disapprovingly. "Not long enough."

I retract my tongue. "Long enough for what?"

"To reach the walnut, obviously." He sighs theatrically. "I guess I'll work with what I've got."

Ugh. Can I slap him? "How about we work on his peen?"

With another sigh, he turns Bill over. "Did you take those lozenges, like I told you?"

Not for the first time, I field doubts about my instructor. The goal for this training is simple: I want to be a spy, which means gaining skills as a seductress/femme fatale. Think Keri Russell's character in *The Americans*. According to her backstory in that show, she attended a creepy spy school that taught seduction. In fact, such schools are common in movies about Russian spies—the latest was featured in *Anna*. Alas, these schools are harder to find in real life. So I figured I'd hire a professional instead, but the prostitute I solicited for help refused. Ditto with the female porn stars I reached out to on social media. As my last resort, I turned to Fabio, a childhood friend who's now a male porn star. Being in gay porn, he claims he's able to please a man better than any woman can.

"Yes, I sucked on the lozenges," I say. "My throat is numb, and I can barely feel my tongue."

"Great. Now get that whole shlong down your throat." Fabio points at Bill.

I scan Bill's length apprehensively. "You sure about this? Wouldn't the lozenges make the penis numb? If Bill were real, that is."

He lifts an eyebrow. "Bill?"

I shrug. "Figured if I'm having relations with him, he shouldn't be anonymous."

Fabio pats my shoulder. "The lozenges are just to give you some confidence. Once you see that it fits, you'll be more relaxed for the real thing and won't require numbing. Don't worry. I'll teach you proper breathing and everything. You'll be a pro in no time."

"Okay." I take off my sexy wig and put it on the couch. Before Fabio says anything, I assure him I'll keep it on during a real encounter.

Now comfy, I lean over and take Bill into my mouth as far as I can.

My lips touch the silicone base. Wow. This is deeper than I was able to swallow any of my exes—and they weren't this big. My gag reflex is sensitive. Typically, even a toothbrush gives me issues when I use it to clean my tongue. But thanks to the numbing, the silicone dildo has gone in all the way.

This is interesting. Could lozenges also help one withstand waterboarding? If I'm to become a spy, I need to learn to withstand torture in case I'm captured. Of course, waterboarding isn't my biggest concern. If the enemy has access to a duck—or any bird, really—I'll spill all the state secrets to keep the feathery monstrosity away from me.

Yeah, okay. Maybe the CIA did have a good reason to reject my candidacy. Then again, in *Homeland*—another one of my favorite shows—they let Claire Danes stay in the CIA with all of *her* issues. Which reminds me: I need to practice making my chin quiver on demand.

Fabio taps my shoulder. "That's enough."

I disengage and swallow an overabundance of saliva. "That wasn't so bad. Should I go again?"

He shakes his head. "I think you need a motivation boost."

I know what he's talking about, so I take my phone out.

"Yeah." He rubs his hands like a villain from the early Bond films. "Show me the picture again."

I pull up the image of codename Hottie McSpy.

An undercover FBI agent took this photo because he was after one of the men in it, but not my target. No. Everyone thinks Hottie McSpy is just a rando—but *I* believe he's a Russian agent.

Fabio whistles. "So much premium man meat."

It's true. In the image, a group of extremely delicious-looking men are sitting around a table inside a Russian-style *banya*—a hybrid between a steam room and a sauna—wearing only towels and, in the case of Hottie McSpy, a pair of non-reflective aviator sunglasses that must have some kind of anti-fog coating. With the sweat beading on everyone's glistening muscles, they look like a wet dream come to life.

"They're playing poker," I say. "That's why I've been taking poker lessons."

"Yeah, I figured as much, since the picture is called Hot Poker Club." Fabio giddily enunciates the last three words. "You realize that sounds like the title of one of my movies?"

I shrug. "An FBI agent named this image, not me. They were after another guy who was in that room, and I was helping out as part of the collaboration between the agencies."

Fabio taps on the screen to zoom in on Hottie McSpy. "And he's the one you're after?"

Nodding, I drink in the image once more. Hottie McSpy has the hardest muscles of this already-impressive bunch, and the strongest jaw. His chiseled masculine features are vaguely Slavic, a fact that first made me suspicious of him. His hair is dark blond and shampoo-commercial healthy. Not even my wigs are as nice.

If I were to learn that this man was the result of Soviet geneticists trying to create the perfect male specimen / super-soldier / field agent, I wouldn't be surprised. Nor would I be shocked to find out that he was the inspiration for the Russian equivalent of a Ken doll (Ivan A. Pieceof?). Even if I didn't think he was a spy, I'd infiltrate that poker game just to rip those stupid glasses off of him and see his eyes. Though I picture them—

"You're drooling," Fabio says. "Not that I can blame you."

I nearly choke on the treacherous saliva. "No, I'm not."

"Yeah, sure. Be honest, are you going after him

because he might be a spy, or because you want to marry him?"

"The first option." I hide my phone. "Spy or not, marriage is out of the question for me. My current attitude toward dating shares an acronym with the name of the agency I work for: No Strings Attached. But that's not what this is about, anyway. If I single-handedly expose a spy, the CIA is bound to take notice and rethink their rejection of my candidacy. And even if they don't take me, I will have made America safer. Russian spies are still among the biggest threats to our national security."

"Sure, sure," Fabio says. "And his hotness has nothing to do with you focusing on him, specifically."

I frown. "His hotness is why he's the perfect agent. Think James Bond. Think Tom Cruise in *Mission Impossible*. Think—"

Fabio raises his hands like I'm threatening to shoot him. "The lady doth protest too much, methinks."

I gesture at the silicone phallus. "Should I go again? I think the numbing is wearing off."

For some unknown reason, I feel super motivated to deep-throat someone.

Fabio takes out his phone. "Sure. You work on that, but I've got to run. My Grindr date awaits."

He shows me a dick pic.

"Dude," I say. "Don't you get enough action at work?"

Fabio playfully flicks at Bill's erection, and it swings back and forth like a naughty pendulum. "This is why I thank heavens for being attracted to men. Their sex drives are so much stronger."

"That's sexist. Just because women don't hump everything that moves doesn't mean we have weak sex drives."

He flicks Bill's manhood—or is it his dummy-hood?—again. "If your cock and asshole aren't always sore, your sex drive is lacking. That's all there is to it."

I cringe again. What do roosters—killing machines that they are—have in common with penises? Why not call the male organ a python, a bratwurst, or a honey dipper? Any of those would be more appropriate.

Fabio grins and flicks the appendage in question once again. "Sorry for saying 'cock.' I'm such a—"

Before he can finish, a blur of fur streaks by. A giant feline lands on Bill's washboard abs and swats razor-sharp claws at the pendulum-like phallus.

Screaming in falsetto, Fabio pulls away from the scene of the unfolding hate crime.

The owner of the claws is my cat, Machete, and apparently, he's not done—because he rakes his claws over what's left of Bill's dummy-hood.

"That's just obscene." Fabio stands crossed-legged, as if he needs to go tinkle. "You should get your cat to a therapist."

As if he understands what my friend has just said, Machete shoots him a feline hate-filled glare.

As usual, I can picture what Machete would say in a nightmarish world where cats could talk:

The silicone male couldn't escape Machete. The softer, fleshy one will be next.

"Come here, sweetie," I croon and swoop down to grab the cat.

Machete must be feeling extremely magnanimous today because he lets me hold him and keep my eyes.

Fabio chuckles, and I give him a quizzical look.

"Your cat was trying to kill Bill," he explains.

Machete hisses at Fabio.

Machete is not amused. Uma Thurman has a lot of range, but she can't play Machete.

I grin. "He must've heard you call that a cock." I gesture at Bill's misfortune. "My sweetie protects me from birds." I pet Machete's silky fur and get rewarded with a deep purr. "When I first got him, he killed what turned out to be a goose pillow for me."

Fabio eyes the door. "All I know is he looks like he'd fought in a lot of illegal street fights before you adopted him. And lost a lot."

It's true. Machete actually looked even worse when I came across him at the shelter. It was also the only time I can recall seeing him vulnerable in any way.

Needless to say, I used my work resources to track down his prior owners, and soon after, they mysteriously ended up on a no-fly list... just before a big vacation.

I stop the petting for a moment, and Fabio gets hissed at again.

"I'd better go," Fabio says, backing away.

I follow him. A videocall window pops up on one of my wall monitors. Yes, I have multiple wall monitors. My home setup is inspired by all the movies where spies watch someone from a surveillance room.

Forgetting the cat danger, Fabio stops and looks at the screen. If my friend were one of Machete's kind, his curiosity would've killed him long ago.

"It's my video conference with Gia and Clarice," I explain. "You can go."

Fabio purses his lips. "Who's Clarice?"

"My poker teacher," I say. "Go."

He looks on the verge of stomping his foot. "But I want to say hi to my girl Gia."

"Fine." I accept the call, and both Gia and Clarice show up on the screen.

CHAPTER
Two

THE PALE-FACED WOMAN who looks like Morticia Addams is my sister Gia—one of my two sisters who aren't part of my litter of identical sextuplets.

Yep, I have five sisters who share one hundred percent of my DNA. Gia also has a sister with whom she shares one hundred percent of her DNA—her twin, Holly.

I'm a little jealous of the twins. For starters, they have fewer identical clones of each other. Also, they're named after our grandmothers, while my litter got the hippity-dippity names that our parents must've come up with during a particularly extensive LSD trip.

Take my name: Blue Hyman. It sounds like what you'd need to break to deflower one of those aliens in *Avatar*. Then again, didn't they have telepathic sex via their creepy ponytails? Same ponytails they used on animals, by the way. Oh, and my name also sucks in my line of work. After I did something—the specifics of which are classified—to a few computers, my colleagues started calling me BSoD, as in the Blue Screen of Death.

Clearing her throat, Gia looks between Fabio and Bill's damaged dick. Her face contorts into one of her signature devious grins. "Kinky."

Fabio rolls his eyes at her. "Gross, as usual."

Clarice readjusts her pirate hat. "Is that your sweetheart?"

"No," Fabio and I say, while Gia says, "Yep."

Well, whatever. It's not an insult to assume I'm with Fabio. He's a good-looking guy, just like the Italian model his mom lusted after enough to give his name to her son. This Fabio's naked chest wouldn't look out of place on a romance novel circa the early nineties, either.

"Fine," Gia says. "Maybe he's not a boyfriend, but Blue blew him back in the day."

"I didn't blow him," I say. "We played *show me yours and I'll show you mine*. Once."

"Yeah. And that was plenty." Fabio grimaces, and I have to resist throwing Machete at his face.

"Oh, yeah," Gia says. "Wasn't that when Fabio realized he's better off gay?"

I narrow my eyes at her. "Didn't you claim to have slept with him in high school?"

A rare expression shows up on Gia's face—guilt. "It was a joke." She looks at Fabio pointedly. "A private joke."

It wasn't a joke, and we all know it. For some reason, Gia went out of her way to make everyone think she was the sluttiest of the eight of us.

"Guys," Clarice says. "That man isn't the sweetheart I'm asking about." She points at Machete. "*That* is."

"Ah." I scratch Machete under his chin, and he closes his eyes, blissed out. "He *is* my sweetheart."

"What's his name?" Clarice picks up a cute Persian and holds him up to the camera. "This is Hannibal, by the way. *My* sweetheart."

Clarice has a cat named Hannibal?

Of course she does.

When Machete opens his eyes and spots Hannibal, he hisses viciously.

Machete doesn't like fluffy, spoiled excuses for cats. Also, isn't that face exactly what's on a can of Fancy Feast? Makes Machete wonder if that whole breed is a bunch of cannibals.

To his credit, Hannibal looks unperturbed. Either he knows the cat in front of him can't reach him through the screen, or he is as brave as Machete.

"So, Clarice," Fabio says. "What's with the pirate getup? Is that a magician thing, like Gia's vampire outfit?"

It is, in fact. My sister and Clarice are magicians, and the way they dress is for their stage personas. Though I have no idea how the pirate outfit Clarice wears relates to her specialty: playing cards. Maybe poker is the link? Pirates played poker, and Clarice knows a lot about that game, which is why she's my teacher.

Before anyone can answer, it's Hannibal's turn to start hissing at Fabio. And—though it could be my imagination—I hear words in the hiss: *Call my understudy a pirate again, and I'll eat your liver with some fava beans and a nice Chianti.*

Mistaking the target of the hiss, Machete doubles down on his hostility. Not for the first time, I wonder if I could train him to be my sidekick spy. He could intimidate in some situations and infiltrate hard-to-reach places in others.

"I really should get going," Fabio says, shifting his gaze back and forth between the two angry cats. "I'm late for my date."

"I'll walk you to the door," I say with an evil grin. He's not escaping Machete so easily.

"No need," he says, but Machete and I follow him anyway. Once he's gone, I lock the apartment door and leave Machete in the kitchen to eat.

When I come back to the living room, Clarice's cat is also missing from the camera's view. Must be off on a hunt, looking for someone to cannibalize.

"So sad he's gay," Clarice says. "I'd also show him mine if he showed me his."

Sad indeed. Fabio is hot, and would be quite fuckable if we weren't attracted to the same gender. Well, almost. Unlike Fabio, who's Team Y Chromosome all the way, I'd also sleep with Claire Danes, Keri Russell, and a few other actresses who've played spies I admire.

In any case, Fabio is a friend all of us sextuplets share, in part because we were collectively his beard back in high school. To this day, I think he sees us as one person with multiple personality disorder.

"I bet Fabio is popular in the genre of porn where a gay guy seduces a 'straight guy,'" Gia says.

I raise my eyebrows. "You watch gay porn?"

Gia shrugs. "I watch all porn. Are you prejudiced with yours?"

I just shake my head. Dumb jokes aside, Gia is the sister who understands me best, despite not being a part of my litter. We both love deception. Magic and spy craft have that in common. Also—and this is a biggie—we've been forever linked by the same traumatizing event, codename the Zombie Tit Massacre.

See, our parents live on a farm where they rescue all sorts of animals—and I'm all for that, except for that one case when they adopted a bird called the Great Tit, or as it's also known, the Zombie Tit. The reason for the second name is as blood-chilling as everything to do with birds. These monsters are thirsty for the brains of bats and, occasionally, other birds—including chickens, which is what I witnessed on that horrible day.

My heartbeat picks up as I relive it once more.

The pecking.

The gore.

The brains splattered everywhere.

The cursed Zombie Tit, with its bloody beak and eyes thirsty for more brains, looking at me.

Hitchcock's *The Birds* had nothing on that horror show.

Since that day, I've been terrified of birds and studiously avoid them in all forms, including cooked.

Hey, at least I won't die of the avian flu.

What I don't get is why I'm alone in this. Birds are dinosaurs. Everyone has seen *Jurassic Park*. Were the velociraptors in it scary? Yes. Could they have been scarier if the movie creators hadn't been humane and had depicted them properly, feathers and all? Sure could've.

Yep, that's right. In reality, velociraptors had feathers and were the size of a big turkey.

Pure nightmare fuel.

"Hey, sis, I was just kidding," Gia says, clearly misunderstanding why my face has gotten as pale as hers. "How about we get down to business?"

"Right." I shake off the terrible memories. "Let's. The game is happening tonight."

"By Houdini's adrenal gland," Gia says. "Are you ready?"

I fold a finger. "Reviewed everything Clarice has taught me." I fold another finger. "Re-watched *Casino Royale*." I fold one more finger. "Saw *Rounders* for the first time—and, as Clarice said, John Malkovich was awesome as Teddy KGB, and young Ed Norton and Matt Damon looked delicious."

"I assume that's a yes, then," Gia says.

I nod. "Now I just want to get your opinion on how I execute the magician moves you've taught me, and hear any last-minute poker tips from Clarice."

Gia pulls their camera closer. "Do the moves."

I grab the wig I designated for the infiltration and pull it over my buzzcut. Next, I take a poker chip with my phone number etched into it and stick it under the wig, near my left ear. Lastly, I get the micro-camera/GPS gadget and hide it by my right ear.

"Here." I sneak my fingers under the wig and take out the chip, holding it in the finger grip Gia has taught me. Apparently, this is a classic move taught in every beginner book on coin magic. Bottom line is, the coin/poker chip isn't visible in my hand.

"And here's the camera move." I sneak the gadget out and hold it in a more advanced grip—again from the coin magic books. I then take a picture of the room, just as I will at the poker game, and surreptitiously attach the device to the wall with some magician sticky wax.

"Great job," Gia says. "It's obvious you've been practicing."

"What's the exact plan?" Clarice asks.

"I'll sneak the poker chip to the target and hope he calls me," I say. "I'm also going to take some pictures with this." I unglue the gizmo from the wall.

"Stealthy." Clarice examines the device admiringly. "But what if they scan you for electronics before the game?"

I take off my wig and show them the mesh on the inside. "This has a Faraday cage sewn in." At Clarice's blank stare, I say, "It doesn't let electromagnetic signals go in or out."

Gia snickers. "Like those tinfoil hats that prevent aliens from listening in."

I put the wig back on. "Tinfoil wouldn't make a good Faraday cage and you know it."

"Children," Clarice says. "It's my turn to give advice."

We both look at her expectantly.

"Don't talk poker strategy at the table," she says. "You might've gotten into that habit with me, but it can bite you in the butt during a real game."

"I won't," I say. "What else?"

"Watch out for the disclaimer tells," she says.

"What's that?" Gia asks.

"It's when someone says something like, 'I'm sick of you winning all the time. I'm going all in.'"

I flush. That example is from a game we played a few weeks back.

"What do you do when someone says that?" Gia asks.

Clarice looks smug. "Obviously, you assume it's an act, and the real reason they're going all in is because they've got a strong hand."

"I'll make sure I don't do that," I say. "And I'll keep an eye out for others doing it."

Clarice gives me more reminders, and I listen appreciatively. Eventually, she says, "Okay, you're as ready as you can be."

"Thanks," I say.

"What does it matter if you win or lose?" Gia asks. "I thought the idea was just to be in the same room with the target."

I roll my eyes. "You mean besides not looking like a fool?"

She nods.

I sigh. "The buy-in for this game is half a million dollars. I'd like to keep that money."

Both sets of eyes on the screen widen to comical proportions. I guess I forgot to mention that little detail. Oops.

Gia clears her throat. "Where did you get so much cash? I didn't realize the NSA paid so well."

"I work for No Such Agency," I say on autopilot. "And no. They don't pay *that* well. I just sold some of my bitcoin."

Since I studied cryptography in college, it made sense to me to invest in—and to mine—cryptocurrencies, and my investments have grown quite nicely in the past few years. For a twenty-five-year-old, I'm pretty well off. Still, I'd feel very sad if I lost that buy-in.

"I didn't realize." Clarice looks crestfallen. "I guess I have no chance of ever going to that game."

"I'll make you a deal," I say. "If I double my money tonight—thanks to your training—I'll back you. The catch is, you'll share your winnings with me."

"Deal," Clarice says, her eyes gleaming. "I'm going to be rich."

"Uh-huh," Gia says, ignoring her. "I can see why you're so proactive with all the prepping. Half a fucking million. I know you have that fancy car, but I had no idea you were so rich. This is the first time I envy you your boring college major."

"I'm not that rich," I say. "At least not usually. Crypto's just been on a tear lately, so I got the car and now this. Forgetting the buy-in for a second, it would simply look suspicious if I showed up at that game and sucked ass. It's obviously a bunch of poker sharks, or people who think they are."

Gia waggles her eyebrows lasciviously. "I'm sure they would cut a *woman* some slack." Seeing Clarice's and my glare, she quickly adds, "I didn't mean that in a sexist way. It's a game full of naked hunks who are apparently rolling in dough. A rich lady might be excused for wanting to go there to feast her eyes… or maybe meet her future husband."

"That reminds me," Clarice says. "Why are the guys who play at that club so good-looking?"

I shrug. "I'm sure unattractive players join from time to time. But I bet after they spot the others, their self-esteem takes a dive, and they probably don't want to come back. I wouldn't like doing Bikram Yoga surrounded by Victoria's Secret models either."

"I guess that makes sense," Clarice says. "I've also been wondering why you're so sure your target will be there. You don't know who he is or what he does. He could've just popped in for that one game."

"True," I say. "But if he's a spy, it would make sense for him to keep going and mingling with those people. Most of them are rich and powerful, which makes them great connections to have."

Gia and Clarice nod sagely.

"Okay, you two," I say. "I should go."

"Last question," Gia says. "Why are you doing this?"

Is this going to lead to a Fabio-like "you want him" statement?

"That's top secret," I say. "Need to know basis, and you don't need to know."

"But seriously," Clarice chimes in. "I also want to know."

I shrug. "I guess I want to show the CIA that they were wrong to reject me."

"Why would you even want to work for them?"

Clarice asks. "They have a bad reputation. The FBI might be a better choice."

"FBI agents aren't spies," I say. "They do undercover work, but it's not the same."

"The NSA spies," Gia says. "And they also have a pretty crappy reputation if that's what you're after."

"Sitting at a computer all day isn't my idea of spying," I say. "I want field work, and tonight, I'll get a taste of the real thing."

"Well, good luck," Gia says.

"Hold on," Clarice says. "You never explained what's up with the well-hung dummy on your couch."

"Oh, no." I create a hissing sound with the side of my mouth. "I think I'm losing you."

Gia chuckles. "Before you go, I meant to ask... Will you come see my magic show?"

"Sure. Send me the details." With that, I hang up before they can delay me further.

It's time to get ready for the Hot Poker Club infiltration.

CHAPTER

Three

FIRST THINGS FIRST. Should I wear my cat burglar suit for this?

No. That would be pointless. You get naked to play.

I put on my best bathing suit instead. Hopefully, they'll let me keep it on.

Clothes decided, I tackle makeup, prioritizing the following: waterproofness, so it doesn't run in the banya, and sex appeal enhancement, so Hottie McSpy wants to call me afterward.

Securing my Faraday cage wig atop of my head, I saunter to the door and check the time.

Crap. It's later than I thought. I'll have to drive instead of walking to the meet.

My phone pings with a doorbell alert.

Odd. I'm not expecting anyone.

Even though I'm standing within reach of my peep-hole, I pull up my phone and check the video feed from my smart doorbell camera.

The person behind the door looks identical to me, especially me in the wig I'm currently wearing.

Strawberry-blond hair, high cheekbones, strong chin, greenish eyes—clearly one of my litter mates. I think I know who it is based on the way she's dressed, but just in case, I ask, "Which one are you?"

"It's Olive," she says.

Yep. As I thought. Olive—or Octopussy as I lovingly think of her. Not because she reminds me of the character from the 1983 Bond film, but because she is obsessed with octopuses.

I open the door, and she steps in.

Oh, no. I don't need twin telepathy juju to determine that she's upset.

"Can I stay with you?" she blurts in lieu of a hello.

"Of course. What happened?"

If my sister needs me, I'm rescheduling the infiltration. Even if it means they'll keep the buy-in I've already sent in.

"Please," Olive says. "I don't want to talk about it."

I grab her hand. "Are you okay?"

"Yeah," she says, even though her eyes are overly bright in that holding-back-tears kind of way. "I just need to rest. Is that okay?"

"Sure," I say, though I'm getting increasingly worried.

"I also need some time to myself." She looks at me pleadingly. "Do you think I could take a long bath?"

"No problem." Something is clearly wrong, but I get that she needs her space. "Take the bath, and we'll talk afterward."

She averts her gaze. "I was hoping to crash on your couch and get some sleep after. Is that okay?"

She doesn't want to talk today about whatever is bugging her. Fine. I'll give her until tomorrow, and then it's interrogation time.

"Do you need me here then?" I ask. "I was on my way out somewhere, but—"

"Please go." The words sound like she's begging—which just makes me want to stay.

"Are you sure?"

"Very sure. I need a place to be, not company."

"Fine. Follow me." I walk her through my apartment and explain where everything she might need is. When we come across the beast, I say, "You remember Machete."

He looks up at us lazily, so I sternly tell him, "This is Olive. Treat her as you would treat me."

He licks his paw, his furry face bored.

All humans look the same to Machete, but especially you two for some reason. Whoever feeds Machete gets to live... for now.

When we return to the living room, Olive spots Bill on the couch and rubs her eyes.

"Oh yeah, can you toss him into the closet in my bedroom?" I ask.

It's a testament to how upset she is that instead of teasing or asking any questions, she simply nods, like putting away dummies with damaged dildos is completely routine.

"You sure you don't want to tell me what's wrong?" I ask.

24

"No. Go, please." Olive puts her hands on her hips. "I've got it from here."

She'd better spill all her secrets tomorrow. I'm not above using sleep deprivation—or hair pulling—to get information. At this point, I'm almost as curious about Olive's troubles as I am about Hottie McSpy's mission.

"Fine." I turn toward the door. "Mi casa es su casa."

I still feel uneasy leaving, but she looks so relieved that I capitulate. Whatever happened, she wants to be alone for now.

An elevator ride later, I step into my building's basement parking lot, and my excitement about the infiltration returns.

I check the time.

Fuck. I'm late.

I dash for my car, an Aston Martin DBS V12. Or, as I think of it, the car Daniel Craig drove as James Bond in *Casino Royale* and *Quantum of Solace*.

As the powerful engine purrs to life, I put the *Mission Impossible* theme music on full blast and mentally plot my route.

The meet is near the Manhattan side of the Brooklyn Bridge, and since I live by Battery Park, the distance I need to cover is but a few blocks. Typically, it would take about six minutes to traverse, depending on traffic. Given that the meet is about to start, I'll have to halve that, traffic or not.

I turn the wheel and floor the gas.

As I fly out of the parking lot, I nearly run over a lady who lives across the hall.

Oops.

At least with the illegal-level tinting on my windows, she can't see me behind the wheel. Hopefully.

Tires screeching, I turn onto Water Street—and nearly crash into a yellow cab.

The cab driver doesn't even blink. He's been through worse. In fact, the guy I took driving lessons from had cut his teeth on one of those cabs.

Torpedoing ahead, I scan for pedestrians before running a red light and praying that no cop saw me. Luckily, I get away with it, and with annihilating the speed limit. When I reach the famous Wall Street, I run another red light. From here, I get all green until I'm zooming up Pearl Street.

If I were really going onto the bridge, I'd take the ramp, but I'm not exactly, so I swerve into a parking lot, my tires squealing and the wheel jerking in my hands. Leaping out of the car, I leave my keys inside and toss a hundred-dollar bill at the nearby attendant.

"Are you nuts?" he asks, mouth agape.

"I'll be back in a few hours," I say. "Keep the change from that, and I'll tip you another hundred if my car is happy."

Before he can ask me to fill out a form, write up a receipt, or do anything else to slow me down, I sprint out of there and beeline for the meet location.

When I get there, panting, I check the time.

A minute late.

My FBI contact warned me that these people are punctual, but hopefully, a single minute isn't a deal breaker.

The meet was arranged on the Dark Web as per my contact's instructions. I was impressed with the Hot Poker Club organizers. They sent me an email that I couldn't trace despite all of my skills. A self-destructing email, in fact—very *Mission Impossible*.

Not to mention, the location is great. A bridge. That's a classic for things like prisoner exchanges à la *Bridge of Spies*, so it makes a fitting place to take me as a prisoner... of sorts.

I make hand signals the way I was instructed, and notice two masked guys exit a black Chevrolet Suburban across the street.

They must be the people I'm meeting.

Yep. One of them makes the answering hand signal.

My contact warned me about what comes next, so I feel a tiny bit apprehensive. I'm the first woman that I know of to do this. What if they decide to keep my cash and do something unspeakable to me instead of playing poker?

But no. Woman or not, that would be bad for business, as it might deter future players. Besides, if anything untoward starts to happen, I can always use my Krav Maga combat skills. And if that fails, I can tell them where I work. Killing government agents is really bad for business—just watch *Sicario*.

Still, no matter what I tell myself, my knees are wobbly as I cross the street. My Krav Maga instructor would call me a chicken right now—a dumb expression. To me, being a chicken means being a feathery monster, not feeling fear. I guess when it comes to chickens, I'm a chicken, but these guys aren't as scary as that.

"Hello," I say when I reach them.

Hey, my voice is steady. Score one for me.

"What's the passcode?" the leftmost guy booms.

I say it.

"Get in," he says.

Yep. I'm getting into a sketchy black van. Time to see if I'm cut out for field work.

The reminder of my ultimate goal puts a spring in my step, and I jump into the car almost giddily.

Hells yeah, I'm cut out for this. In fact, a cut-out of me should be in the dictionary under "kickass spy."

The man sitting shotgun turns my way. Besides his mask, he's wearing a pair of those thick, giant sunglasses that the elderly wear to cut down on glare.

Maybe this goon is going to retire soon?

"Hand me your phone," he demands.

Hmm. He doesn't sound all *that* old.

I hand him my phone, and he turns it off.

"You can keep it in your pocket, but don't turn it on until we bring you back here," he says. "We'll know if you do."

So they plan to bring me back. That's a relief. Of course, he'd say that even if they were planning to turn me into bird feed.

"I'll keep it off," I say.

"Good." He pulls out a black bag from the glove compartment, tempering whatever was left of my enthusiasm. My FBI contact warned me about this part, but still. Black bag over one's head is how you end up in a terrorist dungeon, not at a poker game.

"What are you planning to do with that?" I ask, channeling an indignant—and very rich—poker player.

"Don't want you to see where we're going," the sunglasses guy says. "Until you become a regular, we'd prefer to keep the Club's location private."

Huh. My FBI contact didn't know the bag is a temporary measure. I guess my amazing feminine wiles are already loosening tongues.

I bat my eyelashes prettily. "Please be careful with my hair."

The last thing I want is for that poker chip and camera to fall out of my wig. I wouldn't make it to the game for sure, and maybe not home either.

The guy looks at my impeccable hairdo/wig, then at one of his colleagues.

The other guy shrugs.

The sunglasses man reaches into the glove compartment and pulls out duct tape.

Uh-oh. Is that for my mouth? The FBI contact said nothing about that. Fuck. Have I overplayed my hand before even getting to the poker table? If I'm gagged, I won't be able to tell them I'm an agent.

Before I can say anything, the guy takes off his sunglasses, rips off a piece of tape, and sticks it inside the lenses.

Oh. Is he—?

Yep.

Done turning his glasses into a makeshift blindfold, he puts them on my face.

How accommodating. My Yelp review of the Hot Poker Club has just gone from one star to three.

Next, someone puts earmuffs over my ears. My FBI contact theorized they're of the type used at gun ranges. You can still hear, but the sound is heavily dampened.

"Drive," I hear someone say, but the voice is faint.

We begin moving.

A soothing tune emanates from the car's speakers. Even without the earmuffs, I'm unlikely to hear what's happening outside.

I sneak a peek down and to the side.

Nope.

The glasses are as good as a black bag when it comes to blocking my view.

If I had Liam Neeson's "very particular set of skills" from *Taken*, I'd be able to tell where we're headed even without sight or sound. Alas, I can't do that (yet), but in my defense, neither could my FBI contact.

It's fine. I have a gizmo with GPS. If I live long enough to take it out of my Faraday cage wig, I'll have the Club's location.

A female singer's voice joins the music. "You're beautiful…"

Is that Nelly Furtado? But what song is this?

When the answer comes, it's as unsettling as my situation.

Nelly belts out, "I'm like a bird, I'll—"

I don't want to hear the rest.

A song about birds? What's next, a jingle about Hitler? Charles Manson? Daffy Duck?

I recite cryptographic algorithms in my head to tune out the horror melody for the rest of the ride.

————

We stop in about a half hour. That means we could be in Brooklyn, Midtown, or even Queens if we were speeding and didn't encounter any traffic.

Someone leads me by the hand, and we walk on asphalt, then carpeted floors. Eventually, I feel tiles under my feet.

There's also a smell that grows stronger. Chlorine and lemon. Must be what they use to disinfect the spa at the poker game.

Hey, at least they didn't lower me in one of those dumbwaiter contraptions, or throw me down a laundry chute.

After another short corridor, we enter a room where the chlorine-and-lemon aroma is overpowered by locker room smells. Naked sweaty men must be near.

Someone takes off my sunglasses and earmuffs.

The room is bright, so it takes me a second to adjust.

In front of me is the goon who gave me the glasses, and next to him is another masked person, clearly a woman.

She's holding two towels—a detail I don't like.

"Ms. Black will take care of you," the guy says and leaves, sunglasses in hand.

"For security reasons, we're having you use the men's locker room," Ms. Black says in a chipper tone. "Rest assured, the male players are already at the table, and when you're done, you'll get priority here over a man who decides to cash out at the same time as you."

"Thanks," I say.

"Your chips are on the table, and you can leave them there when done. We'll cash you out electronically." She thrusts the towels at me. "Strip and put this on."

She turns around.

I take everything off but the bathing suit and clear my throat.

She turns.

"Can I play in this?" I ask.

She examines me. "I'll have to check you."

"What do you mean?"

"I'll need to examine your breasts if you want to keep the top, and—"

"Got it." I unhook the bikini top. "I'll wear a towel around my waist."

It's hard to be sure with the mask on, but I think she's relieved she won't need to pat down my vag.

She pats my bikini top, gives my boobs a quick once-over—not much there to look at—and hands the top back to me. "Leave your clothes there and set a combination." She gestures at an open locker.

I have her turn around as I swap my bikini bottoms for a towel. Then I pack my stuff into the locker and let her lead me to the other side of the room.

"There." She points at a large wooden door with a small glass window that's completely fogged up, like the car in *Titanic*.

I look at her. "So I just go in?"

She nods. "Your seat is waiting for you."

I approach the door apprehensively.

After all this, Hottie McSpy might not actually be on the other side. Or he might be there, but turn out to be uninterested in me. Or that room might be filled with evil birds.

No. That last one is against the Geneva Convention.

Taking in a deep breath, I open the door and step in.

CHAPTER
Four

A BLAST of heat hits me in the face as the door of the sauna closes behind me. I blink and fight the urge to cough at the steam. The poker table in front of me is just like the one I saw in the picture. The half-naked men around it also look the same, at least at first. When I examine them closer, I spot a few new faces, including an unattractive guy who, as I would suspect, appears very uncomfortable in his skin given the male beauty surrounding him.

Speaking of male beauty, there he is.

Hottie McSpy—chiseled face, aviator glasses, and all. He looks even bigger in person, and more lickable with all those beads of sweat running down that hard-muscled torso.

My heart jumps into my throat.

Not only is he *here*, the only empty seat is right next to him.

My seat.

Moving as though in a daze, I plop blindly into that

chair. It's a miracle I don't end up on his lap.

A disappointing miracle.

"Hello," I say, almost knocking over the pile of poker chips someone prepared for me.

The sweaty men study me intently as they greet me, but I only care about attention from my target.

Turning my way, Hottie McSpy lifts his sunglasses. "Welcome."

Whoa.

I've dreamed of seeing his eyes for so long, yet somehow, they surpass even my impossible expectations. Instead of blue or gray, the colors that typically accompany blond hair, they're a dark forest-green, with flecks of honey that take them to the very edge of hazel. And those dark brown lashes.

I need to get my FBI contact on the case, because I'm pretty sure it's a felony for a man to have lashes of that length and thickness.

"Thanks," I manage to say, belatedly realizing that the one word he's uttered so far didn't have any hint of a Russian accent.

Not that this proves anything. He could be a deep cover agent, like in *The Americans*.

Someone grabs the cards and begins to shuffle.

Shit. I need to get my head in the game.

Scanning the room with that in mind, I take notice of everyone's stacks of chips.

A few guys, including McSpy, have neatened theirs. According to Clarice, that means they'll be more organized and methodical in their play, while the sloppy-looking stack of the pale guy across from me means the opposite.

I take particular note of one player. He's built a sculpture from his chips, a sure sign of someone who lives and breathes poker.

As the cards are dealt, I neaten my chip stacks—which causes my elbow to touch McSpy's.

Holy shit. It's like a jolt straight to my nipples, code-names Sergeant and Captain.

I sneak a peek at McSpy.

His nostrils are flared and a bead of sweat rolls down his forehead, but otherwise, it's hard to tell if he's been affected by the touch, or has even noticed it. Curse those sunglasses that hide his beautiful eyes.

On my end, the already-hot temperature in the room seems to skyrocket. I'm sweating as liquid heat pools between my legs—this had better be the effect of the sauna and not of that elbow touch. Oh, and the yummy scent of my delicious table neighbor doesn't help in the between-legs department either. I detect something woodsy—maple, I think—with just a hint of lavender.

As the last card is dealt, my arousal cools. Further helping in that is the sloppy-stack guy. I catch him staring uncouthly at my breasts.

I take a peek down to make sure Sergeant and Captain aren't showing. The last thing you want in a room full of men is a nip-slip.

Nope. Sergeant and Captain are hidden, but thanks to that encounter with McSpy, they're standing at attention, ready for battle—a situation visible even through all the padding in my bikini top.

The game starts, so I put Sloppy Stack out of my head.

Thank goodness for Clarice. In an eyeblink, I make five thousand dollars. The dopamine hit is strong, though McSpy's proximity might deserve some of the credit. No wonder some people get addicted to gambling.

In the next round, McSpy takes the pot, and in the round after that, it's Sloppy Stack—though I suspect he's just gotten lucky.

He pulls his chips into his messy pile. "Kind of wish this was strip poker," he says without breaking eye contact with my breasts.

"Shut it," McSpy growls.

Is he defending my honor? Is that nice or sexist of him? I can certainly speak for myself.

"It's fine," I say, my voice laced with honey. "Though, if I wanted to play strip poker, I would've brought my magnifying glass."

For the first time, Sloppy Stack looks up from my boobs, his expression confused.

"You know." I look at his towel. "To see your micro penis."

Sloppy Stack clenches his jaw, and everyone looks uncomfortable except McSpy—who turns my way with a grin on his face, lifts his glasses again, and winks at me.

Fuck me, he's got a dimple on his left cheek. Hotter yet, there's a light dusting of hair on his knuckles— something the picture of him didn't prepare me for.

I feel tingly between my legs, and it's definitely not the sauna.

I *love* knuckle hair to the point where I once put Rogaine on my ex-boyfriend's knuckles—and when that didn't work, I glued fake eyebrows there for my birthday sex.

It all started after watching Sean Connery and Pierce Brosnan as James Bond, and Elijah Wood as Frodo in *Lord of the Rings*. Frodo wasn't exactly a spy, but he did (spoiler alert) sneak into Mordor.

Thank goodness there's a towel between me and the chair. Reminiscing about the various Bonds isn't helping me keep my fluids in.

What would McSpy do if I reached under his towel and pleasured his walnut? Maybe also stroked his—

What am I thinking? I'm the one who's supposed to seduce McSpy into telling me all his secrets. I can't let his dimples and hairy knuckles—or his walnut—do the same to me.

Also, it's getting ridiculously hot in here. In addition to practicing with Clarice, I should've made sure to develop sauna temperature endurance.

Well, no helping it now.

With an effort of will, I force myself to focus on the game.

Thankfully, the deception at the poker table comes naturally to me—like it did for James Bond in *Casino Royale*.

I soon lose a hundred grand but learn a lot of people's poker tells. Sloppy Stack overacts being disinterested but then keeps on betting when he's got something. The unattractive guy sighs to make it seem like he's got a bad hand, but it's an act every time. Another dude sits up straighter when he gets strong cards. Another slides his chips daintily, pretending to be acting weak when he's actually strong.

I even catch the tell of the sculpture-building player. He sneaks a peek at his chips whenever he has a strong hand.

The only person whose tells I still don't know is McSpy, but knowing everyone else's is enough.

Using my knowledge, I start to win, and by the time I'm about to faint from heat stroke, I'm up a quarter of a mill.

Okay. If my feminine wiles haven't impressed McSpy, my poker skills might have. True, he's doubled his chips, but he should at least see me as his card shark equal—and call me to chat about poker, if nothing else.

Time to pass him my number and skedaddle.

On the next deal, I sneak my hand near my wig, and when no one is looking, I slide the engraved poker chip out.

My heartbeat is insane. There's a reason people with heart conditions are told to avoid saunas. They should avoid shady business in saunas even more.

If I get caught with this chip, I could be in huge trouble. My phone number aside, bringing your own chip might be seen as fraud. Plus, once they start wondering where I hid the chip, they might find the gizmo—and getting caught with that would be even worse.

The good news is that no one is looking at me except Sloppy Stack, and his gaze is still on my breasts. The bad news is that this is much harder to do with sweaty hands.

Still, I manage not to drop the chip as I grip it the way Gia has taught me.

Since the cards are dealt, I check mine.

Two aces and two sixes. Nice. Thanks to the stats Clarice has drilled into my head and my ability to mentally crunch numbers, I have a reason to be happy. This would beat a single pair and any high cards. Also, if I get another ace or six, I'll have a Full House—which isn't just the show where the Olsen twins got their start.

The betting starts, and I use that as a cover to sneak my hand over the nearest stack of McSpy's as I release the phone number chip.

McSpy darts a barely perceptible glance at it, then continues on as though nothing's happened.

Whew.

I haven't been busted.

At least I don't think I have.

Still, security might run in at any moment. Or he might bet my chip, and it could end up—

Nope.

As I hoped, he's caught on quick.

He slides my chip from the pile and sneaks it under his towel.

Fuck me.

I get a glimpse of his upper thigh. I didn't know I was a leg woman, but I guess I am.

Also, is he going to keister it? By his walnut?

Time to leave.

But wait.

I get the ace to go with my pair.

I have a Full House.

I'd be crazy not to jump on this opportunity. Only three other hands are stronger than this. I just need to be careful not to telegraph my glee to everyone at the table.

Fuck. McSpy must know some tell of mine. That or there's some other reason he folds.

The others do not, though, so I end up doing two very pleasing things at once: I more than double my money and leave Sloppy Stack without any chips.

If I liked bird-related expressions (which I definitely don't), this would be a perfect example of "killing two birds with one stone." Actually, that expression isn't the worst. Killing two birds is a good start, after all. "A bird in hand is worth two in the bush" is much worse. First, kiss that hand goodbye. Second, "two in the bush" sounds vaguely sexual, evoking ménage à trois, bestiality-style. And speaking of sex, why is it called "the birds and the bees," two species that reproduce so differently from humans? Is egg laying supposed to be part of that conversation? Relatedly, do you want to have nightmares? If so, read up on duck reproduction. Spoiler alert: genitals shaped like screws and what is politely termed "forced copulation" feature prominently. Do I even need to go into something like "the early bird gets the worm," or is there a more frightening way to measure distance than "as the crow flies?"

"This is bullshit," Sloppy Stack (or should I say Nonexistent Stack?) says, glaring at me. "You don't belong here."

I give him my most withering look. "Seriously? 'The woman doesn't belong here?' Maybe if you hadn't been staring at my boobs the whole game, you'd have some chips left. Next time, don't let your micro penis guide your poker strategy."

"Bitch." He stands up. "I'm out of here."

Everyone stares at him, and to their credit, the men look unanimously disapproving.

McSpy pushes to his feet, the muscles in his broad shoulders flexing. His deep voice is low and dangerous. "There's only one whiny bitch in this room, and I'm looking at him."

While the attention is away from me, I sneak my gizmo out and hide it in my hand. "You're not leaving yet," I tell Sloppy Stack as I also rise to my feet. "I'm cashing out, and I get priority when it comes to the locker room."

There. I *could* play another hand or two, but he called me a bitch, so I'll have him wait at the table without any chips, like the loser he is.

"Fuck that." He starts toward the door. "I'm going."

McSpy steps in front of him, blocking his way. "Everyone agreed the lady would get priority when it comes to the locker room. Sit or you will be seated."

Damn. Usually, I'd find it patronizing for a man to do that on my behalf, but in this case, it's panty-melting hot—not that I'm wearing any panties.

Since everyone's attention is still on Sloppy/No-More Stack, I take a picture of the room with my gizmo.

One of the players from the FBI picture tosses a chip at Sloppy Stack.

"There," he says. "You're back in the game. Pay me back later."

Grumbling, the asshole sits back down.

Big mistake. The man he now owes money to is one of the regulars—and, according to the FBI file on him, might be a member of the mob. Sloppy had better have the cash to pay him back.

"Thanks," I whisper into McSpy's ear as he sits back down, and then I skedaddle before I catch second-hand testosterone poisoning.

———

When I'm back in the locker room, I realize how overheated I actually am.

I could faint at any moment.

Crap. I still have one more thing to do.

Leaning back as if to catch my breath—which I need to do anyway—I attach my gizmo to the wall with the wax.

There. Now I have a video feed into the men's locker room, like a perv.

I'd better get out of here ASAP. They claimed they'd know if I turned on my phone, so they might detect the gizmo too.

Grabbing nearby towels, I wipe the sweat off my face and body. I don't dare shower under the circumstances. Instead, I dress as fast as my overheated state allows and stick my head out of the locker room.

One of the masked guys tells me to wait and disappears. A minute later, he returns with the makeshift blindfold from before, and its owner.

The way back feels quicker, probably because it's blissfully free of songs about birds.

When the earmuffs and sunglasses are removed, the guy who owns the sunglasses asks me where to drop me off.

I point at the parking lot.

They drive me inside.

My car is ready to go. I guess the guy I tipped earlier wants the other hundred.

"You can go," one of the masked men says.

I'm about to leave when I see it.

A pigeon.

It's sitting right above my driver-side door.

I'm glued to my seat. There's no way I can get near that car now.

"I said you can go," the same guy growls.

"I heard you, but there's a problem. That." I point an unsteady finger at the pigeon.

"What?" He looks out the window, eyes narrowing.

"The bird," I say. "Can you get rid of it, please?"

Muttering something unintelligible, he exits the Suburban and starts shooing away the pigeon.

My Yelp review is now five glowing stars. I just hope the guy doesn't pay too dearly for his bravery.

Anyone who calls pigeons "rats with wings" is wrong. Compared to pigeons, rats are cute and cuddly; they're also a lot cleaner, and carry fewer diseases. Even for birds, pigeons are creepy. Their eyes are beady and always seem to glare at you, and they have zero fear.

Here is a horror movie idea. Say a pigeon wanted you dead. You could transport the evil creature, in isolation (without sight or sound), as far as 1300 miles away, and it would find its way back. Scientists don't know how they do this, which makes sense. Pure evil works in mysteriously creepy ways.

And let's not forget, if your child has asthma, the stuff pigeons carry on their wings will set it off. If a pigeon touches you and you manage to live, you'll at the very least get scabies. And if you were to actually befriend one, you could get an emphysema-like condition called bird fancier's lung.

I could go on, but that would be cruel.

Wait a sec. Did I just see him take out his gun?

Unclear, but something he does finally scares the monster away, so I exit and thank my hero profusely.

"Can I tip you?" I ask at the end.

He gives a grim shake of his head.

"Well, if I ever meet your boss, I'll make sure to tell him about your amazing customer service skills."

My savior grunts something and returns to his black Suburban. They drive away, fast.

As I get into my car, the parking lot attendant from earlier turns up. "A deal is a deal."

I give him the money as promised and start the engine.

Before pulling out, I decide to check the live feed from the gizmo—and it's lucky I do.

In view of the camera is none other than Hottie McSpy himself, and he seems to be up to no good.

CHAPTER

Five

In McSpy's hands is a device I've seen before. It's an outdated way to infiltrate someone's cellphone, and at No Such Agency, we've been told to be careful lest someone uses it on us. Side note: such gadgets aren't necessary for my agency. We can get into most smartphones with our hands tied behind our backs.

As I suspected. He's a spy. Why else would he own a device like that? The better question is: where did he hide that thing during the game?

Moving furtively, McSpy walks up to a nearby locker.

I'd bet my buy-in money that locker isn't his. He's clearly after the phone of someone who's still in that game.

If so, how does he know someone else's pin?

Suddenly, the locker room door opens and a masked person steps inside, holding some kind of device as well. If I had to guess what it does, I'd say it notifies the

Hot Poker Club people when someone turns on their phone.

Is McSpy about to get caught spying?

Reacting with impressive speed, he drops his infiltration tech onto the tile floor beneath his feet. It shatters. He swiftly steps on one of the pieces with one bare foot and covers the rest with the other.

That will hurt, but the evidence of his sneakiness is gone.

I cringe as I watch him drag his feet over to another locker, the one that must be his.

To my surprise, the security person isn't going for McSpy.

Instead, he beelines for me—as in, the camera.

Oh, shit.

Yep. He grabs my gizmo, making my view go haywire.

"Is this yours?" the security guy asks Hottie McSpy, examining the tiny piece of tech.

"No," McSpy says. "I've never seen that before."

The security guy drops my gizmo and stomps on it, so I don't get to hear the rest.

Fuck. I knew there was a chance the device would be found, but I didn't think it would happen so quickly.

Will Hottie McSpy talk his way out of that predicament? If not, what will they do to him? Not kill him, surely? That seems too severe a reaction, but you never know.

More importantly, why am I worried about a stranger who's most likely a foreign agent?

I'm not. This ache in my chest is just guilt over the

fact that it was my gizmo that brought the heat down on him.

Yeah, that must be it.

Still, for a second, I consider embarking on a rescue mission. After all, in addition to the video, my gizmo has captured the GPS coordinates of the Hot Poker Club location.

I plug in said coordinates into the GPS.

It's in Midtown. Specifically, it's smack in the middle of a hotel called The Palace.

Interesting. Hotels do have steam rooms and saunas, so why not a banya?

Do I go there and save a fellow spy, even though he's working for the other side?

No. My strength is stealth, not brawn. He'll be fine. They'll probably check the security camera and see that he hasn't been near the spot where the gizmo was glued.

Crap.

Could they figure *me* out?

I'll know if they don't pay me.

For now, I drive home.

———

Entering my apartment, I tiptoe into the living room.

Olive is snoring on the couch, with Machete cuddled next to her.

Traitor. That's how he usually sleeps with me. No doubt he can't even tell the difference between us.

I grab a blanket and cover my littermate.

Now that I'm back, I have to fight the temptation to wake her and make her tell me what happened to her.

Machete opens one green eye and hisses at me.

Never wake up Machete like that. He can kill you with but a swipe of his hind paw.

Rolling my eyes at the cat, I go to the kitchen and drink a whole bottle of water.

Bathroom and shower are next.

Once I'm clean and somewhat rehydrated, I crash on my bed and pass out.

CHAPTER
Six

WAKING UP, I grab my phone.

Nope.

Hottie McSpy hasn't called.

That doesn't mean he got hurt—or that he lost the chip with my number. It's only the morning after. Some guys wait three days or longer to call.

Tapping on the screen, I check the bank account I used to provide the buy-in for the game.

Score! The money is all there. Clarice will be happy. Since I've more than doubled what I put in, I'll back her as promised.

I guess the Hot Poker Club peeps either didn't realize the gizmo they found belonged to me, or they didn't let that stop them from paying.

Leaping off the bed, I run into the bathroom and brush my teeth. Then I locate Olive in the living room. She's awake and holding a bottle of industrial-strength sunblock in her hand.

"Hey, sis. How did you sleep?" I ask.

She smiles at me—a good sign. "Your cat is better than Ambien. As soon as I hugged him, I was out."

"He's good like that. So…" I put my hands on my hips. "I've given you your space. Now it's time to dish."

She squeezes a glob of sunblock into her hand and covers her face with it. I tap my foot as I watch her diligently apply the lotion all over her exposed skin.

I sigh. "Seriously? I'm worried about you. How would you feel in my shoes?"

She extends the sunblock toward me.

"No, thanks," I say. "We're indoors."

She doesn't pull the bottle back. "There are still harmful light rays indoors. They pass through glass, are emitted by your lightbulbs and electronics, and—"

I snatch the sunblock. "Will you tell me what happened to you if I use this?"

She nods.

I smear myself with the white goo. "Spill it."

"Brett and I are over," she says, her voice catching.

"Brett, as in the guy you moved in with?" I massage the sunblock into my cheeks.

"I caught him cheating." She balls her hands into fists. "When I said we were over, he yelled at me and called me names."

I squeeze the sunblock tube so hard it makes a slurping sound that reminds me of the noises that came from Bill's silicone butthole—though the anal association might have something to do with me wanting to tear her ex a new one.

"What did he say?" I ask, hiding the menace in my voice in case she has residual feelings for Brett.

"I don't care what he said." She sniffles. "He didn't let me take Beaky with me."

"He what?" I growl. In a more normal tone, I ask, "Who's Beaky?"

"My octopus," she says.

Confusion makes me forget my rage at Brett for a second. "Why would you call an octopus Beaky? That sounds like a bird name."

A horrible name, on par with Freddy, Jason, and Chucky.

"Octopuses have beaks," she says. "And Beaky has a big one."

"Why would you tell me that?" Now I need brain bleach. Being afraid of birds is hard enough. I don't want to also avoid mollusks. Some of them are delicious.

"Can you help me get Beaky back?" she asks, looking miserable. "I don't think Brett will give him back willingly."

"Trust me, you're getting your octopus back." I rub the remaining sunblock into my uncovered skin. "We can go together to make Brett give him up, or—"

"Let's do the or," she says. "I don't want to see Brett ever again."

I give her back the sunblock. "I can go without you."

"Then he'll think you're me and yell at you."

I snort. "I'd like to see him try. I've been itching to use my Krav Maga skills."

She shakes her head. "What's plan B?"

I think quickly. "We wait for him to leave for work on Monday, and then—"

"I don't want to wait two days. He doesn't know how to properly care for Beaky."

"Fine. I can make it so he's forced to leave the house today. Then we go get Beaky."

"I like that plan."

"Good. Let me talk to some people."

"Thanks," she says as I turn to go to my bedroom. "And here." She shoves the sunblock into my hands. "Don't forget to reapply every two hours."

———

Half an hour later, I'm done with step one of my evil plan.

"Brett is going to get arrested for a cybercrime and taken to the FBI offices adjacent to my work building," I tell Olive.

She blinks at me from the living room couch. "What cybercrime? How? Why—"

"Details classified. Mission starts in four hours."

She claps her hands excitedly. "Thank you. Beaky must—"

My phone rings.

It's an unknown number.

"Sorry, sis," I say. "I need to take this."

Without waiting for her reply, I lock myself in the bedroom and pick up.

"Hello?"

"Hey there," a deep, sexy male voice says. "Nice poker chip."

CHAPTER
Seven

My pulse jumps. "Hey! Your poker chips weren't bad either."

Wait, what? That doesn't make any sense.

He chuckles. "What's your name?"

"Blue," I say.

"Like the color?"

"No," I say. "Like a depressing mood."

"Well, it's nice to meet you, Blue. I'm Maxim."

Damn. He's not even trying. Maxim, in a variety of spellings, is a common name in Slavic countries such as Mother Russia. The origin for it is the Roman *Maximus*.

I like that name. The Roman version makes me hopeful for what he might've been packing under his towel.

"Maxim," I say. "Like the magazine that objectifies women?"

He chuckles again. "You can call me Max if that sounds more feminist."

"Max," I say, tasting the word and wishing it were

his lips. "That's a little better, but it does make you sound like a man's best friend."

Actually, Max makes me think of the Min-Max Theorem and its applications in cryptography, and then I'm back to hoping that whatever he had under his towel was Max and not Min.

"Don't you mean a woman's best friend?" he asks. "I'm shocked you'd use such a sexist expression."

"I'm sorry if I offended your delicate sensibilities with such blatant sexism, Max. I'll be more careful in the future."

I can practically hear him smirking as he says, "I'd appreciate that, Blue."

"What's your last name?" I ask, trying to sound nonchalant.

Once I have his full name, I'll own him.

"Stolyar," he says.

Seriously, the lack of effort he's putting into hiding his Russianness is insulting. Has he watched too many James Bond movies, like I have? Bond also tells everyone his actual name for some reason, even enemy spies. But yeah, Stolyar is a typical occupational surname back in Max's homeland. It means either "joiner" or "carpenter"—I'll need to double-check my Russian dictionary. Furthermore, the way he pronounced it was exactly how a Russian would. The "L" in the middle was a soft consonant. A native English speaker would have to break his tongue to say it like that.

Great. Now I'm thinking about Max's tongue. And,

relatedly, sitting on his face. What's next, moaning like a phone sex operator?

"Stolyar," I say and make a point of touching my tongue to the roof of my mouth as I say the "L," as my Russian teacher drilled into us—mostly fruitlessly, I should add.

"And what is *your* last name?" he asks.

Interesting. He didn't comment on my pronunciation of his name. Maybe my "L" sucked so bad he didn't even notice my effort? Or maybe that's where he draws the line when it comes to hiding his Russian origins?

"Hyman," I say and tense. If he makes a virgin-related joke, I'll tell him to stick his commie—

"That's pretty," he says.

"It is?"

He's clearly been through one of those spy schools that teach seduction. With barely any effort, he's making me feel like bursting into that *West Side Story* song, since I also feel "Oh, so pretty," and maybe even "witty," but absolutely not "gay."

"Blue is also pretty," he says.

Damn. He's good. I've got to be very careful here.

"Max isn't that bad either," I say. "Canine associations aside."

"Thanks. So what's the deal with that poker chip?"

I shrug before I remember that he can't see me. Hopefully. If I had a few minutes, I might be able to see *him* through his phone's camera.

"I brought that with me because I was told there would be lots of attractive men at the game," I say. "I'm single, so I figured I might want to pass my number to one of them."

Hey, I'm not going for subtle here.

"I feel special," he says. "Thanks for giving the chip to me."

"You were the obvious choice." I grin evilly. "Close enough for me to slip the chip into your pile without anyone noticing."

He laughs. "So it was like in real estate: location, location, location?"

"Not only. Your chips were neatly stacked. Also, your overall lack of hideousness helped your cause somewhat."

"I pride myself on my lack of hideousness," he says. "I'm glad you noticed it."

"It's your best quality. Cherish it."

"I like talking to you," he says, making me feel like bursting into that song again. "But I think I'd like to see you even more."

Okay, I need to track down that school he attended. They clearly know more about seduction than Fabio does. Then again, we women are simpler creatures when it comes to this: no walnuts in the crevices of our butts, no need to choke people with our genitals—the list goes on and on.

"You want to hop on a videocall?" I ask.

"How about we meet in the real world?"

Is that because he doesn't do videocalls? Maybe the no-video is a spy thing? Maybe he doesn't want his face captured? Or maybe he thinks a webcam might steal what passes for a Russian spy's soul.

"The get-together would need to happen in a public place," I say. "We know nothing about each other. I could be a serial killer taxidermist who likes making trophies out of non-hideous men."

"Given how specific that is, I concur with the public place idea. How about Central Park?"

He's asking me on a date, right? If so, am I really going along? Well, why not? That's what the chip was for. This is my chance to learn if he's a spy.

Yep. That's why I'm excited. It's purely professional. That's my story, and I'm sticking to it... unless there's some torture-by-sparrow involved.

"Sure," I say. "We can meet on the steps of the Metropolitan Museum. When did you have in mind?"

"You know... it's a beautiful Saturday morning." He sounds extra delicious all of a sudden. "I'm free if you are."

Now? He wants to see me now? I'm not ready. I need to further hone my seduction skills and form a plan of action. For example, maybe I could kidnap him, take him to a private island, and wait for Stockholm syndrome to kick in? But no. Come Monday, I have to work, and No Such Agency doesn't let me work remotely.

"I have something in a few hours," I say, remembering Operation Saving Private Beaky. "Maybe another—"

"That's great," he says. "I only have two hours before a business engagement. If we get moving, that gives us plenty of time for a stroll."

My heart hammers in excitement. I guess it's happening. "Okay, when can you be there?"

"Fifteen minutes?"

"Make that a half hour for me," I say. It'll have to be the quickest getting-ready in all of my years as a woman, but I'm up for the challenge.

"Deal," he says. "I'll see you then."

He hangs up, and I jump up and down in (purely professional) excitement.

I hurry to get ready. Since he saw me in the Faraday cage wig, I'll have to wear that, or something similar to it in terms of color and hair length. I'm not ready to tell him about my buzzcut—a convenience for wigs that I'm suddenly regretting. Well, as luck would have it, I happen to have an even better version of the wig from last night. With me in it, Max won't be the only one who could star in a shampoo commercial. Hair determined, I choose a skirt, shoes, and makeup that should make codename Maximus twitch in Max's pants, assuming he finds anything about me attractive, which is likely, given the call and the date and all.

"Wow," Olive says when I strut into the living room. "That's a pretty fancy look for an octopus rescue."

"This isn't for Beaky," I say. "I'm going to a quick get-together with a friend first. Don't worry, I'll be back in time for our mission."

She looks me up and down. "Hundred bucks says your friend has a nice penis."

I grin. "I'm so optimistic I've already dubbed it Maximus."

She pulls out a bottle of sunblock from I have no

idea what orifice. "Want to take this with? You'll want to reapply if you're going out in the sunlight."

"I'm good," I say and sprint outside to hail a cab.

———

Getting out of the cab, I scan the MET steps and nearly choke on my tongue.

Max is already waiting for me, a sunflower in his hand.

How does his hair look even better today? Does he also wear a wig?

As if the gorgeous mane weren't enough, he's dressed in a bespoke suit—which is now officially my second-favorite suit of his, the first being his birthday suit.

Oh, and have I mentioned the tie? It makes him look like he's about to order a martini, shaken not stirred, or vodka straight... from the bottle.

"Hi," he says, handing me the flower as I approach.

I wish I could shush the butterflies in my stomach. The sunflower is sweet, though this particular plant is a strange choice for a date. A rose or a lily would be more traditional. It almost feels like spy tradecraft. Maybe if I were a fellow Russian spy, I'd give him a pumpkin in return—since both produce seeds that are great for your cardiovascular health.

"You're wearing clothes," I blurt.

He flashes me that devastating dimple. "So are you."

Brilliant conversation. Maybe I should tell him the sky is blue, which might also sound like tradecraft.

"I'm Blue… still." I extend my hand.

"Max." He shakes my hand, his honey-flecked eyes gleaming.

Holy fuck.

The earlier elbow touch didn't properly prepare me for this.

My palm feels like it's just turned into a clit and he's licked it. And sucked it. My whole body is humming with sexual energy. Captain and Sergeant give Max a crisp military salute, and my real clit—whose codename is classified—yearns for the treatment my palm has just received.

Before I have a public orgasm—or start speaking in Slavic tongues—I pull my hand away.

"Want to go that way?" I point in the direction of East 80th Street.

"Sure." He offers me his arm as if we're a married couple out for a stroll. "Shall we?"

Well, I guess when in Rome, do as the Russians do. I loop my hand through the crook of his elbow, the feel of his muscular arm nearly sending me back into an orgasmic frenzy.

We begin walking. The greenery, trees, and benches everywhere remind me of those movie scenes where spies have a covert rendezvous. Unlike in those movies, though, we're not pretending not to know each other.

A gaggle of women with baby strollers looks at me with unabashed jealousy.

Yeah. Just keep walking. He's mine.

"So," I say. "How did you end up at that poker table?"

He slows down. "Don't you think that's more of a third-date kind of question?"

Third date? I plan to have seduced him by then, and if that happens, he'll tell me everything I want to know during pillow talk. Or—if my skills in the bedroom are up to snuff—he might actually turn. My pussy needs to be *that* good. For my country. The turning bit happens in spy movies all the time, usually when an enemy femme fatale sleeps with the hot hero, especially if he's James Bond.

"Sorry," he says. "I'm a private person, and as you know, the Club involves the Dark Web. Hypothetically."

Private person. Understatement much?

"Hypothetically, of course," I say. "What *can* you tell me about yourself?"

He shrugs. "Help me narrow it down."

"You're single, right?"

Better be.

"Yes, and you said you were as well." His dimple shows. "Are you still?"

"Yep. Though I had a bunch of marriage proposals on my way here. Your turn. Where do you go to school?"

Surely, he won't just blurt "Moscow."

"York University," he says. "What about you?"

York University? As in Toronto. As in Ontario. As in... Canada?

I guess it's cold there, so a Russian would feel at home.

"I went to California State University," I say. "What did you study?"

"International Relations," he says, stopping in front of a statue of three bears.

Huh. International Relations is exactly what a spy would study. Should I be insulted by his lack of subtlety?

"What about you?" he asks, his eyes on the bears.

"Cyber Security," I say.

More specifically, I have a Master of Science in National Cyber Security Studies, but going into that much detail is too close to admitting what I do for a living. Not that I plan to hide it. If anything, my job might help the seduction bit. If he decides he wants to turn *me*, the chances of that third date go up. Besides, if he works for the Russians, he might already know where I work, since I've told him my name.

The only reason I haven't looked up his name yet is that I was in a hurry to get here.

"What do you do?" He turns from the bears and cocks his head, regarding me with those gorgeous forest-green eyes.

Huh. Maybe he *doesn't* know. Or he's good at pretending.

"My job is related to my major," I say. "Most of it is classified. Sorry."

"Say no more," he says without batting an eye.

Aha. He understands the need for secrecy—yet another clue he's a spy.

Turning back to the bears, he murmurs, "Isn't that an amazing statue?"

Sure. If you're homesick for Mother Russia, where—as everyone knows—bears roam the streets and swim in rivers of vodka.

"They're okay. I like the Alice in Wonderland statue more." I point the way we're headed.

"Yeah," he says, flashing me a sidelong glance. "The rabbit is well done. The mouse too. And the cat."

Oh, so he's not only into bears. It's all animals, apparently?

That or he's realized the bear was a giveaway.

I hope it's not a cover. Growing up on the farm, I, like most of my siblings, developed a love for animals, and I appreciate it in other people. Worth noting: though taxonomy claims birds are animals, I think they should be in a kingdom of their own, like mushrooms. Mushrooms seem like they might be plants, but are really fungi.

As we resume walking, I ask, "What about you?"

He runs his hand through his dark blond hair. "What about me?"

Nice try.

"What do *you* do for a living?"

He slows down again, but it's barely noticeable.

Is this a tell when he lies? If so, he's lucky that at the poker table, he sits still.

"I'm a corporate consultant," he answers.

Am I imagining it, or does he sound a little cagey?

"What kind?" I ask.

"Oh, different projects in different industries. All boring—"

I don't hear what he says next because I see a big problem in our path.

We're talking a shit-one's-pants and run-away-screaming type of problem.

It combines the worst words in the English language.

A murder of crows.

CHAPTER
Eight

THIS WALK HAS JUST BECOME a horror movie, like *The Crow*, which I haven't seen, or *28 Days Later*, which I did see despite my aversion to zombies. I wasn't at all surprised that (spoiler alert) a crow carried the virus.

"You okay?" he asks as I freeze in place.

I'm struck mute, facts about crows swirling through my mind, each more terrifying than the next.

Crows are among the most intelligent birds. Yes. They are so smart that they can make and use tools, and what's more terrifying than a bird smart enough to do that? And it gets worse. They will eat just about anything, including human flesh, even rotting human flesh. Crows are commonly regarded as symbols of ill fortune in many cultures, and for good reason.

"Seriously, what's the matter?" Max clasps my shoulders and gives me a gentle shake.

"Let's go back," I choke out. I'm so rattled I barely register the fact that he's touching me with those big, strong hands of his.

"Sure."

Releasing me, he turns and I follow his lead—only it's too late.

Behind us, a lady is throwing bird feed on the ground, and a flock of pigeons is already attacking it. They have only a small window to feast before the crows notice and pounce.

Operating on pure instinct, I press myself against Max. "The birds. I don't like birds."

"Got it," he says, and wrapping one arm around my shoulders to hold me against him, he starts shooing away the crows.

"Don't be a hero, go for the pigeons!" I shout, but he isn't listening and keeps waving his free arm at the murder. Shuddering, I tell him, "They will remember your face and hold a grudge." At least I've read blood-chilling research to that effect.

If I were Max, I'd sleep with one eye open going forward and hope it doesn't get pecked.

The crows caw angrily, but my savior makes a sharp, caw-like sound, which finally scatters the murder.

I blow out a relieved breath. This reminds me of movies about spies who can do impossible feats, like making a bomb from a microwave, a donut, and a tampon.

"Let's go." Holding me pressed against his side, Max leads me through the area that the crows occupied just a second ago.

Then he releases me, and we run.

Crows caw angrily, and one even tries to dive-bomb

Max's head, but my savior proves his spy bona fides again with a few martial-arts-like moves that scare off the crows at last.

That's it. I'm investing in a hat with a scarecrow on it, assuming such hats exist. At least the crows' intellect and long memory could work in my favor this time. They might've just learned not to attack Max or anyone he's with.

Or so I tell myself in order to calm down as we slow to a walk.

"Want to watch model boat sailing?" Max asks, gesturing at the attraction ahead. He doesn't seem to be nearly as affected by the crow attack as I am.

I shake my head. "There might be ducks there, and I'm not recovered enough to face birds with genitals shaped like screws."

He lifts an eyebrow. "Maybe there's something you want to explain to me?"

I sigh. "Fine. But you'll make fun of me."

"I swear I won't," he says, pressing a hand to his chest.

Ahhh, those hair-dusted knuckles. He so knows how to push my buttons. Do I dare give him ammunition in case he needs to torture me later? Could he use it as kompromat?

Screw it. He's already seen how I react to crows.

I tell him about the Massacre, and he listens without a hint of amusement. If anything, he looks angry at the Zombie Tit on my behalf.

"So, since the Zombie Tit Massacre," I say in conclusion, "I've been afraid of birds and zombies, and I'm not a fan of the word 'tit.'"

He levels a hungry glance at my chest. "What term do you prefer?"

"Depends if they're big or small," I say.

He squints. "I'd guess B cup."

Damn. That's exactly right—assuming we're talking about mine. "I call them twins, but that's mostly to annoy certain siblings. To you, they're babushkas."

And that's how you catch a spy. He laughs, which means he knows that *babushka* is Russian for "grandmother." Right?

"Babushkas," he says, dragging his gaze up to my face. "I'll refer to them thusly going forward."

"Do that." I reach my hand toward his elbow, and he puts his arm in position for me.

As we resume walking, I say, "So, what were we talking about before the crows?"

He smiles. "What we do, where we went to school—stuff like that."

"Right," I say. I'm actually amazed he didn't take the bait and change the subject. Unless… is he eager to run his cover by me, flimsy as it is? "Whose turn was it to answer a question?"

"Yours," he says.

"Convenient."

He grins. "What was your favorite subject back in school? Or is that classified?"

"I can tell you which was the most mind-boggling." I squeeze his elbow. "Quantum computing."

"Quantum computers… They split computations between multiple universes, right?"

I really hope this question doesn't mean that Russia is working on this too. In class, we learned that mature quantum computing (which is not here yet) could become a threat to modern cryptographic algorithms. We also covered some algorithms that *could* withstand future quantum computing, but I'm not sharing that with him. In fact, I'm taking the conversation far away from here.

"Multiple universes is just one interpretation of the weirdness that is quantum physics," I say. "Do you personally believe they exist?"

There. No more talk about my education or work.

He slows slightly, which might mean it's his thinking tell instead of his lying tell. "Yes. I think there are infinite universes out there."

"You don't find that weird?"

He shrugs. "Why should I?"

"Infinite means that there's another Earth out there, with another version of us walking just like this—or one where we're talking crows." I shudder at the horrific image.

He chuckles. "Are we lovers in some of those universes?"

You sly spy. If the goal was to make me tingly—or *tinglier*—mission accomplished. "I bet in some, we are, and in some, we aren't. That's the problem with infinity. It allows crazy options, like a universe where you're a girl and I'm a guy with a very, very big dick. You like it rough, and we're really into doggy style."

He laughs. "I guess I like the universes where you don't have a dick. In this one, you don't, right?"

"I don't have a dick." I sigh wistfully. "But hey, that was an extra personal question, out of turn. Now you owe me two answers."

"I didn't realize this was quid pro quo. What would you like to know?"

"For starters, you have to tell me something you're afraid of," I say. "I told you mine."

What are the chances I get some kompromat on *him*?

He looks up at the nearby trees. "This isn't exactly a fear, per se, but when I was vacationing in Florida, I grew concerned about palm trees... or more specifically, a coconut falling on my head."

I spot a pigeon in the distance and take a turn into a shadier part of the park. "You're afraid of palm trees?"

That makes some weird sense. Russia is too cold for him to have ever encountered a palm tree there, so when he finally saw one for the first time, it must've looked like this exotic plant that he didn't understand—and people tend to fear that which they don't understand.

"It's falling coconuts, and I'm not afraid of them," he says. "My original concern was actually sharks, but I was told it was a non-issue, and that ten times more people die from coconuts falling on their heads than from shark attacks. I think they meant to make me fear sharks less, but I started to watch out for the palm trees instead."

Should I tell him how deadly birds can be? A kick from an ostrich can kill a lion. Can a shark or a palm tree do that? An ostrich once nearly killed Johnny Cash, and yet they're not the worst birds. Emus have claws that can eviscerate, bearded vultures know how to open their victim's bones to retrieve the marrow inside, and the clutching force of a great horned owl is enough to permanently disfigure, blind, or kill.

Yeah. No. He's better off fearing only docile palm trees, not the real evil that is birds. That is my burden to bear.

"You've got one more question," he says.

Do I dare ask him what I've been itching to?

Fuck it. As they say in his homeland, she who doesn't risk doesn't drink champagne.

I take in a deep breath and, as casually as I can, ask, "Where are you from?"

CHAPTER
Nine

"I was born in Edmonton, Alberta," he says. "That's in Canada, in case you—"

Canada again? That's what he's going with? Seriously? I get that it has weather similar to Russia, but that's the only—

"What about you?" he asks, bringing me back to the conversation.

"I was born in upstate New York," I say. "That's where my parents' farm is. But can we go back to your alleged Canadian origins?"

He quirks an eyebrow. "Alleged?"

"You haven't said 'eh' once," I say. "You're no more polite than most other guys, you haven't mentioned hockey during this walk at all, and last but not least, you haven't offered me any poutine."

"You seem to know a lot a-boot us Canadians, eh?" he says. "I think you forgot to ask me if I have Wi-Fi in my igloo, whether I ski or skate to work, what my favorite item is on the Tim Horton's menu, how severe my maple syrup addiction is, and last but not least, what the names of all my pets are—the polar bear, the moose, and the dogs I use for sledding."

I chuckle. He's done his homework, I'll give him that. "Growing up, did you know Justin Bieber or the two Ryans—Reynolds and Gosling?"

His dimple makes an appearance. "No, but I *am* a big fan of Celine Dion."

A guy liking Celine Dion? His cover could get blown by a puff of air during a glaucoma test.

Should I tell him how much Grandma Gia likes Celine Dion?

No. I have a better idea.

"Who is Celine Dion?" I say, doing my best to keep a poker face.

He stops and turns my way, eyes wide. "She's one of the best-selling artists of all time. Have you never seen *Titanic*? She sings the theme song."

"Ah." A devious smile lifts my lips. *"It's all coming back to me now."*

"Whew." He resumes walking. "You were joking. I almost had a heart attack."

"Sorry," I say. "I'm glad that *your heart will go on.*"

He chuckles again and points at the lake nearby. "Want to rent a boat?"

I squint at the lake. "Maybe. Depends on the duck situation."

Is he using my fear of birds to stop talking about his supposed homeland?

"Let's go check." Picking up his pace, he leads me as close to the water as we can get.

I scan the water.

No ducks, and the spot is extremely romantic too.

Why do I suddenly want something Canadian in me? Bacon, Max's Maximus... No. What am I talking about? Maximus, like his owner, is as Russian as Tolstoy.

As if reading my mind, Max turns my way, his eyes hooded.

I swallow hard.

Thanks to my Krav Maga training, I'm keenly aware of how close we are—just a few inches apart. A dip of his head and a rise onto my tiptoes, and we'd be able to kiss.

Both realizing this truth, we sway toward each other, drawn by the same force as Russians toward vodka.

My heart races madly. This is it. This is my first venture into femme fatale land. Fabio didn't tell me when to whip out the walnut-pleasing maneuver, but I figure it's not a first-date type of thing. A kiss is the classic first move in seduction. Speaking of seduction, who's seducing whom right now? Or is this the beginning of one of those duels of seduction from spy fiction?

When our lips are but a hair width apart, I hear it.

A horrific sound that is a hybrid between a honk and a bark, with an evil cackle thrown in.

I jump away from Max, spinning on my heel.

My gaze lands on the source of the sound, and my already overactive heart threatens to leap out of my chest.

No.

Please no.

But there can be no mistaking it.

It's the most aggressive and scary monster you're likely to meet, serial killers and Komodo dragons included. A truly insane creature that doesn't know the meaning of fear. Honey badgers with their crazy reputation have nothing on these terrible things.

Its mere name turns my insides into frozen goo.

The loud…

The terrible…

The goose.

CHAPTER
Ten

I BACK AWAY.

Max steps between us. As established earlier, the man is foolishly brave.

The goose flaps its massive wings and opens its crushing beak, exposing its horror-movie serrated tongue that looks like it's sprouted teeth.

Oh, and geese have something called *a nail* on their bills, and also boast real nails—or claws—on their webbed feet.

The beast shrieks again.

My skin breaks out in gooseflesh. No doubt this penultimate fear reaction got its name from a fateful goose meeting.

A dozen courses of action flit through my brain in an eyeblink, thanks to my martial arts training.

Play dead? No, that's what you do with bears—and if this were a bear, Max would just dance with it. Problem solved.

Run? No, these fuckers are famous for chasing

people. Trying to outrun one is futile—hence the expression "a wild goose chase." Plus, it wouldn't be cool to leave Max behind and all.

Jump into the lake? I think that only works with bees in cartoons.

What then? No eye contact, obviously. No sudden movements—not that I'd be able to make any if I tried.

Are there goslings nearby? These creatures can become especially murderous when protecting their young.

Crap. Did I summon this evil by mentioning Ryan Gosling earlier?

Also, this is definitely a Canadian goose—the least welcome export from Max's alleged birthplace. In fact, if Canada weren't a friendly country, I'd suspect them of genetically engineering these beasts as weapons of terror.

"Shoo," Max says.

Shoo? If he were really Canadian, wouldn't he know how ineffective that is? Surely, geese attacks are part of everyday Canadian life.

And indeed, the goose gets more agitated and rushes forward.

"Blue, stay behind me," Max says.

Yeah. You don't have to ask me twice.

The goose's beak opens again, its tongue looking like a nightmarish eel.

Moving with cobra speed, the goose flies up into the air for a second and pecks Max's eyes out.

Or at least, that's how it appears for a moment.

What the goose really does is snatch Max's tie, and then doesn't let go.

Holy shit.

Max now sports a goose-shaped necklace reminiscent of those giant clocks Flavor Flav wears—only from hell.

Why is the goose not letting go? Does it think it's a pitbull?

I can't even fathom how scared Max must be with the goose hanging off his neck.

Well. This is it. If I don't want Max to get choked to death, I must act.

Overcoming my paralysis, I grab a nearby rock. Only I'm still too scared of approaching the bird to get within head-bashing distance.

Maybe I could throw the rock?

No. This is like one of those hostage situations. I'm just as likely to hit Max as I am the goose.

Laughing, no doubt hysterically, Max pulls out a butterfly knife from his pocket and unsheathes the blade with a showy flick of the wrist.

Is this another clue as to his spy nature? Why would a corporate consultant carry an illegal knife and possess the skills to use it so expertly?

"Yes," I shout. "Stab it in the brain through the eye!"

Shaking his head, Max goes for a much less violent solution. He slices off his tie.

Landing with the tie piece in its beak, the goose looks confused for a second. I guess we got lucky, and this one isn't as inclined to dismember its victims as the rest of its kind.

Glaring at us, but unable to shriek without losing its hard-won souvenir, the goose takes flight, tie piece in beak.

"You think it will eat it?" I ask when I can speak again.

If so, is it mean of me to hope that it chokes on it?

"Maybe it'll be used to make a nest." Max turns and looks me over, his expression turning serious. "Are you okay?"

"I could use a Xanax."

"How about we go to the zoo here?" he says. "I find looking at a red panda to be an extremely soothing experience."

"I haven't been to this zoo," I say cautiously. "Do they have birds?"

He runs his hand through his sleek hair. "Parrots, I think. Maybe a peacock. Definitely a few varieties of penguins. We can avoid those exhibits, though."

"Okay, let's go there," I say, mostly in an effort to save face. I'm representing the American intelligence community, after all.

Still, it takes all my willpower not to tell him how I feel about the birds he's just mentioned.

Let's start with parrots. They are scary as fuck. They remind me of clowns—evil, Stephen King-style clowns of the avian world.

Penguins? There's a good reason that Batman's bitterest nemesis was the Penguin. They are openly evil. What's the most popular movie about them? *March of the Penguins.* Who else likes to march? Nazis. Who looks like they might correct your grammar? Penguins.

And don't get me started on peacocks, with their blood-chilling honor of being among the largest flying birds. They're also the most sexist bird—so much so that only the males are allowed to be called peacocks. The females go by peahens, or female peafowl, both pretty foul and derisive terms. But it doesn't stop there. A peacock will have up to five female partners, so it's not a surprise that a group of peafowl is known as a harem. Yep. The Ancient Greeks knew what was up. They believed that peacock flesh did not decay after death—as in, they thought these birds were zombies. Last but certainly not least, the fancy tails of these patriarchy-supporting birds contain microscopic crystal-like structures that reflect wavelengths of light that you don't even see. Do peacock tails shoot x-rays that give innocent people cancer? Nobody knows. Big Peacock doesn't want you to learn the truth.

Max reaches out and takes my hand, sending a jolt of pleasurable energy right into Captain, Sergeant, and my clit—whose codename is still classified.

If the idea was to take my mind off the birds and put it firmly in the gutter, mission accomplished. But I'm not just horny. I'm calm too. Who needs a Xanax and red pandas when you can hold the hand of a super-sexy Russian spy?

"Whose turn is it to ask questions?" he asks.

"Mine," I say. "Do you have any siblings?"

The more he tells me, the easier it'll be to penetrate his cover. What are the chances he was inserted into Canada with a gaggle of relatives?

Wait. *Penetrate. Insert.* Clearly, his hand and that

dusting of hair on his knuckles are overloading my brain with hormones.

He nods. "I have a big family. Three brothers and a sister."

I scoff. "Four siblings? You consider that a big family?"

He shrugs. "The average family size in Canada is 2.9 people."

Canada. Right.

"I have seven sisters," I say.

His jaw drops, so I tell him about my litter and the twins.

"And everyone is monozygotic?" he asks incredulously.

"Yeah. The twins, Holly and Gia, look like each other, and I'm identical to the other sextuplets."

"Do the twins look like you?" he asks, giving me a heated once-over.

"We share a lot of features, more than usual for sisters, I would say. How about you? Do you look like your siblings?"

"Some joke that my brothers and I are quadruplets, but we're not. Thankfully, my sister looks nothing like us."

I grin. "Let me guess, your sister is the youngest."

He nods.

"Your parents were going for a girl, right?"

"You got it."

"Mine tried for a boy and got six more girls," I say. "We were a case of assisted reproductive technology gone awry."

"I don't know." The heat in his eyes intensifies as he gives me a penetrating stare. "I think you're a case of assisted reproductive technology gone very right."

My cheeks burn. "No one has complimented me as a product of reproductive technology before."

He flashes a set of white teeth. "I aim to please. What was it like growing up with your sisters?"

I tell him, and he reciprocates with stories that aren't all that different. Throughout the exchange, I wonder if he really did grow up with a large family, or if it's purely a cover. He certainly gets a lot of details right, so at the very least, whoever wrote the script for his cover story must have a fair number of siblings.

I'm in the middle of a story about Gia's evil pranks when a couple walks up to us, holding a map. They're covered in sun protection that even Olive would find overkill: Darth Vader-esque visors, parasols, really big hats, long sleeves—you name it, they have it on.

"*Sillyehamnida*." The woman taps the map. "Where MET?"

Was that "excuse me" in Korean? I have minimal experience with that language. "Gangnam Style" and a few other K-Pop songs are about all the exposure I've had.

Smiling, Max launches into what sounds to me like fluent Korean—if that's what this language is. The tourists look as impressed as I am as he points at a spot on the map and, I presume, recruits them to be his sources in their home country.

When the tourists leave, he grabs my hand again

and resumes walking, like what happened was completely normal.

"What language was that?" I ask.

"Korean," he says.

Score. At least I identified it correctly.

I slow down. "So you just happen to speak Korean? If it were French, I'd be less surprised—you being from Canada and all."

He shrugs. "I wanted to be a diplomat, so I learned several foreign languages in my youth." He looks at me. "Do you only speak English?"

This is my chance. I watch his face closely as I switch to his native tongue and say, "No. I also speak Russian."

"*Da*," he says. "*Neploho*."

Damn. I thought he'd pretend not to know it, but he didn't. His pronunciation is just a touch off—unless that's a trick to make me think he's a Canadian speaking a language he's learned.

"What other languages do you know?" I ask.

"I don't like to brag."

I squeeze his hand. "Come on. Tell me."

He frowns.

Shit. Did I sound too insistent there?

"I've been meaning to ask you." He clears his throat. "I get that your work is classified, but... are you perchance looking into me for your job?"

This is what I get for playing twenty questions so persistently on the first date.

What the fuck do I say? I've been trying to be honest with him. On the minuscule chance that he isn't a spy and we end up married with children, I don't want any secrets weighing on us.

Well, if I answer this carefully, I will not lie. Making my face as earnest as possible, I say, "I'm not looking into you for my job."

It's true. I'm doing it more as a hobby, and as a way to maybe switch jobs in the future.

I can't tell if his exaggeratedly relieved exhale is a joke or not.

"We're here." He gestures at the zoo entrance. "How are you doing on time?"

I check my phone. "I'm good. You?"

He glances at his watch. "Sadly, this will have to be our last stop today. But I think we can see all the animals."

We proceed to do exactly that: sea lions first, then lemurs, then red pandas (which are as soothing as advertised), grizzly bears, snow monkeys, and finally, snow leopards. Afterward, we head over to the gift shop, where he lingers next to a display of stuffed snow leopards.

"Do they make you homesick?" I ask, nodding at the toys.

"Why?" he asks. "We don't have them in Canada."

It was worth a shot. I know perfectly well that snow leopards are found in the mountains of Central Asia.

"What about the bear?" I point at a teddy.

He shrugs. "We have grizzlies in Canada, but I've never really met one, so they don't make me homesick either."

Wow. It's admirable how earnest he looks as he

claims to have never met a bear. I bet he would've have looked just as earnest if he'd said he's never danced with one.

"Speaking of bears, did you like the red pandas?" he asks, gesturing at a stuffed white-and-black panda.

I teasingly wrinkle my nose. "They're okay. If you're into that sort of thing."

"You mean adorableness?"

I pick up the toy and examine it closely. "Well, for starters, red pandas have nothing to do with regular panda bears. They're closely related to raccoons, skunks, and weasels."

"Every creature you've just listed is insanely cute," he says.

"If you say so." I take out my phone and look up an image of a naked mole-rat. I shove it toward him. "Now here's a real cutie. I have no idea why they don't have a stuffed toy of it here."

He looks at the image with a grin. "I love animals, but that's a creature that's lucky to be nearly blind. Otherwise, they'd stop reproducing immediately."

"They actually have a unique reproduction process, with queens that mate with multiple males, and sterile females—a bit like ants and bees." I put my phone away. "Pandas are reluctant to reproduce. Does that mean they're hideous?"

He chuckles. "That's regular pandas, not red ones. Besides, they're cute too." He grabs the toy and show-cases it to me. "They only have trouble with reproduction in captivity—probably because they need that fancy mating ritual they do in the wild."

"I bet their small penises don't help," I say. "They have the smallest penises relative to their body size of all the animals on the planet."

"That settles it." He takes two stuffed pandas and walks up to the register. "I'll get one for me and one for you."

Aww. Warmth and cuddliness overload. When he hands me the panda, I clutch it to my chest. "It's no naked mole-rat, but I'll take it."

He glances at his watch. "I have to go."

"I get it." I cast a look around. We're indoors, so no geese, pigeons, crows, or any other horrors. Only me, him, and the gift shop clerk.

I close the distance between us with a single goal—to seduce. I'm not sure if I'll drag him into the gift shop bathroom and have my way with him there, or if I'll bribe the clerk to leave.

All I know is that any resistance to my wiles will be futile.

My voice is just the right amount of husky with a dollop of flirtatiousness. "I guess we'd better say our goodbyes… properly."

He steps into my personal space, his maple-lavender scent intoxicating. "We do owe ourselves a proper goodbye." He tucks a strand from my wig behind my ear, giving me a glimpse of the hair on his knuckles.

Damn, he's good.

By the time he leans down, I'm already on tiptoes, my lips needy.

He pulls me to him and expertly claims my mouth.

CHAPTER
Eleven

THE WORLD AROUND US DISAPPEARS.

His lips are soft, his tongue delicious.

Before I realize what's happening, my free hand is on his butt, but I don't go into his pants and look for his walnut... yet. In a duel of seduction against a formidable opponent, a girl needs to keep some cards close to her chest.

In the far distance, someone pointedly clears their throat.

Ignoring the distraction, I lose myself in the kiss again. Max's tongue is doing that Russian squat dance in my mouth, and I'm on the verge of a mouthgasm. This is the best kiss of my life, no ifs or buts. If I burst from joy, I'll die a happy woman. Fieldwork is even more amazing than I expected.

The throat-clearing gets pointier.

Max pulls away and readjusts what's left of his tie.

Panting, I level a death glare at the clerk.

Max's eyes look ravenous. "I'll be in touch."

Nooo. I'm not done seducing him. This will greatly delay those pillow-talk revelations, not to mention my femme fatale license.

Before I can do or say anything, he turns on his heel and leaves the shop.

I check my phone.

Still some time before Operation Saving Private Beaky. Maybe I can still learn a thing or two about my mercurial date. After all, what is this urgent business of his?

Yeah. Maybe I can catch him talking to his handler.

Teddy panda clutched firmly in my hand, I sprint outside and look for Max.

Whew. He's not far.

I use a nearby tree for cover as I wait for him to put more distance between us.

When it feels safe, I run over to the next tree, then the next. I don't care if my tradecraft is inspired by cartoons. Thus far, he hasn't spotted me, and I haven't lost him.

He leaves the park.

Crap.

I take off my wig and hope that's enough to disguise me. I've got to be more careful from here. If he catches me, I could be in big trouble. Spies have a policy not to leave witnesses alive—as seen on every episode of *The Americans*. You'll know what's coming if they ask you, "Have you told anyone what you've seen or heard?" At that point, you might as well kiss your life goodbye and give them a list of people you hate enough to want killed soon after you.

The good news is that New York is a crowded city, which makes it easy to stalk someone—a fact that's usually to a woman's disadvantage, but which helps me now. Still, next time, I'll need to bring a reversible coat and maybe a change of wigs to make this safer. If only those latex mask disguises from the *Mission Impossible* franchise were real... Unless they are?

My phone dings with a text.

I check it.

It's from Gia, and it's the details about her magic show later today.

No, wait. Can't get distracted.

When I frantically look up, Max is missing.

Ugh. How could I be so stupid? I guess stalking someone requires the same rules as going to a wedding or the movies—your phone must be off.

Wait. There he is. Across the street, sitting in a coffee shop.

Thank goodness I didn't lose him—and that I'm running this op on my own. If someone found out I'd almost lost my target due to a text, I would have to follow the spy tradition and eliminate them.

I dive into a salon right across the street from Max's location. Its front window is tinted with a mirror sheen that should make it hard to see me inside.

"How can I help you?" a lady asks me.

I scan the options: manicure, eyebrow wax, Brazilian, fish pedicure... Weird, I could've sworn Olive told me this last one was recently banned in NYC. Since other options involve nosy technicians, I go for the fish treatment anyway and vow never to tell my sea-life-loving sister about it. As the lady leads me to my fishy doom, I ask for a spot that faces the window.

When the special fishes attack my feet, it feels tickly, in a disturbing way. I sure hope no one lets them out into the wild. They now have a taste for human skin, and it would only be a matter of time before they started eating all the flesh from people's bones, like the piranhas used by the villain from *The Spy Who Loved Me*.

Max is still sitting there by himself.

Odd.

I take my phone out and start the camera app. This marvel of modern technology has a camera that can zoom in up to a hundred times—something even James Bond would envy.

With the phone aimed at Max, I'm able to see him clearly on the screen, and I'm glad. He's talking to someone without turning his head—a classic spy maneuver.

Fuck. Now I wish I had a device to overhear what he's saying, but alas, I do not. Hopefully, I'll be able to turn his phone into a listening device later.

Hey, at least I can see whom he's talking to.

It's a woman with her back to him, one wearing sharp business attire.

An annoyingly attractive woman who'd better be his handler or his mark and not, say, his girlfriend or wife.

I take a picture so I can research her later and make sure her last name is not Stolyar.

Am I jealous? No, that's ridiculous. This is purely professional interest. Besides, why would he talk to his wife or girlfriend in that way? They're clearly trying to stay on the down low. At most, they're having an affair, and she is someone else's wife. But hopefully, they have a platonic handler-and-agent or mark-and-spy relationship.

Or could I be mistaken entirely? What if they're both wearing a Bluetooth earpiece that I can't see and are talking to different people on the phone?

But no.

When the conversation is over, they both get up at the same time and go separate ways. What are the chances their phone calls ended in sync like that? Plus, I didn't see Max put in an earpiece.

Cutting the work of the man-eating fish short, I towel my feet dry, tip generously, and rush back home.

On the way, I get a notification from my contact at the FBI.

Olive's ex has been detained, so Operation Saving Private Beaky is a go.

CHAPTER
Twelve

WHEN I WALK into my apartment, my littermate is lying on the couch next to Machete, playing with her phone— and when I see the game on her screen, I wish I hadn't looked.

Its title is a nightmarish tautology: *Angry Birds.*

"Hey, sis." Olive locks her phone, sparing me from witnessing the massacre of innocent pigs and the vicious destruction of property that is at the core of the terrible game. I don't usually side with people who say video games are the reason for a rise in violence among young people, but if someone were to ban *this* game on those grounds, I'd be for it.

"Hey," I say.

She pushes Machete away and stands up.

He glares at her.

She snorts. "Your pet reminds me of that Grumpy Cat meme."

The glare turns deadly.

Screw you, Octopussy. Machete eats Grumpy Cat for

*breakfast. Then he assaults all cats who look like Hitler...
anally.*

Did that escalate too quickly?

"Ready to go?" I drop my wig and the gift panda on the coffee table.

"One minute." Olive proceeds to take ten minutes that feel like an hour to slather herself with sunblock. Then she puts on a long-sleeved shirt and grabs a parasol. "Ready."

————

"You're going to kill us." Olive lifts her sunglasses to give me a narrow-eyed stare. "The speed limit is twenty-five miles per hour, not twenty-five hundred."

I wink at her. "We have a limited-time window for the operation, and you used up a chunk of it on sun protection."

She jabs her finger at the windshield. "For the love of Cthulhu, look at the road."

I do as she says—just in time to avoid smashing into a yellow cab.

"Cthulhu?" I ask, my eyes now firmly on the road.

"A fictional cosmic entity from the writings of H. P. Lovecraft," she says. "It's supposed to be shaped like an octopus."

"Wasn't he—or it—also a giant humanoid... with dragon wings?"

She huffs. "I prefer to think of the Ancient One as predominantly octopus."

I shake my head. My sister doesn't just have an

octopus fetish; she's a marine biologist and loves sea creatures of all types, just not as much as she adores her tentacled favorites. Hey, at least she's not an ornithologist—a profession as dark and macabre as necromancy.

Unlike me, who discovered her calling as a spy later in life, Olive's obsession goes back as far as I can remember. One notable summer day, she peed repeatedly in a pool filled with the chemical that makes urine turn blue, while happily screaming, "I'm shooting ink."

For the rest of the ride, we play a game of *I spy with my little eye*, and I win, naturally.

"Pull over there," Olive says, pointing ahead.

I park.

"I'm driving back in my own car, praise Cthulhu," Olive mutters as she opens the door.

"You have a car?" I ask.

She points across the street at a white van. "I got it for Beaky."

Beaky needed a van? How large is this octopus?

Before I can voice my question, Olive and I enter the building. As we walk to the elevator, I get a text from my FBI friend:

The guy lawyered up, so we had to let him go.

"Shit," I say and explain the situation to Olive. "He might catch us. It might be safer to abort the mission for now and regroup."

Her crestfallen expression tugs at my heart.

"What if he hurts Beaky?"

I grit my teeth. "Fine. Wait here."

"No," she says. "You'll need my help. Plus, Beaky can be skittish with people he's never met."

I roll my eyes. "Won't he assume I'm you?"

She stands straighter. "Beaky is smarter than some humans. I'm going, and that's that."

I let out a long sigh. "I don't have time to make you see reason."

"Good."

I hurry into the elevator, and she follows.

When we get to her ex's floor, we sprint to the door.

Olive sticks her key into the lock and frowns as she tries to turn it.

I look around furtively. "Hurry up."

She stops messing around with the key. "I think he's changed the locks."

"Move over." I reach into my pocket and pull out my lockpicking kit. Gia has mastered this skill as part of her magician repertoire, and I had her teach it to me— along with safe cracking, which hopefully won't be needed for this heist, as I'm not as good at that as I am with locks.

"What's taking so long?" Olive asks just as I finally hear something give inside the lock.

I push the door in and give her an "are you kidding me?" look.

Olive doesn't seem to care. Diving into the apartment, she sprints through the living room so fast I have trouble keeping up. As I follow her, I can't help but notice a broken picture frame on the floor. The photo is one of Olive and a guy who must be the ex, Brett.

Did someone throw a hissy fit after my sister left? Now I'm doubly glad she *did* leave.

When I catch up with her in the bedroom, Olive is

standing next to a silvery dresser-like thing that houses one of the biggest aquariums I've ever seen.

An empty aquarium.

"Hi, sweetheart," Olive croons at the water.

That's it. She's finally lost it. If it weren't for the FBI and that picture I just saw, I'd start doubting the existence of the ex-boyfriend too.

Suddenly, what looks to be a rock turns into a giant cephalopod.

Startled, I draw back.

Though not exactly bird-scary—nothing is—Beaky is freaky. It's no wonder his kind inspired the looks of Cthulhu, the Kraken, and hordes of alien invaders.

I guess the rule is if it has a beak, it's officially nightmare-worthy.

"—and we're going to take you out of here," Olive says, making me realize I've missed the monologue she's just delivered to her dearest.

I examine the aquarium skeptically. "That looks like it weighs a ton. Maybe if Brett has his own pet, we steal it and do a prisoner exchange later."

"I told you, you need me." She gestures at the bottom of the dresser-thing, and I realize there are wheels there.

"That should help," I say. "Still, even with that, it looks heavy."

She leans down and grabs a little remote that was attached by a magnet to the bottom of the tank. "This thing is motorized. The only reason we'll need to push is to speed this up."

She unlocks a security latch on the wheels and activates the motor before she has me push as she pulls the contraption through the apartment. Even with the motor helping our manual labor, the thing moves slowly, and I worry her ex might catch us in the act.

"What about your other stuff?" I ask as we pass the living room.

"I don't care about anything but Beaky," she says. "I was going to get all new clothes anyway. Most of my shirts don't have enough UV protection."

I nod at what must be her ex's stuff. "Do you want to quickly ransack the place, like they do in spy movies? Brett would come back and shit a brick."

She shakes her head. "Not if it means I see his stupid face again."

Oh, right. Our time is limited.

"What's Brett's last name?" I ask, doing my best to sound casual.

She tells me, and I file it away for later. That broken picture frame doesn't sit well with me, so I plan to take some steps to protect my sister—steps she doesn't need to know about.

At first, Beaky seems to enjoy the ride—in that he floats around and examines everything. When he tires of that, he decides to fuck with me, or so I assume. What he really does is stare right at me with his slitty alien eyes. Eyes that seem to gleam with an other-worldly intellect.

When we enter the service elevator, I realize a problem. "This aquarium won't fit into my car."

She nods. "That's what my van is for."

Makes sense.

When we reach the van in question, Olive frowns—and when I see why, I curse under my breath.

Someone—and it's not hard to guess who—scratched the word "bitch" on the passenger door.

Eyes narrowing, Olive closely examines the aquarium lid where it locks in place. "Fucker," she shouts, shoving a hand through her hair. "He tried to get to Beaky too, but couldn't figure out how."

Looks like her ex's penis isn't his smallest organ. His brain takes that prize. Olive's side business is making puzzles for octopuses, as well as making sure they don't escape their homes—something they like to do, as seen in a documentary called *Finding Dory*.

"So," I say derisively, "I guess now we know Brett isn't smarter than an octopus."

"Not even close." Olive pulls out a ramp that was clearly designed for this aquarium on wheels.

As we push Beaky up the ramp, he spreads his eight legs threateningly and turns an angry red. At least I assume it's angry. For all I know, he might just be telling Olive he loves her.

Once the mobile aquarium is up the ramp, I snap a picture of the octopus—just as he changes his color once again.

"Okay," Olive says when Beaky is secured. "I'll see you there?"

I nod and head over to my car.

A text arrives on my phone just as I buckle up.

My heart begins fluttering.

It's from Max. He's sent me an image of the most adorable sleepy kitten I've ever seen, along with:

THIS is what cute looks like.

Grinning, I reply:

No. That's what LAZY looks like. Don't let that thing drive. If you want to see cute, check this out.

I attach the image of Beaky.

Max's reply is almost instant:

Thanks. I didn't need to sleep tonight anyway.

I reply with a smiley face, and he sends me a, *Let's make more plans soon.*

The giddiness I feel is ridiculous. You'd think I were a middle schooler sexting her first boyfriend.

As I turn on my car, all the excitement makes me wonder if the vehicle will explode. When it doesn't, I make a mental note to watch fewer spy movies. If someone starts a car in those, it's kaboom time.

Also, I need to get a grip on my emotions. Just because Max sent me a cute text doesn't mean he's any less of an enemy agent. In general, I need to be very careful in keeping my feelings toward him appropriate. He's the target of my femme fatale wiles, nothing more. Falling for one's mark—especially by an assassin—happens a lot in spy fiction, so I have to stay vigilant. Even if I wanted a boyfriend, which I don't, he sure as hell wouldn't be a Russian spy.

A potentially married spy. I still need to research the woman he was chatting with.

Also, am I sure he wants me? And if he does, would he still if he saw me without my wig? I don't exactly have time to grow out my buzzcut.

To keep my mind away from treacherous Max

thoughts, I practice the art of tailing someone using Olive's van as my target.

"Did you see me follow you?" I ask after we park and I walk over to her.

"You followed me?" Olive asks. "I thought you were going to reenact *The Fast and the Furious* again."

With an eyeroll, I help her wheel Beaky into my building.

When we enter my place, Machete eyes the aquarium with unabashed greed.

Finally. Fish. Machete will feast on its blood and brains.

As if he were waiting for a new audience, Beaky spreads his tentacles to make himself seem the size of a sea monster and changes colors a couple of times, his weird eyes hypnotizing my cat.

I didn't realize cats could go pale, but Machete comes close—which is odd, as he's never been scared of anything, not even giant cucumbers.

Machete is not afraid. Machete figures that fish is broken. Possessed by evil. It will make Machete's stomach hurt.

With a half-hiss, half-whimper, my tough-as-nails cat runs away with his tail tucked between his legs.

"Now I've seen everything," I say with a grin.

"Where do you want him?" Olive asks.

"The only place this tank will fit," I say. "The living room."

Maybe Machete will now cozy up next to the correct sister—the one who feeds him.

"Are you going to Gia's show?" Olive asks once Beaky's aquarium motor is deactivated and the wheels are latched.

Oh, right. That's soon. "Of course I'm going, but we should get dinner first."

We proceed to argue about the restaurant. I don't like the ones that serve a lot of poultry, and she's not keen on seafood. We settle on a steakhouse and get ready, or at least I do. She looks the same when I'm done.

"Like old times," she says, eyeing my wig.

I knew she would get a kick out of this. Back in high school, I colored my hair to match my name, and this navy-blue wig looks exactly like my hair did back then.

"Ready?" I ask her.

"One sec," she says and reapplies sunblock to her face. "You want some?"

"No, I've already applied mine," I lie.

Should I remind her it's after four p.m., and therefore, the UV index is almost nonexistent?

Nah. Not worth the lecture I might get.

We exit my apartment, but then she refuses to get into my car.

"What's the problem?" I ask.

"Let me drive," she says.

I purse my lips. "You break it, you buy it."

She shakes her head. "Even if I weren't broke, which I am, I wouldn't be able to afford this car."

"That settles that," I say, opening the door.

"Yep," she says. "We're taking my van."

I arch an eyebrow. "A van over an Aston Martin?"

"No," she says. "Surviving over crashing."

I slam the door and shlep over to the stupid van.

My phone dings with a text, and when I see who

sent it, my mood lifts dramatically, even though a part of me knows it shouldn't.

Lunch tomorrow? Max is asking.

Fighting a loony grin, I reply in the affirmative and ask him where and when.

Where is good for you? he replies. *And when?*

Does that mean his schedule is more flexible... like that of a spy?

Hmm, should I suggest a place near my work? Nah. I work in a building that's not publicly acknowledged to be my agency's headquarters. I mean, it's a windowless skyscraper that everyone suspects of being what it is, but nobody knows for sure, and I don't want to be the reason the secret gets out.

How about 1 p.m., I reply. *And you pick a place, either Downtown or Midtown.*

There. That should obscure things somewhat.

Deal, he replies. *Meet me at this address.*

The address he comes up with is almost perfect— just a quick cab ride away from my office.

When I look up from the phone, I catch Olive shamelessly reading off my screen.

"Who is Max?" She waggles her eyebrows.

I sigh. "Let me tell you on the way."

———

I'm still explaining all the details when we get seated in the steakhouse, so I take a quick break to order.

"I think you've finally watched one too many spy

movies," Olive says when I'm done. "What if he's just a guy?"

I sip my water. "He's not just a guy."

"But what if?" she asks.

I shrug. "In that very unlikely scenario, I might date him."

Of course, I dare not even hope he's just a guy. All the evidence points to the contrary.

She almost jumps up and down in excitement. "I knew it. You like this guy."

"No, I don't," I say, wishing I could convince myself.

"You liiiike him." Olive is clearly devolving back to our middle-school years—something my littermates tend to bring out in each other. If I don't act fast, she's bound to sing something along the lines of, "Blue and Max are sittin' in a tree. K. I. S. S. I. N. G."

"Enough about me," I say. "What are your plans?"

She reacts as if my question were an ice bucket to the face.

I instantly feel bad, so I say swiftly, "Mind you, you can stay with me for as long as you need."

I know the sea animal refuge she was working at recently went out of business, and she's been struggling to find a similar job in her field.

"I've applied to a bunch of jobs out of state," she says. "Now that I'm single, I can go anywhere, which really helps."

I gape at her. "You're leaving New York?"

The waiter comes with our food, and Olive waits to reply until we have privacy again.

"As much as I'll miss you and everyone, not to

mention this city, the jobs I need almost never open up here," she says.

I cut into my steak. "So where did you apply?"

"All over the country, but funnily enough, the most promising job posting was in Palm Pilot."

I grin. "Have you told them yet?"

She shakes her head. "I'll only tell them if I get the job."

Palm Islet—or Palm Pilot as we jokingly call it—is the town in Florida where our retired grandparents live. It's also the place where those of my siblings who can't afford a real vacation go when they want to take a break.

If Olive got this job, it would be perfect for her.

Well, almost perfect.

Florida is the "Sunshine State," and she's been over-concerned with UV protection recently.

I don't bring up this point, and not just to avoid raining on her parade. I'm a little scared to learn what all the sunblock business is about. I'm worried that if Olive explains it, I'll end up joining her in the dark. Avoiding the topic is my general strategy when my siblings develop strange quirks—and they seem to be prone to them. It's never something logical, like my perfectly understandable wariness of the killing machines that are birds.

Come to think of it, has Gia become as pale as a vampire from talking to Olive? She said it was for her stage persona, but it makes me wonder if—

"Earth to Blue," Olive says pointedly.

Crap. "Sorry," I say, and we return to our meal, only

to switch to the subject our litter cannot live without: gossiping about each other.

After dinner, we head over to Gia's show, and Olive gets behind the wheel again. When we pull up next to a giant hotel named The Palace, I frown.

Why does this name sound familiar? Have I seen it in some TV show? It's not just named The Palace; it looks like one too, so I can see why it might get featured.

We open the van doors, and a valet wrinkles his nose at Olive's keys.

Well, that's dumb. His generous tip has just shrunk.

As we head toward the front doors, it finally hits me.

The Palace is where my GPS gizmo marked the location of the Hot Poker Club.

This is awesome. Not only do I get to support my sister, but I can also snoop around after the show and learn more about the club.

Except when we step into the hotel lobby, I realize that I won't get the chance to snoop at all.

Or to see Gia's show.

Or to take another step.

Not with the horrors surrounding us on all sides.

Birds. Lots of birds.

CHAPTER
Thirteen

MY HEART RACES so fast my chest hurts.

The lobby is teeming with cages full of parrots that are shrieking like banshees hungry for blood. This is the one area where parrots are much worse than killer clowns. Since they're smaller, more of them can be crammed into a given space, and some suicidal sadist has done just that.

As bad as that is, it gets worse.

There are peacocks roaming free.

Countless peacocks, with those horrific tails open tauntingly, without a care for anyone they might hurt.

Knees weak, I take a trembling step back. Then another and another. Once I clear the doors, I turn on my heel and flee. At some point, I stop and attempt to even out my supersonic breathing.

"What the fuck?" Olive pants when she catches up with me.

"Birds," I grit out.

"Oh, right." She puts a hand on my shoulder. "Are you okay?"

I shake my head. "Please tell Gia that I'm sorry. I'm not going to make the show."

"Tell Gia?" She snatches her hand back. "You know what she does when she's upset?"

"Pulls pranks, I know, but what can I do?"

"Go to the show?" Olive ventures.

"Not this one. I'll go to another show of hers."

"I think this venue has given her a long-term show. There might not be another elsewhere."

I shrug. "I'll take Gia's wrath over birds any day."

Olive looks thoughtful. "How about you give me your wig? I can put it on and come talk to Gia as you after the show."

"Thank you, but no," I say. "If it were anyone else, I'd risk it, but Gia is tricky."

"You're right," Olive says. "Best not to risk it. Are you okay enough for me to leave you alone?"

"Yeah. Go."

She reluctantly leaves me be, and I head over to the sidewalk to hail a cab.

"Hey," a familiar voice says from behind me. "I think you're going the wrong way."

I turn and smile.

Only one person I know dresses like a pirate.

It's Clarice, Gia's magician roommate and my former poker instructor.

"I'm not going to the show," I say. "Not this time."

As she often does when nervous, Clarice pulls out a

deck of cards and begins playing with them. "How did your poker game go?"

Ah. I know what this is about.

"The game was amazing," I say. "I was going to text you the great news. I doubled my buy-in, which means I'll stake you. That is, assuming you still want to go after I tell you about the security precautions they take."

I describe the black bag over the head and the rest of it, but it doesn't dampen her enthusiasm in the slightest. I debate telling her she's going into the building where the game is to take place, but I decide against it—for her protection. Fewer people get killed for knowing too little than for knowing too much, at least in spy movies.

"I can't believe I'm going to the game." Clarice performs a super-fancy cut with the cards that must've taken a year of practice to master. "I don't know how to thank you."

I wink at her. "Half of your winnings will be thanks enough. Talk details tomorrow?"

She pockets her cards. "Yep. Now I'd better go catch the show."

"Enjoy."

She rushes off, and I grab a cab.

When I get home, I realize something retroactively horrible.

To bring me to the Hot Poker Club, the security team must've taken me through the lobby with the parrots and the peacocks. I was blindfolded, so I didn't know the danger I was in at the time, but I'm lucky to have survived.

Unless… they have a secret entrance into the hotel and brought me in that way.

Yeah. That must be the case. After all, other hotel patrons would look askance at someone being dragged through the lobby with a bag over their head. Also, I would've heard those parrot screams even in the earmuffs.

But wait, if there is a secret entrance, could I use it to get to Gia's show?

Nah. It's probably guarded. Plus, it's already too late. By the time I return to the hotel, the show will be almost over.

Fine. I guess I'm done for the day.

I turn on the light in the living room and catch Machete peering at Beaky from around the corner. Beaky stares right back with his otherworldly eyes, then makes what looks like a rude gesture with his tentacles.

The cat backs away.

Machete isn't running. Machete wanted to see if the fish is still broken, and it is. Machete refuses to eat it. Or look at it. Or be in the same room with it.

With a grin, I pour Machete's food into his bowl.

Yeah. That's right, little human. Magnanimous Machete will let you wake up one more day with your face uneaten.

Just as I'm about to head to bed, I get a text from Max. It's a picture of the cutest creature yet with a caption: *That's a bearded emperor tamarin.*

Is his evil plan to make me produce oxytocin by

looking at these creatures, so I associate the feel-good sensation with him?

Because it might be working.

That's a posh name, I reply. *Especially considering that the thing looks like a hipster monkey with an ironic mustache. If you want something cute, here.*

I do a quick search online and send him a picture of a lemur from Madagascar called an aye-aye.

Max replies with a face-screaming-in-fear emoji and: *If Nosferatu were a monkey and had spidery hands, that's what he would look like.*

Seriously, I need to watch my oxytocin production. Maybe I should get on Atosiban, a drug that inhibits said production. It's usually used to halt premature labor, but this could be an off-label spy usage—a bit like sodium thiopental, an anesthetic that some in the spy world use as a truth serum.

But no. That's probably overkill. Willpower will have to suffice.

Going to bed, I text him. *See you tomorrow.*

He replies right away:

Now I'm picturing you in bed. Sweet dreams.

Damn. Why am *I* picturing him in bed now? Or more precisely, us together?

Stupid Russian seduction schools. They've prepared Max a little too well.

With a sigh, I turn off my phone. I have an important decision to make.

To masturbate or not to masturbate—that is the question.

If I masturbate, I might think of Max while doing so,

which would be bad, but if I don't masturbate, I'll be more sexually charged when I see him tomorrow. Also bad.

I bet Hamlet's decision wasn't this hard.

No. Must not think of Max at all. Nor masturbate. Keeping him out of my mind if I did masturbate would be a feat I'm incapable of, like resisting an enhanced interrogation technique using birds.

Thus decided, I climb into bed and try to sleep, only to fail for a while. Eventually, though, Machete cuddles up to me, and his purring puts me under.

CHAPTER
Fourteen

THE NEXT MORNING, I walk into my work building.

To say it's not cozy would be an understatement. Besides being windowless, it's dreary and cold, but hey, it was built to withstand a nuclear blast, so I can cheer myself up with that factoid on a beautiful sunny day.

Like much to do with my job, I can't say more about the building because it's classified, but it might or might not have appeared in *The X-Files* episode titled *This*, as well as in season three of *Mr. Robot*, where it posed as the storage facility for Evil Corp.

Yeah. That last one was subtle.

When I get to my desk, a colleague—name classified —asks, "How was your weekend?"

The rest of the exchange is not classified but is so boring I'll be kind and strike it from the record.

When I log into **classified message software**, my boss—name classified—gives me some work to do, the details of which, you guessed it, are classified.

As often happens, I finish faster than my boss

expected. I'm good at my job. I just prefer field work to crunching numbers—or whatever my hypothetical and highly classified work happens to be.

I request that my boss give me another project to work on, and as I wait, I do something I shouldn't: I utilize work resources—most of them classified—for personal use.

I begin with the low-hanging fruit.

Using **classified**, I'm able to verify that one Max Stolyar did graduate from York University. Next, I look up everything else Max told me, like his being born in Canada and having four siblings.

Yep. All true. Then again, I didn't expect it to be otherwise. He wouldn't be a spy worth his salt if such basic info didn't check out.

I dare not dig deeper myself. Instead, I reach out to an expert on Canada, name classified, who owes me one. I make the subject line "Personal Favor" to make it clear this isn't official agency business.

The reply is quick:

Got a lot on my plate this week. Sorry. I'll get to this when I free up.

Sucks, but not unexpected. For now, there's something else I can try. Since I know Max's number, I use **classified** to get into his phone.

It fails.

I use **classified** instead.

Same lack of results.

I'm disappointed but not surprised. This is just another clue that he's part of the intelligence community. Getting access to our hardware is not as easy as a regular civilian's. If he tried to get into my phone, he'd fail too. Hopefully.

There are, of course, other methods I can use to force my way in, but that might give me away.

I'd better move on to something else.

Furtively looking around, I pull out a flash drive from my Faraday cage wig and transfer the photos I saved there to my work computer.

As soon as I'm done, I hide the flash drive back in my wig. Bringing recording devices of any kind is a huge breach of protocol, since that's how you get Snowden situations. Fingers crossed no one asks me about this on the next pop-up polygraph interview... Wait, are *those* classified?

I proceed to link the faces of all the men at the Hot Poker game I attended to their names, and then I do the same for the woman Max had spoken with.

Armed with the names, I learn more about these people, starting with the woman.

Odd.

She's an executive at JP Morgan. What does investment banking have to do with Russia?

No clue. Maybe she's involved in the financing of terrorism, or maybe this has to do with some conflict Russia is in? Didn't they upset Ukraine again the other week?

Alternatively, Max could've set this whole thing up as a ruse. Maybe he knew I'd follow?

Nah. I'm being paranoid.

The other possibility—that the meeting with her was

personal—is also still on the table, and I hate how much it bugs me.

To distract myself, I look up the Hot Poker Club men. After all, one of them seemed to be Max's target.

I start with the only unattractive player and learn that he's an owner of an oil company.

Could Russia be interested in him?

Unlikely. They have plenty of their own oil.

The next guy—the one who built a sculpture from his chips—is named Bogdan Velik and doesn't have a listed occupation. Could he be a professional poker hustler? I'll have to ping my FBI contact to see if they know.

Another guy turns out to be an owner of a hedge fund. Would Max care about him? Maybe this fund trades in Russian stocks?

Then there's the real estate magnate. Was he the one Max was after? Maybe Russia wants to invest in some prime Manhattan property? But why do it secretly?

Hmm. Maybe this next guy was Max's target. He's the CEO of a biotech company. It doesn't seem like the company makes anything that can be weaponized, but you never know what Russia might find interesting. For all I know, they're looking for a drink that's stronger than vodka—or for the ultimate cure for hangovers.

The next person I look up is Sloppy Stack, whose real name I don't bother to memorize because he will always be Sloppy Stack to me.

Interesting. Sloppy Stack is a software engineer. Not exactly a job that pays well enough to be at that game. Could he be Max's target?

I check **classified** and see that Sloppy Stack's software company makes trading platforms, which isn't something Russia would be interested in.

I send all the names I've discovered to my FBI contact—in part to see if I can learn more, but also to give my actions more legitimacy in case I'm caught. Agencies collaborating sounds good; a rogue employee snooping around on her own, not so much.

The next bit I have no excuse for, so I doubly hope I don't get caught doing it. Using **classified**, I locate Brett's phone and put a tracking app on it. Now I'll get an alert if he comes within fifty feet of Olive—or more specifically, her phone.

Last but not least, as payback for scratching Olive's car, I arrange it so that he'll get audited by the IRS next year.

Crap. It's already lunchtime.

I'm about to sign out when I get a message from my FBI contact.

It's info on Bogdan, the guy who built a sculpture from his chips. The FBI thinks he's the organizer of the Hot Poker Club. Also, I'm strongly advised not to get on his bad side. According to an informant, this guy has a reputation for being extremely dangerous.

Is he the one whose phone Max wanted to bug?

No, doubt it. Why would the person who runs the club keep his phone in a locker? It would be in his office or someplace like that.

My heart skips a beat as I think back to that night. If this Bogdan really *is* dangerous, Max could've gotten hurt.

Speaking of Max, I'm going to be late for our lunch.

———

Running out of my building, I jump into a cab and rattle out the address Max texted me.

The cab drives too slowly, making me wish I'd taken my car today. The reason I decided not to is that my work building is in walking distance from my apartment, and Manhattan parking can be a real headache.

To kill time, I videocall Gia.

"Hey, sis," she says.

"Hey. I'm very sorry."

Gia clears her throat. "What are you sorry about this time?"

Is this a trick? Probably. Gia's whole life is.

"There were birds in that lobby." I do my best to sound as apologetic as possible.

"You missed the show?"

Fuck. She didn't know?

Also, why does she sound guilty instead of pissed? This has to be a trick.

"I'm sorry," I say. "I couldn't enter. It would be like you going into a hospital. If you perform anywhere else, I'll be there, I swear."

"Actually, I'm the one who should be sorry," Gia says. "When I go into that lobby, I always think about how much you'd hate it, but when I invited you, I totally forgot."

I gape at her. Seriously, is this a trick?

"Still," I say cautiously. "I should've overcome it, for you."

Gia's smile is devilish. "I appreciate your honesty. It just so happens I'll have a show in a different venue soon, and I could use friendly faces in the audience. You're coming to that, right?"

I can almost hear the "or else."

"I'll be there," I say solemnly.

"Good," she says. "And we should get together so you can repay the favor you owe me."

I forgot about that. No wonder she's so forgiving. She still needs me alive.

"Whenever you want," I say.

"I'll get in touch with the details. Both for the show and the get-together."

"Right." I switch to a form of Pig Latin I developed when we were kids—my first cryptography-related accomplishment. The idea behind it was to speak secrets in front of our parents, but it will also keep the cab driver out of the loop. "I was wondering… how did you get that venue? The Palace, I mean?"

"Why?" Gia asks.

"The Hot Poker Club is in the same hotel."

Is that shocked silence?

"No way," she says.

"Yes way."

"Well, I got the show because that hotel belongs to my boyfriend's brother."

"Is the brother's name Bogdan Velik?" I ask.

"No," she says. "His name is Kazimir Cezaroff, or Kaz for short."

Right. She mentioned this when she told me about her new beau. I just didn't remember the name of the hotel.

"Who's this Bogdan then?" I ask.

"Not sure. I'll ask, though."

"Thanks. When you find out, let me know."

She says she will, and I hang up. I dial Clarice next, and we arrange everything so she can join the Hot Poker Club at her convenience.

"Can I do it soon?" she asks.

"Your call."

"I don't want to step on your toes," she says.

"I'm not going there again. They're all yours."

She chuckles. "Thanks."

I warn her against messing with Bogdan while she's there and hang up as the cab pulls up to the curb.

I stare at the sign of the restaurant Max picked.

Сало.

Written in English letters as *salo*, that's a Russian word for a dish that, as I understand it, is pure animal fat—as in lard. Allegedly, it goes well with vodka on a cold day. I guess if you want to make sure you die of a heart attack before your liver gives out, it's the perfect dish.

I can just picture the Russian inventor's thought process as he was coming up with this delicacy. Americans eat bacon? Pussies. Bacon has *some* meat in it. Being Russians, we'll get rid of any meat. They fry theirs? We'll eat ours raw, or cure it at best.

Does this mean this is a Russian restaurant?

When I step inside, I hear voices speaking in what

sounds like Russian, and the faces of the servers share Max's Slavic features.

What the hell? Does Max have zero faith in my abilities to see through his soap-bubble-thin cover? Or is this some weird reverse psychology?

Maybe he hopes I'll fall in love with the food and want to defect to Russia?

"Hi," a familiar deep male voice says from behind me.

CHAPTER
Fifteen

I turn and almost gasp.

It's only been a day, but I already forgot the full effect of Max's proximity.

I'm not sure about Russian food, but that hair and those lips might just have a chance at making me turn.

He comes closer.

My heart rate speeds up.

Are we about to kiss again? It wouldn't be very conducive to keeping my wits about me, but—

A waitress steps between us, her blinking eyes glued to Max. Coquettishly, she rattles out something in Russian while I fight the urge to put her down with a Krav Maga kick to the liver.

At least I think she's speaking Russian. It sounds a little off. Maybe she's not fluent?

Max steps back before walking around her to take my hand. "Any table is fine," he says in English as tingles run up my arm from where our palms are touching.

The waitress glares at our joined hands, then plasters on a fake smile as she seats us by the window. Without saying a word, she slaps a menu into my hands and gives Max his in a gentler fashion.

"Do you know her?" I ask when the waitress leaves.

"Not by name, but I've seen her before. I know everyone here. I come here all the time."

A Russian restaurant where he comes all the time.

It's like he's taunting me with his Russianness.

"Do you work nearby?" I ask.

He shakes his head. "It's just a place I frequent when I feel homesick."

Okay, there's not trying, and there's that answer. What's his game? Maybe I should just openly ask him if he's a Russian spy at this point. Is that what he wants?

Tired of being confused, I glance at the menu. It's English on one side and Russian on the other.

Borscht, salo—obviously—and *blini*, all Russian cuisine staples.

But hold on. Is that actually Russian on the menu? Some dishes have the lower case "i" in their names. That's not a letter that's in the Russian alphabet. Also, are potato pancakes a Russian dish?

"Do you want me to order something for you?" Max asks, probably misunderstanding my expression.

"What cuisine is this?" I ask.

He shows me his dimple. "Ukrainian. Have you ever had it?"

Ukrainian?

Russia and Ukraine aren't exactly on good terms. Is that the subtle angle he's playing?

I decide to just go for it. "Why does Ukrainian food make you homesick?"

If he tells me that borscht has replaced poutine as a traditional Canadian dish, I'll just flat out accuse him of being a spy.

He puts down his menu. "I'm a Ukrainian Canadian."

"Huh?" is my genius reply.

"My parents immigrated to Canada from Ukraine. It was part of the USSR at that time."

"Oh." I'm on a roll with the witty repartee.

"Ukrainians are Canada's seventh-largest ethnic group. There are more than a million of us."

How come I've never heard this? It must be true, though. He wouldn't drop a statement so easily verifiable otherwise.

I take back all my earlier digs at his cover. It turns out to be devilishly clever. With this one twist, he has an explanation for his Slavic facial features, his ability to pronounce soft consonants, and his cravings for borscht.

"Huh," is my latest pearl of conversation.

"Yeah. We have a lot of parallels with Italian Americans," he says. "Did you know they're also in seventh place in the US?"

I shake my head.

"It's true. And like them, we maintain the traditions from our home country, especially when it comes to food." He lifts the menu. "That's why, when you said we could eat anywhere, I chose this place. Is that okay?"

"Of course," I say, glad to have finally recovered my wits. "I like trying new things."

He gives me a heated once-over. "That's good. I think you should give Ukrainian a try."

Gulp. Why am I picturing something other than food entering my mouth? Something with the noble name of a gladiator.

I clear my strangely dry throat. "To circle back to your earlier offer, please order something for me that you think I might like."

"Good choice, *sonechko*," he murmurs.

I turn my menu over. "What does *sonechko* mean?"

"It's Ukrainian. It means the sun."

Resist. Swoon. Overload.

The waitress comes back.

Max animatedly talks to her in what I now know is Ukrainian. On occasion, I can make out a word or two, like *borscht, salo,* and *holodets*.

As they talk, I ponder if he could be a Ukrainian spy instead of Russian. Their intelligence agency is called the SBU, and it has a checkered past when it comes to Russia. Initially a branch of the KGB, the SBU was deeply infiltrated by Russian spies after Ukraine became independent. That means that even if he *is* a Ukrainian spy, he could also be a Russian double agent. Or not. A few years back, they cleaned up shop and now claim to have much stricter protocols to prevent infiltration, going so far as to regularly perform loyalty tests via interrogations and lie detector tests.

Either way, a foreign spy is a foreign spy.

The waitress leaves, and I decide to subtly probe him for spy knowledge.

"What kind of movies do you like?" I ask.

Before he can answer, the waitress comes back and puts two bowls of dark red soup in front of us.

Borscht. Of course.

"I don't have a specific genre I like," he says. "But all of my favorite movies have animals in them. In case you didn't pick up on it, I really like animals."

Is there a correlation between liking animals and being an animal in bed?

Asking for a friend.

"You didn't hide it too well," I say. "Which is your favorite? *The Jungle Book*? *The Lion King*?"

He dips a wooden spoon into his borscht. "You'll make fun of me, but my favorite movie is called *Max*. It's about a war dog."

Is this a clue? Would a spy see himself in a stressed-out war dog?

"Me, make fun of you? I'd never." I fan myself. "Just because that sounds super-narcissistic doesn't mean it's funny. Right?"

In his defense, if there were a spy movie with a lead named Blue, it would be my favorite also.

He grins and brings a spoonful of soup to his mouth. "What about you? What kind of movies do you like?"

Jackpot. "Spy movies," I say, watching his reaction.

He doesn't flinch. Instead, he swallows the borscht and closes his eyes in pleasure.

Fine. Two can play this game.

I take in a spoonful of borscht—and then spit it out, instantly.

Borscht is supposed to have beets, potatoes, cabbage, and so on, but the main, and maybe the only, ingredient in this one is garlic.

Enough garlic to kill every vampire in Transylvania and Sunnydale combined.

"What's wrong?" Max asks.

"Too little borscht in my garlic," I croak out.

He frowns. "There's almost no garlic in mine."

Is he insane?

He tries my soup, and his frown deepens.

Waving over the waitress, he speaks to her sternly. She looks innocent when she replies to him, but when she darts a glance at me, I'm certain she was the one who tossed all the garlic into my borscht.

After she grabs my bowl and leaves, I say, "Maybe we get another waitress. I think she might like you too much not to add rat poison into my next portion, along with some spit."

He puts his borscht in front of me. "I have a better idea."

He waves at the waitress while I give the soup a taste.

Wow. The savory deliciousness of it almost makes me moan out loud.

What did they do to these beets? Massage them and give them beer, like the Japanese do with Kobe beef?

The waitress comes over and looks at the plate switcheroo with concern.

"Before you bring out the next dish, I wanted to

remind you that I'm good friends with the owner," Max says to her in English. "Also, we'll be sharing everything going forward."

She pales. I guess she wants to keep this job.

I'm certain now that the garlic was her doing and not some snafu in the kitchen. Was she trying to sabotage our post-lunch kiss? I've heard of women who feed their husbands garlic to make sure they don't cheat, but to do this to a female rival is a new level of deviousness.

Damn it. How will I kiss him now?

I decide I have to retaliate.

"Thanks." I move Max's soup over to his side. "Why don't we share it, like you said?"

He grins and picks up his spoon.

I sneak out my phone from under the floor-length tablecloth.

The apps I'm about to use are not classified because I made them on my own. They're probably illegal, though, so the less said about them, the better.

First, I get onto the local Wi-Fi for guests, and from there, onto the restaurant's private network.

People like me are the reason using public Wi-Fi isn't secure.

Only a small number of devices are hooked up to this network, and even fewer of them are phones. I jump onto the first phone—nope, a guy's name. I get on another. Female. Good. And has social media apps installed. Even better.

I run the Twitter app first.

Yep. The profile picture is that of the waitress. I'm inside her phone, as intended.

Mysteriously, her next tweet is the following, in English and then Google-translated into Ukrainian:

I just pooped my pants again!

This very informative info becomes an update on her Facebook profile as well.

"Your turn." Max moves the soup back.

I hide my phone and eat another spoonful.

So good.

I give it back to him. "Is there a difference between the Russian and Ukrainian borscht recipes?"

"I'd say there's a little difference in every family recipe." He swallows another spoonful with relish. "The reason I like this place is how close their recipe is to my mother's. Hers is just a tiny bit thicker."

What are the chances his mom has the recipe stored in a digital form that I can steal? Then I could make this for him. Seduction through the stomach isn't something I've seen movie femmes fatales do, but why not?

The waitress is back. She's carrying another borscht. Looking confused, she puts it in the middle of the table.

Max grabs it first and tastes it pointedly.

"Thank you," he says, looking up.

As she starts to walk away, she pulls out her phone and her eyes widen.

I open a translation app on my phone and type in, "Like you, karma can be a real bitch." Then I make the app say that out loud in Ukrainian.

She turns my way, her eyes even wider.

"Oops," I say. "This translation app is clearly incompetent. I wanted it to say, 'Thank you for being so accommodating.'"

With a huff, she turns on her heel and storms away.

"What was that about?" Max asks.

I shrug. "Someone seems to have a bigger crush on you than we initially thought."

He pushes the new borscht my way. "I don't care what she thinks."

Great answer. He gets to live.

"What were we talking about before?" I ask, curious if he'll dodge the topic of spy movies, for obvious reasons.

"You said you like spy movies," he says. "Do you have a favorite?"

Bold.

I tell him about the shows and movies that I love, perhaps a little too passionately.

A male waiter comes over, holding two plates. "Since you have an English speaker in your party, I was asked to take over your table."

Sure. That's why. Not because that waitress is pooping her panties in fear (again?) thanks to yours truly.

When the guy leaves, I check out the new entrée. It looks like pancakes. Must be those potato ones I saw on the menu. I taste one.

Yum.

"What's the most realistic element you've seen in a spy movie?" Max asks. "Without going into anything classified, of course."

I chew my pancake thoughtfully before I say, "Numbers stations."

I watch his reaction again, but his poker face makes it impossible to gain any advantage this way.

"Numbers stations," he repeats.

"Yeah. You know what those are?"

How bold is he?

"Aren't they radio stations that broadcast a bunch of numbers?" he asks. "For intelligence officers operating in foreign lands, right?"

I nod. Bold indeed. That's exactly what they are— and the fact that he knows this means he uses one... unless he doesn't use one and this is a red herring that he's throwing my way. With spies, you have to watch for plots within plots.

The waiter comes back with something new, a breaded round shape that looks fried.

"What's that?" I ask when he leaves.

"Not sure if the best analogy would be a burger or a patty," Max says. "It's made from chicken and is in Kiev-style, which means it has melted butter in the middle."

I pull away from the table. "Did you say chicken?"

He looks at the thing and winces. "Afraid so. I didn't realize your dislike of birds extended to culinary preferences. I figured you might actually enjoy eating them as revenge."

I shake my head vehemently. "Think tarantulas. Flying ones that can peck your eyes out. Would you eat a tarantula?"

"Say no more." He hails the waiter and the dish is taken away.

"Oh, I didn't mean for *you* to miss out," I say.

His dimple peeks out. "I don't want you to be grossed out by me later."

Fuck. He's open about his plan to kiss me. Best distraction from a cooked bird ever.

I moisten my lips. "If anyone will be grossed out, it'll be you. Remember all that garlic?"

He looks at my lips hungrily. "Don't care."

Check, please.

The waiter comes back and sets down a plate that has bread and a chunk of lard on it—salo. He also provides two shot glasses, which he fills with a clear liquid that looks like vodka.

"That's *horilka*," Max says. "Are you okay having a drink at lunch?"

I nod.

He slices a piece of salo, puts it on a piece of bread, and delivers that to my plate. He then does the same for himself and raises the glass. "Watch out—this one has chili peppers in it."

I raise my glass. "I'm sure I can handle it."

"*Budmo!*" He downs the drink.

"Cheers." I swallow mine.

Holy fucking burn. If he hadn't warned me about the chili peppers, I would think the evil waitress was at it again.

Why would you take vodka, a drink that already burns, and add capsaicin to it? Are Ukrainians masochists? Are they trying to create the feeling of herpes, but full body?

Max bites into his salo sandwich, so I do the same.

It helps.

A little.

I think I get the idea behind horilka now. If you want to stomach a piece of lard, you need to burn out your taste buds first.

Max covers my hand with his large one. "Thoughts?"

His touch matches the burn in my belly, and the warmth of the alcohol spreads through my every cell, settling in my core—and I'm not sure if this is Max's influence or the horilka.

How strong is this drink? Eighty proof? I'm instantly feeling a buzz.

"I'm getting a taste for Ukrainian." My voice is hoarse, and not just from the horilka.

The waiter comes back with another dish.

Max pulls his hand away. I miss it instantly.

The new item is stuffed cabbage rolls called *golubtsi*, and I discover that I'm a big fan of them, especially when I add a dollop of sour cream as instructed.

"Do you have any pets?" I ask when I recover from another mouthgasm.

"Sadly, no."

So he likes animals but has no pets? I guess it's hard to keep them with the busy schedule of a spy. That or he's trying not to have too many attachments.

"How about you?" Max asks.

"I have a cat." I get my phone out and pull up a picture of Machete.

He grins. "Very cute."

I'm glad Machete isn't here to claw his face for such an insult. "Fierce, you mean."

133

"Of course." He smiles.

I grin. "I also currently have an honest-to-goodness octopus at my place. Remember the picture?"

"Seriously?"

"Yep." I pull up the image once more and show him. "His name is Beaky."

He shakes his head. "Now I really want to visit your place and see him. And your cat."

Sure. Visit my place to see my pussycat... not my pussy.

I clear my throat. "Beaky is my sister's pet. She's crashing with me for the moment." As in, if any hanky-panky were to transpire, your place would work better.

His gaze is heated. He's caught my drift. I bet he's about to—

The waiter comes back.

Nooo. Max was just about to come up with some excuse for me to visit his place. I'm sure of it.

A dish is placed on the table.

I blink at it. And blink some more.

It's Jell-O, but unlike any I've ever seen in my life, and I thought I'd sampled them all—all colors and flavors, with and without fruit inside. Even Jell-O shots.

This one has meat in it. And carrots and celery—you know, things everyone associates with Jell-O.

The waiter also puts a side dish consisting of a reddish-purple paste on the table. Clearly something with beets. And why not at this point?

Max points at the meat Jell-O. "That's *holodets*." He then gestures at the paste. "And that's *hren*, a horse-radish that goes really well with it."

I keep my doubts to myself. I'm hoping that if I eat this, he'll get back to the topic of inviting me to his house.

"Should we have another shot?" I ask.

I need liquid courage to eat this holodets thing.

He looks at his watch. "I have a meeting soon, but one more shot should be okay." He gestures at the waiter and says something about horilka in Ukrainian.

Before I know it, we have two more shots in our hands.

"Let me service you." Max places the meat Jell-O on my plate and adds some horseradish on the side.

Service me? I know he's talking about the table chivalry that Russians—and I guess Ukrainians—are known for, but I can't help hearing the dirty version.

"*Budmo.*" I grab my shot and down it in a single go.

"*Hey.*" He downs his.

Even expecting it, I still feel like a dragon just gave me mouth to mouth.

He eats a piece of holodets covered in the beety horseradish, and I follow his lead.

Oh, come on. The garnish is wasabi-strong and makes the burn triple.

Desperate, I eat a chunk of meat Jell-O plain.

Whew. I think I can breathe again.

The dish isn't as bad as I expected. Reminds me of soup. A cold, very thick soup with a gelatinous texture that melts when you put it in your mouth. Also, very garlicky, so hey, we both have garlic breath now.

Why does even that not make me any less horny? If anything, I'm getting hornier by the second. Not masturbating last night was a tactical error, one that every femme fatale rulebook warns you about.

"Do you like Ukrainian cuisine?" Max asks.

There. I bet if I say yes, he'll invite me over for dinner with an offer of "getting more Ukrainian into me."

"Love it." My words come out husky, a total femme fatale move.

"I'm relieved," he says. "I was worried that the chicken thing ruined it."

Grr.

Where is my invite?

It might be time to take matters into my own hands and activate full-on femme fatale mode. Or rather, given the idea I have, to take matters into my own feet.

Scooting my butt to the edge of my seat, I toe off my shoes.

My heart picks up pace.

Am I bold enough to do this?

Buzzed enough?

Don't care. Going for it. With the thick tablecloth, no one will be the wiser—and Max will finally fall into line.

Gently but decisively, I sneak my left foot to his calf and run it up his thigh before placing it on his crotch. Playing coy footsie is for virgins, nuns, and IRA agents. A femme fatale CIA agent doesn't mess around.

She goes directly for the dick.

CHAPTER
Sixteen

I MOVE my foot until I feel it.

Hardness.

Major hardness.

Wow. Either Maximus is as big as the name would imply, or my foot isn't good at gauging size.

Max's eyes widen.

Bingo.

I stroke Maximus up and down.

Eyes darkening, Max reaches out and places his hand over mine.

There we go.

I wiggle my toes.

His breath audibly catches. Leaning forward, he says huskily, "Touch yourself."

So bossy.

I love it.

I scan my surroundings. No one seems to be paying any attention to us.

Sliding a little farther down, I sneak my right hand

into my soaking panties and nod at Max to let him know I've obeyed his command.

His eyes go beastly.

My left foot tap-dances on his dick.

His nostrils flare, and Maximus feels on the verge of hulking out of Max's pants.

My clit is oversensitive to the touch, my folds slippery. I move my fingers faster as an orgasm begins to build in my core. Sliding lower still, I pull my hand from under his so I can grab onto the corner of the table. Then I reach up with my other foot and grasp Maximus on both sides, monkey style.

Max sucks in air and leans forward again. His voice is a low, deep growl. "Will you come for me, sonechko?"

I nod and mean it.

I'm close.

So close.

Speeding up, I squeeze the edge of the table until my knuckles go white.

He grunts approvingly.

Does that mean he's close too?

I slide down a tiny bit more so I can grasp Maximus from—

A strong scent of garlic hits my nostrils as a waiter passes close to our table, holding a plate.

When I see what's on it, my blood chills.

It's a small bird that someone crucified for some unthinkable reason. At least that's what it looks like.

The uncanny sight breaks my concentration—and my butt slips off the edge of the chair.

Everything happens at once.

I try to get my hand out of my panties, but no luck.

My free arm flails, but it doesn't grab the table in time.

Yelping, I crash hard, landing on my butt as one of my feet squishes Max's balls and the other kicks him in the dick.

CHAPTER
Seventeen

MAX'S FACE turns a shade of green that almost matches his eyes, and a pained grunt escapes his throat.

Oh my God. Did I break his dick?

My ears are ringing, and my coccyx bone feels like it's gotten a horilka injection.

Before anyone can bust me for public masturbation, I finally jerk my hand out of my pants. Clutching the edge of the table with the clean hand, I prop my other hand on the floor and pull myself halfway up, only to nearly fall again because the floor hand is slippery—for reasons.

This is when strong hands pick me up.

The waiter?

No. It's Max.

How is he moving after what I've just done to him?

In Krav Maga, we learn how to devastate an attacker as brutally as possible, and the cornerstone move for that is the groin kick, which is essentially what I did to him.

Yet he's helping me up.

Must be another clue about his spy origins. In *Casino Royale,* James Bond's balls get brutally tortured. Did that scene give someone an idea to train their operatives to withstand that?

Hopefully not. Hopefully, I didn't hurt Max's balls or dick at all. I still have big plans that involve them.

"Are you okay?" he murmurs, settling me on my chair.

"Me?" I leap to my feet. "Are you okay?"

He glances down. His voice is a bit hoarse, though his face is less green. "I'll be fine."

"Everything all right here?" the waiter asks.

I turn. He's still holding the crucified atrocity on the plate.

"What is that?" I ask in horror.

"In English, you'd call it *chick tobacco*," the waiter says. "We press the chicken like a panini and fry it with garlic and spices."

This chick could use a smoke after seeing it, that's for sure.

"Can we please get the check?" I say, averting my eyes.

"What about dessert?" the waiter asks.

Shaking my head, I slide my feet into my shoes.

"Next time." Max throws some cash on the table and helps me out of the place.

Crap. He's not fine. He's walking as if I've pleasured his walnut a little too enthusiastically. If I had a femme fatale license, it would officially be null and void after that so-called seduction attempt.

"Seriously, are you okay?" Max asks.

"Seriously, are *you*?"

"I'm fine." He shifts from foot to foot. "I do think I should head over to my appointment now. Maybe grab some ice on the way."

"I'm sorry." I resist the urge to say I'm willing to kiss it and make it better.

"Nothing to be sorry about." He kisses me on the forehead. "I'd better go."

And just like that, he's gone.

CHAPTER
Eighteen

A KISS on the fucking forehead? After my feet had a BDSM orgy with his dick and balls?

Unless... maybe he's avoiding a passionate kiss because it would majorly arouse him—as only a kiss with me could—and thus hurt his damaged privates?

That had better be it. I'd hate to think I blew this. Or *blue it*, as my siblings would tease.

Well, whether he's fed up with me or not, I still have spying to do. Whatever his meeting is, I need to follow him and see if I can learn something new.

I realize this just as he gets into a cab.

Sprinting, I hail a cab of my own and catch a break. A cab stops right away. Great. This is my chance to do something I've always seen in movies. Taking out a hundred-dollar bill, I toss it at the driver. "Follow that cab."

The driver looks at me like I'm crazy—and driving in NYC, these guys have a high tolerance for crazy. Thankfully, greed wins out and he obeys.

The good news is that we're traveling downtown, toward my work building, so my lunch break won't be two hours long.

As the cab winds its way through traffic, I reverse my jacket. It's red on the outside and yellow inside. Then, like the last time, I take my wig off and tweak my makeup.

There. A totally different person.

When Max's cab stops, I get mine to drive a little down the block to make sure I'm not seen. Then I tip generously and get out.

Max's gait seems more normal as he strides down the block. Good. The less his balls hurt, the lower the chance he'll ghost me.

Using other pedestrians for cover, I follow him for half of a long block.

He rounds the corner next to a new-looking blue storefront.

This is weird. Why have the cab drop him so far from the meet? Is he that paranoid, or could this be a trap for me?

I picture myself turning the corner and getting confronted by him.

Nope. Not falling for that. Plastering my chest against the wall, I peek a single eye over the corner.

Aha.

Max is sitting down in a coffee shop.

Wait. What's this sticky crap on my boobs? Also, do I smell paint?

I pull away from the wall and look down.

Yep. I'm covered in blue—of all the ironic fucking colors.

I sigh. My stealth skills today are on par with the proverbial bull in a china shop.

Whatever. I need to know what Max is up to.

Taking out my phone, I put it on camera mode and hold it out so I can see behind the corner while remaining hidden. This is the maneuver I should've done in the first place.

Boom. Gotcha.

Max is doing the exact same thing as with the woman from JPMorgan. Only this time, it's a man he's speaking back-to-back with.

That's a pleasant change. I hope that means the woman from before was business, and not that Max is bi and this is how he talks to all of his lovers.

What are they talking about? Too bad I failed to turn Max's phone into a listening device.

When they finish talking, Max heads my way.

Shit. Covered in paint that bears my name, I'm extremely conspicuous. Before he can so much as glance at me, I jog away through the throng of pedestrians.

When I'm sufficiently far away, I catch my breath and grab a cab.

I have to go home. I can't show up to the office like this. My coworkers already make puns and jokes related to my name, and unlike my sisters with their semi-clever pearls like "yesterday, the wind blue strongly," my colleagues suck at this. I'm not sure if it's all office workers, or just cybersecurity professionals, but I've heard it all, most of it extremely cringey.

Blued to your seat. Give credit where credit is blue. I'd hate to be the bearer of bad blues. I haven't got a blue. Goody blue shoes. Show us your blue colors.

The combinations and permutations are infinite, but they don't stop there. I've also heard things about teal and azure, along the lines of: Fake it teal you make it. A done teal. Nerves of teal. Get teal. For teal. Head over teals in love. Teal your fate. That's a teal. Teally? Hope you teal better soon. Three square teals. Chasing your own teal. A tell-teal sign. Teal the deal. Telling tall teals. Rest azured. Azure aware. Azure headed into town.

The worst one was probably "Cyanara!" and "What's blue and not very heavy? Light blue." The best joke anyone at my office has ever came up with is, "Purple is better than red and blue combined."

But hey, at least every time I go to a bar with them, I get unlimited beers… as long as they're Blue Moon. Bar outings would be especially great if they stopped trying to order me buffalo wings (not made from buffalo) with *blue* cheese dressing, or playing that song on the juke-box: *"Blue (Da Ba Dee)"* by Eiffel 65. Also, for my birthday last year, they all chipped in to get me tickets to see the Blue Man Group.

At least they don't ever make fun of my last name, probably because of sexual harassment training.

My phone rings, taking me out of my office blues. It's Gia, and she tells me that Bogdan is a good friend of her boyfriend's brother. She confirms that he's got a bad reputation and suggests I don't mess with the guy.

"Why does your boyfriend's brother allow him to use the hotel for poker games?" I ask.

"It's good for business. Many of the Hot Poker Club regulars stay in the penthouse suites."

The cab stops next to my building, so I thank Gia and hang up.

When I enter my apartment, Olive isn't there, which is good. Otherwise, if she saw me covered with paint, she'd probably quote the line from *Arrested Development* that's caused me to cringe plenty of times: "I'm afraid I just 'blue' myself."

When I step into the living room, Beaky locks eyes with me, and—though it could be a coincidence—turns blue.

In my bedroom, Machete is lounging on my pillow. When I open the creaky closet door, he cracks open one eye, managing to imbue the small gesture with the kind of grump people get after years on a low-carb diet.

How dare you, puny human? Wake Machete again, and he will skin you.

I change my clothes and load the picture of the guy I saw with Max onto the flash drive from my wig.

After all, I got blue for this.

———

When I get back to work, an assignment is waiting for me in my inbox. After I'm done, I sneak the flash drive out of my wig and check on who the guy is.

Hmm. He works at Bank of America, also in the investment banking division. It's safe to assume this is related to Max's meeting with the woman.

But what would a Russian or a Ukrainian spy need

with investment bankers? Is Max an agent provocateur? Is he trying to engineer another financial crisis? That sort of thing could hurt this country more than some physical threats.

I need more info to go on. If I ever get a chance to visit Max, maybe I'll find a clue at his place.

Yeah, that's it. Spying is why I want to go to Max's place. Not lust.

A new assignment arrives in my inbox, and I work on it for the rest of the day before heading home, where I find Olive dropping a new puzzle into Beaky's tank.

"Hi," I say.

"Hey." She seals the tank. "How was your day?"

"Fine." I peer at the tank. "Can you make puzzles for cats? Maybe Machete could use one?"

Hearing his name, Machete sneaks a glare at me from around the corner.

Have you seen the movie Saw? *Those are the kind of puzzles Machete will build for you if you piss him off.*

"I've never tried making toys for felines, but I think they're easy to entertain," Olive says. "Just put on one of those YouTube videos for cats."

I grin and walk over to the dresser to take out my old iPad. "This is what happens when I try."

She examines the mangled iPad in openmouthed fascination. "I can understand how he shredded the cover, and even the grooves in the metal on the back make sense. But how did he manage to leave claw marks on the glass?"

I shrug. "I think those are cracks. I hope so anyway."

The doorbell rings.

I check the app. Yep. It's Fabio, here to train me on how to please a man.

When I let him in, he looks from me to Olive with slight disapproval. "Which is which? And who's going to be doing the lesson?"

I take off my wig. "I'm Blue."

He narrows his eyes at Olive. "And you?"

"Olive," she says with an eyeroll.

"Come to my bedroom," I tell Fabio quickly.

I'm not sure Olive needs to know what we're about to do.

Fabio looks at the wall of monitors. "Are Gia and her pirate friend joining today?"

"No," I say.

He pouts. "I had jokes prepared."

Great. Fabio's jokes are usually older than my grandparents.

"You want to hear them?" he asks me.

I shake my head.

"What about you?" he asks Olive.

She nods.

Traitor.

"A vampire—I mean Gia—walks into a bar and orders hot water," he says. "The bartender obliges, then says, 'I thought you drank blood.'" Fabio grins. "The vampire pulls out a used tampon. 'I'm making tea.'"

Double standard much? The one time I uttered the word *tampon* around him, he nearly threw a fit.

"Want the other joke?" Fabio asks.

I say no, but Olive betrays me again.

"A pirate walks into a bar with a ship's steering

wheel sticking out of their pants. The bartender looks at the wheel. 'Doesn't that hurt?' The pirate tugs on the wheel. 'Arrrr, I know. It's driving me nuts.'"

"Dude," I say. "Was that supposed to be about Clarice?"

He nods.

"You realize she doesn't have nuts?"

"She could," Fabio says defensively. "If she were trans."

I nod. "I haven't seen her naked, so I guess anything's possible."

Olive grins like a loon. "Speaking of seeing people naked, didn't Fabio see your bearded clam before he swore off women forever?"

Fabio makes a gagging sound. "Blue doesn't have nuts. She *is* nuts."

This topic reminds me of Bill. Whoever molded him didn't bother giving him silicone testicles. More importantly, his dick is still damaged, so I hope Fabio has a plan for that.

Relatedly, I hope Max's parts are okay.

"Ready?" I ask Fabio.

With an eyeroll, he prances in the direction of my bedroom.

"Later," I tell Olive and follow him.

When I enter the room, Fabio is already taking out Bill from the closet—which makes me think of the "Bring out the Gimp" line from *Pulp Fiction*. Before I can ask, Fabio pulls out a roll of tape from his pocket and wraps Bill's silicone dong with it.

God. I really hope Max didn't have to do any repairs like that.

"Much better." Fabio looks over his masterwork like a sculptor. He then pulls out a condom and hands it to me. "Might as well show me your skills with this."

"There are skills for this too?"

Should I unwrap it with my teeth or something? But that carries a risk of breaking the latex.

He gapes at me. "Of course there are skills. The best way is to put it into your mouth and roll it on him that way, but it takes some practice."

"How about we make that a separate lesson?" I use my hands to unseal the thing and cover Bill with it. "Blow job stuff is more important, don't you think?"

Fabio nods. "Have you done your deep-throat homework?"

"Yeah," I lie. I've been a bad student.

"A coworker gave me an idea that should help you with that," he says. "Learn to play a wind instrument. A flute would be great, but an oboe would work too, or a bassoon. Maybe even a clarinet."

"What about a saxophone?" I ask sarcastically.

"It could work."

"How?"

"It would teach you to control your throat muscles, which can help with the gag reflex."

"Got it." I check if Machete is around. The coast looks clear. "Should we start?"

"Are you well-hydrated today?" Fabio asks.

I frown. "Yeah. I think so."

"Proper hydration is extremely important. Helps

saliva production. When it comes to blow jobs, you're going to need drool. Lots and lots of drool."

I giggle. "Would it help if I fantasized about a juicy steak?"

He looks at me sternly. "Absolutely not. That way lies biting the man meat—the worst thing you can do during a blowjob."

"Chill, I was kidding."

"Blowjobs are not a joke." He moves Bill farther up the bed. "They're the cornerstone of a relationship."

Isn't communication the cornerstone of a relationship? Or attraction?

"Okay," I say. "How about I take a drink, just in case?"

He nods. "Also, bring back two toothpicks and two avocados."

"I don't have any avocados."

"What about lychees?"

"As in the fruit or the bug? Either way, I don't have any."

Fabio shakes his head. "Rambutans? Apricots? Figs?"

"Nope."

He sighs. "You need to have fruit in your diet. And veggies. That's key for anal sex, which is a lesson for another day, but I might as well tell you now."

"I have fiber in my diet." I put my hands on my hips. "I've got cherries, grapes, and kiwis in my fridge. Tomatoes too, and onions and—"

"Fine," he says curtly. "Bring two kiwis."

I think I know why he needs them, so I don't ask.

Rushing to the kitchen, I chug some water, wash the kiwis in case I'm right, locate the sandwich toothpicks, and hurry back.

It's as I suspected. Fabio takes the toothpicks, jams them under Bill's dick, and attaches the kiwis under there, giving Bill what looks surprisingly like balls.

"The proper handling of balls is fundamental for blowjobs," Fabio says, taking on a professorial tone. "But that's an art that will be unique for each pair of balls. Take tugging on them—some love it, some hate it. Or slapping—some guys get extra hard from a little slap on the balls, while others go completely soft and might punch you in the nose."

Is there a chance Max liked what my foot did?

Nah, doubt it. More likely, he's upset and will ghost me, so this training is for someone else.

Must not think about that.

I point at Bill's kiwis. "What's a safe move? Something to do before I go into a 'what do you want me to do to your balls' conversation."

"You can't go wrong with gentle sucking and licking," Fabio says. "But you should start every relationship with a 'what do you want me to do to your balls' conversation. I do."

Not for the first time, I'm having doubts about the practicality of Fabio's advice. "Is there a specific pace guys like? Fast, slow?"

"Depends on the guy," he says. "Watch him masturbate in front of you, and you'll know."

Yeah. That's super easy. I'm sure every femme fatale

asks a guy to jerk off in front of her before she seduces him.

"Should I blow Bill now?" I ask.

"No, a few more tips." Fabio points under the kiwis. "That's the perineum. You should make sure to give it a lick from time to time."

"Got it."

"Also, lick the butthole, but closer to the prostate massage."

"Wouldn't I do that at the same time?"

He cocks his head. "Learn to walk before you run."

"No finger in butt when distracted." I salute Fabio. "Got it."

"Good." Fabio playfully flicks Bill's erection again. Now that it's bandaged, the swinging is much slower.

"Dude," I say, wrinkling my nose. "That's going into my mouth."

"Sorry," he says sheepishly. "Should we swap condoms?"

"Did you wash your hands?"

He nods.

"Then no. I'm not Gia-level paranoid about germs. Just don't touch it again."

"Deal." He steps away from the bed, like distance is the only way to fight the temptation to flick a dick. "Have we talked about angles?"

I shake my head. Gia told me angles are important for magic, but Fabio is talking about turning a different kind of trick.

"Depending on the way a dick curves, you want to approach it from different positions," he says. "If it curves down, you can be on your knees. If it tilts up, sixty-nine would be better."

"Why?"

He gestures toward his neck. "A throat has a downward curve, so to reach it, down curve or straight works best. If the dick points up, you'll get it in your sinuses."

"Oh. Right."

"You particularly don't want cum in your sinuses." He makes a grossed-out face. "Unless he's into that and you want to accommodate, in which case I pity you. Personally, I think I'd rather take it in the eyes."

"I don't think I want it in either the eyes *or* the nose," I say.

"Limits are okay, but some things you'll want to do, even if you're not going to like them."

"Like what?"

He pulls out a jar and dumps a green slimy thing out of it. "This is Cra-Z-Art Nickelodeon Slime. It should give you an idea of what cum is like."

I flush. "I've seen cum before."

He tosses me a little chunk of the green substance, but I fail to catch it, so it sticks to the wall.

"Are you sure you've seen it outside of porn?" He tosses me some more.

This time, I catch it. "Of course." I squeeze the gooey substance. "This feels more like Hulk's snot than cum."

"It's the closest non-toxic thing I could find." He puts the jar of "cum" away. "Do you know how to properly interact with it?"

I stretch the gooey green substitute. "There's a proper way?"

"Yeah. For example, don't spit it out with a grossed-out expression on your face. That's the worst thing you can do."

"Well, duh."

"Seems obvious, but many people make that mistake," he says. "And nothing is a bigger turnoff. Swallowing is best, but if that's not your thing, you can ask him to come on your ass instead. But seriously, if you want to use me as your reference, learn to swallow."

Sure, I'm totally going to put him as my reference on my resume. I can just picture that call between him and Max.

"—it's even good for you," Fabio is saying as I tune back in. "Semen has protein, yet it's not very caloric. You get sugars, both fructose and glucose, as well as citrate, zinc, calcium, lactic acid, magnesium, potassium —the list goes on."

"Yum." I hold the green goo between two fingers. "What if it's on your hands?"

"With a straight guy, you don't want to Spiderman him without checking to make sure he'd like it. Maybe ask before snowballing him also."

Snowballing is sharing cum mouth to mouth, but I've never heard of Spidermanning before.

"That's when you have some on your hands and flick it into his face." Fabio demonstrates, causing my wall to have another green goo spot.

"Not doing that," I say. "Worry not."

"Okay." He takes a step forward, then back, clearly fighting the urge to flick that dick again. "The last and most important rule about a blowjob is don't give up when things get *hard*."

I roll my eyes, pointedly.

He chuckles. "That's the blowjob spirit. Now you're ready for this."

He takes out his phone and starts a song. Two seconds into it, I recognize 50 Cent's "Candy Shop."

Fabio grins. "To set the mood."

With the trepidation I typically experience when sparring in my Krav Maga dojo, I kneel next to Bill and take him into my mouth.

CHAPTER
Nineteen

THE CONDOM IS STRAWBERRY-FLAVORED. The kiwis feel surprisingly like the real thing when I cup them—just weirdly separated without a scrotum. Maybe we should've put them inside of a balloon first?

The music halts.

I keep going.

"Stop!" Fabio sounds irritated.

I pull away.

He crosses his arms over his chest. "What was that?"

"A blowjob?"

He shakes his head. "Where's the feeling? Where's the emotion? Didn't you hear a word I said?"

I flick Bill's dick. "It's hard to work up feelings and emotions when you're pleasuring a headless dummy."

"So think of someone else," he says. "You have an imagination, don't you?"

That's a good idea.

Returning to the dummy dick, I close my eyes and imagine it's Max I'm pleasuring.

A part of me knows he's probably never going to call me again, but it doesn't stop the fantasy, and just like that, my hand is a lot gentler as I caress his kiwis. I suck on the tip, picturing him groaning in gratitude, and jerk the shaft with my hand at the speed I imagine he'd like.

Should I reach around for the walnut? No. Fabio said that's an advanced move.

I suck the left kiwi, then right. Getting into the spirit of things, I lick the taint under the kiwis, then go back to my strawberry lollipop. Deep-throating it, I alternate between fast and slow.

Fabio's voice reaches me as if from a distance. He's telling me to stop again.

Fuck. Am I that hopeless?

When I pull away, Fabio is looking at me like a proud father.

He mimes wiping a tear and says in a mockingly breaking voice, "The student has become the master."

"I was good?" I'm bursting with pride.

"Better than some men I know." He walks over and flicks the dick, causing some drool to fly at my bed. Gia would kill him for that.

"Dubious compliment, but I'll take it."

He flicks the dick again. "I meant it as the greatest—"

Fabio doesn't finish his sentence because in that moment, Machete pounces from under the bed.

He must've been sleeping through our lesson, but he's awake now.

Murderously awake.

Claws out, he shreds the condom on Bill's dick in an eyeblink. Two more swipes of his paw, and he leaves Fabio's tape in tatters. I don't even see the next swat of his paw, but the kiwis are now fruit salad.

"Is he trying to give him a sex reassignment surgery?" Fabio whispers, horrified.

Machete turns from Bill to Fabio with unspeakable intentions in his feline eyes.

Machete is not a surgeon. Machete is a butcher. And now, he will cut a bitch.

"Bad cat!" I shout and grab Machete in a special hold, one that makes it possible to give the evil creature a bath without losing my limbs. I had to consult my SEAL Team Six contact to learn it—and why they possess special cat-grappling skills, I don't know. Still, even with this hold, I only dare give Machete a bath once a year, and only if he's really, really dirty. I'm not suicidal.

Machete must think I'm going to wash him now because he's hissing, snarling, and growling, his paws clawing at the air, each like a Freddy Krueger kill strike.

Fabio's face turns ashen.

The door to my room opens, and Olive walks in, her eyes the size of uncut kiwis.

"This isn't what it looks like," I pant.

She examines the green goo on the wall, the headless dummy with damaged privates, petrified Fabio, and me with a homicidal cat in my arms.

"Whatever it is, it looks very kinky," she says. "We're talking praying mantis cosplay meets serial killer orgy."

"Stop talking and help," I grit out.

"How?"

"Get the laser pointer in that drawer." I point with my foot. "Hurry."

She does as I say, and as soon as Machete sees the little red dot on the wall, he turns into a ragdoll.

"Leave the room," I tell Fabio.

I don't have to ask twice. He escapes so fast he nearly trips on the way out.

Olive keeps playing with the laser, and I slowly place Machete down.

The cat follows the pointer's every move. As always, the world doesn't exist for him anymore.

Whew.

That red dot is Machete's only kryptonite. It's how I get him into the bathroom when I brave the horrible process known as washing a cat. It's also what I use to get him into a crate to go to the vet.

Watch your words carefully, insignificant human. Machete is not afraid to get wet. He prefers not to. He's protecting water from his wrath.

I walk over and grab another laser pointer—this one is a fully automated version I recently got online. I set it to "tire out" mode and wait until Machete switches his attention from Olive's thin red dot to the thicker one from the device.

At that point, I tell her the coast is clear, and we tiptoe out of my room.

"Seems like you do have toys for your cat," she says.

"No puzzles, though," I say.

We find Fabio in the kitchen, fanning himself.

"Next time, we're doing this at my place," he states.

"Fair," I say. "Sorry about the scare."

"You owe me dinner," he says. "With drinks."

"Sure," I say. "Olive, you want to join us?"

"Where?" she asks.

Fabio grins. "Olive Garden?"

Olive grimaces. "Har, fucking har."

"There's also that Mediterranean place nearby." Fabio's grin turns evil. "They have an olive bar."

"Stop it," I say sternly. "We'll go to Loopy Doopy Rooftop Bar."

"Sounds good to me," Fabio says. "Once there, I'll buy Olive a Blue Moon… as an olive branch."

———

When Olive and I get home from the bar, we're both tipsy. Fabio is a lot bigger than we are, and we made the age-old mistake of keeping up with him on the number of drinks.

"Good night," I say to Olive.

"Sleep tight," she says, her speech slightly slurred.

I go to my room and find Machete passed out on the floor.

Huh. The laser pointer is still dancing around the walls. I guess the "tire out" option is meant for an energetic kitten and is too much for this large beast.

Machete is not sleeping. He's in stealth mode, looking for a victim to shred.

I hide poor Bill in the closet and am reaching up to take off my wig when my phone pings with a text.

It's Max.

Are you awake?

My heart rate skyrockets. I'd almost accepted the possibility of him ghosting me, so this is an exciting surprise.

Grinning, I type out: *Nope. I'm just snoring so loudly my phone spontaneously texts people.*

Max's next text tempers my enthusiasm:

Do you have a minute to talk?

Is this it? Will he tell me we're over? He does seem like too much of a gentleman to simply stop calling.

Fine. We might as well talk. Hopefully, this will be like ripping off a Band-Aid... from an aroused clit.

Phone or video? I ask.

Video.

So he does do videocalls. Or maybe he's making an exception for me. That's not consistent with a breakup —or is it?

Which app? I text back.

He suggests Signal Private Messenger, the app that Snowden believes to be the most safe and secure. Is this a coincidence? Snowden does live in Russia now, so he and Max might've had vodka together.

Sure, I reply.

Propping my laptop on my bed, I set everything up. When Max's face shows up on the screen, I take in a deep breath.

Here goes nothing.

CHAPTER
Twenty

MAX LOOKS DANGEROUSLY hot in a tight blue T-shirt. Did he go for that color because he subconsciously wants me all over him? Fingers crossed.

"Hi," he says, his deep voice an aural caress.

I try to play it cool. "Hey."

"There was something I didn't get a chance to tell you at lunch."

I arch an eyebrow. "And what's that?"

"I'm leaving town for a week."

I blink at the camera. Leaving town is a good story if you want to break up with someone gently, but you'd make the move permanent, not have it last a mere week. What game is this?

"Where are you headed?" I ask.

"Home."

So... Russia? Maybe Ukraine. "You still think of Canada as home?"

He rubs the stubble on his chin. "Good question. I think my home is my New York apartment. But since

I'm going to stay with my parents and they still live in the house I grew up in, it's not wrong to call that home too."

I guess. It would be like me calling the farm my home. Speaking of the farm, he'd probably enjoy seeing all the animals there. Except my parents are at the farm. If he met them, he'd run away, maybe all the way back to Russia.

"Why this specific week?" I ask.

"Two of my brothers have their birthdays," he says. "And it's my parents' anniversary."

I bet it's actually some important assignment or a meeting with his handlers.

I run my fingers through my wig. "How badly will you miss me?"

He gives me a wicked smirk. "Like a panda misses his favorite bamboo shoot. How badly will you miss *me*?"

I grin back. "Like a raccoon misses her favorite trashcan."

He chuckles. "How very flattering."

"Racoons are relatives of the red panda," I say. "And they're called trash pandas."

"I see." He gives me a heated once-over. "We'll miss each other like pandas."

Hopefully more, given how reluctant they are to reproduce. I doubt any panda is as horny as I'll be for him.

"How are you doing?" I level a pointed look at his crotch.

He waves his hand dismissively. "Fine. I wouldn't

worry about it."

"It's *hard* not to worry."

He laughs. "All fine, really."

This is my chance. Activating femme fatale mode. "I need to be sure," I say seductively.

He draws in a sharp breath. "What are you saying?"

"I want to know if your equipment functions."

I can't believe I just said that.

His nostrils flare. "Oh, sonechko, everything functions very well… for you."

The words come out breathlessly. "Show me."

Wow. Liquid courage or not, I've never been prouder of myself than I am in this moment.

His gaze is pure heat. "Sure. I'll show you—but I have to make sure you weren't harmed either. That was a bad fall."

I swallow audibly. "What do you want to see?"

"Everything."

Damn. It's very, very hot in here.

Get a grip, Blue. A femme fatale would be naked already. Or stripping seductively.

In that case, I'm on it.

I start with my top.

Max's eyes roam hungrily over my exposed skin before he rips his own shirt off, revealing hard, exquisitely chiseled pecs and abs, along with seriously buff arms.

This is the best game ever.

I peel my pants off. He steps out of his.

Wowzer.

Sergeant and Captain pebble in my bra, eager to be freed. Obliging them, I take it off. Then, more hesitantly, I slide my panties down.

I can feel my face burning, and it makes me want to growl in frustration. A true femme fatale wouldn't blush like some maiden, not unless it was the role she decided to play. I'll have to practice blushing on command only because currently, the blood vessels in my face are traitors to the United States of America.

Staring at me like he wants to eat me through the camera, Max pulls down his briefs, exposing an engorged Maximus.

I forget all about my treasonous blush.

As pompous as the name is, it doesn't do Maximus justice. Not even feeling it with my feet has prepared me properly for the glorious reality of it.

Like its namesake, this dick could stand against lions and fierce warriors in a gladiatorial arena, bring down the evil emperor of Rome, and shout, "Are you not entertained?" at a huge gathering of excited vaginas.

"As you can see, everything is intact." Max cups his heavy balls with his hand. No mere kiwis could simulate those puppies.

I swallow an overabundance of drool. "I think I need a proper demonstration."

Fabio said a good blowjob could benefit from having the guy jerk off in front of you, so here's my chance for reconnaissance.

Yeah. That's my goal here. Not lust. No way.

"You never came for me," Max says roughly. "Do it now."

Fair.

I want to. Need to.

I lick the fingers on my right hand.

He groans, and his dick twitches.

I pinch Sergeant and then Captain.

Max grabs Maximus in a tight fist.

I slide my fingers down my stomach until I reach my core.

Eyes widening, Max gives Maximus a slow stroke.

I pinch my aching clit. Then I rub it, the orgasm I was denied earlier coiling with the speed of a cheetah.

He strokes himself again, his pace picking up.

My mouth waters, along with other places. I'd give all my poker winnings to be in that room with him right now—and to have him in me somewhere. Everywhere.

"Slide a finger in." His words are a stern command, and I love it.

I lick my left index finger and gently push it into my heat.

"Fuck," he grunts.

"Yes," I say breathlessly. "That's exactly what we'd be doing if this weren't cyber fucking space."

His eyes darken, and he picks up his pace.

I'm closer.

His pace is frantic now. Desperate.

A moan is wrenched from my lips.

Hungry to be filled, I let my middle finger join my index.

Did he just growl?

Whatever that sound is, it's so hot it pushes me over the edge, and I come all over my fingers.

With a grunt, he comes too. His seed shoots out, and a droplet lands on the phone's camera, creating a strange bukkake effect.

He releases his dick. "That was... wow."

"I second that," I say, fighting to catch my breath. My heart is racing like the aforementioned cheetah chasing a gazelle. Speaking of chasing... "How about we get together now and do this for real?"

He wipes the cum blocking my view with a tissue, his face a mask of regret. "My flight is in two hours. I have to rush to the airport. Rain check?"

More like a downpour check. "I'll hold you to it."

"It" being my clit.

He looks me over. "I'll be looking forward to our meeting every second that I'm away."

A very un-femme-fatale shyness comes over me as the orgasmic afterglow fades. Stepping out of the camera view, I dress swiftly. By the time I look back, he's dressed as well.

Neither of us have hung up for some reason.

Why do I have the feeling that he's going to break up with me after all?

"I have to go," he says, but he still doesn't hang up.

"I get it." I refuse to hang up also.

"I'll stay in touch," he says and still doesn't hang up.

He'd better stay in touch, or else.

"Enjoy your trip," I say and don't hang up.

Am I acting like he's my first boyfriend?

"Good night, sonechko." He blows me an air kiss.

Fighting the urge to giggle like a horny middle schooler, I mime catching the kiss and attaching it to my butt.

He chuckles and finally hangs up.

I stare at the Max-less screen. My emotions are in turmoil, and I'm not sure why. Maybe because that was intense, especially for the heartless seduction that it was meant to be.

I hate to admit it, but I think I'll miss him the week he's away—assuming it *is* a week. I'm still not convinced this isn't some weird game.

What the hell am I thinking?

Just because Max and I have just had orgasms in front of each other doesn't make him any less of an enemy agent. I need to be careful when it comes to keeping a lid on my feelings for him. What's just happened was femme fatale reconnaissance / practice— not intimacy. The last thing I want is to be like those assassins who bungle a perfectly nice murder contract.

The key thing I have to remember is that despite appearances, he might be trying to do to me what I've been trying to do to him. He might be seducing me with some long-term goal in mind. Hell, this "week apart" might be something they've taught him in spy school, inspired by the Russian version of the English proverb "distance makes the heart grow fonder."

How can I tell if I'm a job or not? His attraction to me seems genuine. Erections don't lie. Or do they, when a spy is involved?

Also—and this is pretty shallow—I'm still

wondering what he'd think if he saw me without a wig. What if he wouldn't be attracted to me anymore... or would be unable to fake it?

Hmm. Maybe I'll "get a haircut" the week he's away. My last buzzcut was a couple of months back now. I'm beyond the fuzzy-growth stage but not at the pixie-cut stage. Still, with some product, I can make it so Max won't throw up when he sees me. Hopefully.

My phone dings.

It's a text from Max—a picture of an adorable creature with a caption:

This is a chinchilla, in case you still need to know what cuteness looks like.

Grinning, I do a quick online search and reply with an image of a horseshoe bat's face.

THIS is cute. Chinchillas are actually close relatives of the naked mole-rat, the noble creature you didn't approve of. Did you know that naked mole-rats never get cancer?

His reply takes a few seconds to arrive.

Maybe the cancer refuses to kill the horrible little beasts? Also, do you realize this bat looks like what Nosferatu turns into... once he's done looking like the Aye-eye thing you sent me before?

I chuckle. He's actually got a point.

Have a safe flight, I tell him.

Thanks. Talk to you tomorrow.

Tomorrow? I guess I'd better go to sleep so tomorrow comes that much sooner.

When I'm almost asleep, Machete snuggles at my feet.

Kick Machete at night, and Machete will cure your rest-

*less legs syndrome in the most direct way possible
—amputation.*

CHAPTER
Twenty-One

WHEN I WAKE UP, I check if Max has left any messages.

Not yet.

Maybe not ever again?

Trying not to think about it, I get ready and feed my beast of a cat.

Machete is happy his bowl is full. Machete doesn't think the alternative—human meat—is as Fancy a Feast.

As I head out for work, I catch Olive watching something disturbing on the TV in the living room.

Birds.

CGI birds, but still.

Also, is Beaky watching that with her? It sure looks like it.

When I confront her about the horrific imagery, she pauses the picture. "I'm watching *Rio*. It's about a blue macaw whose name is Blu."

Abomination.

"New houseguest rule," I say sternly. "No bird movies. At least not when I'm home."

"Deal," Olive says. "I'll watch something about octopuses instead."

I fight a smile. "Octopuses" sounds too much like Octopussy, my nickname for her.

"What's a collective noun for octopuses?" I ask her as I put my shoes on.

"They're solitary creatures, so they don't really have one," she says. "I've heard the term 'shoal' be used, but that's really for a group of squid. Some people use the term 'clutch,' but I hate it."

I shudder and head for the door. "A clutch makes you think of chickens. You're smart to hate that."

———

At work, I use **classified** to see if Max really flew to Canada.

Yep. He did.

My boss gives me a large project to work on, which helps me not think about Max obsessively. So, by end of the day, I've only thought of him two-thousand and fifty-seven times. But who's counting? Fortunately, tonight is my Krav Maga training. Maybe I can burn off some of my sexual frustration on the mat.

I do my best, but no luck. Another few hundred thoughts of Max happen.

As I walk home, I fantasize, not for the first time, about what I'd do to a mugger if one tried to rob me.

A text from Max takes me out of my violent reverie. My pulse leaps, but he's just sent me a picture of a porcupine with the following caption:

Your cute image of the day.

My chest feels warm, and not because this proves he hasn't ghosted me.

I text him back: *You realize that's another close relative of the naked mole-rat, right?*

What image should I send him? I consider the platypus but decide against it. Even though these creatures are mammals, with their duckbills and suspicious egg-laying reproductive practices, they could trigger bird nightmares, and I don't wish that even on our country's enemies.

Ah. I know. I locate a pic of the Titicaca giant frog and send that to him.

Will he compare it to a scrotum? The scrotum frog *is* this species' alternative name. Or will he make fun of the word Titicaca—which sounds vaguely like a scat fetish where someone goes caca on titties?

Was that the inspiration for Jabba the Hutt? Max asks instead.

I grin. *No. For Ewoks.*

He replies with a smiley face and: *Video chat in an hour?*

Hells yeah.

I reply with a coy okay and a winky face.

————

Entering my apartment, I eat a quick dinner with Olive before rushing to the bathroom to strategize for my upcoming date.

Should today be the day I "get my haircut?"

I take off my wig and examine myself in the mirror.

Maybe.

I get my buzzer and give myself an undercut. Just as I'm finishing up, Machete waltzes into the bathroom and heads for the kitty litter.

Don't even think of shaving Machete or he will scalp you, pathetic human.

I look at my new hairdo in the mirror.

Much better. The top looks longer somehow.

I shower and muss my hair with some product.

Yep, I'm going for it. If this is a deal breaker for Max, so be it. Still, as a heads up, I text him:

Got a haircut. Don't faint when you see me.

Exciting, he replies. *Can you jump on the call now?*

I ask him for a few minutes. I need to apply copious makeup and clean up the parts of my room in view of the camera.

Got to frame this hairstyle properly.

————

When he shows up on the screen, he's sitting on a bed, and there are posters of animals behind him—an elephant, a zebra, and a moose.

Does he realize only one of those actually belongs in Canada?

"What do you think?" I point at my hair.

"Amazing," he says, and if he's acting, it's Oscar worthy. "Didn't Kristen Stewart have that kind of haircut at one point?"

I shrug. I have no idea if she did, but I'll take it as a

compliment. She's played spies in movies on multiple occasions, and was even one of Charlie's Angels in that one adaptation.

He frowns. "Just to double check... this isn't health-related, right?"

"Oh, no. Nothing like that."

"Good." The relief on his face deserves another Oscar if it's fake. "Maybe I should shave my head to be in sync with you?"

I look at his mouthwatering locks in panic. "Don't. You. Dare."

A sexy smirk appears on his lips, causing the dimple in his cheek to pop out. "Should I grow it out then?"

I cock my head. "I'd be curious to see that."

More importantly, I like it that he's making such far-reaching plans with me.

He leans back, blocking the zebra. "How was your day?"

"Mostly classified. Yours?"

"I had lunch with my parents," he says. "And dinner with my sister."

"That's nice. I had dinner with my sister also. What's it like being back in Canada?" I narrow my eyes theatrically. "Run into any old girlfriends?"

He leans toward the camera. "Nope. You?"

I grin. "My girlfriend and I are not on speaking terms after a certain scissoring accident. Long story."

Did his face just flush?

Of course. Turned on by the mere idea of me with another woman. Such a guy.

The Femme Fatale Association of America—if such a thing were to exist—would give my response an A+.

"I don't actually have a girlfriend," I say, just in case, as I run my hand over the stubble on the back of my head.

"That's a relief. I was just about to ask you to go steady." He gives me a heated once-over. "And I don't share, with men or women."

Sooooo, he doesn't want me to investigate other spies? Ours will be an exclusive spy versus spy game.

Crap. He's looking at me expectantly. I need to answer and quickly, or else my silence will speak volumes.

"I really like the sound of that." Gah! Did that sound too eager? "I'm not a big fan of sharing either. Just ask my five identical sisters."

Yeah, even with that save, the Femme Fatale Association of America would give this response an F-.

He flashes me a panty-incinerating smile. "It's settled then."

Is it too soon to get naked to consummate this arrangement?

No. I'm too rattled right now. Should chat some more to get my equilibrium back.

Oh, I know. "Tell me about your past relationships," I say. "Under the circumstances, I might as well learn what baggage you're bringing to this going-steady setup."

It might all be a bunch of lies that are a part of his cover, but you never know what will be useful.

"There's not much baggage, unless that's baggage in

itself," he says, not batting an eye. "I had a few girlfriends in college. Not many after that because I trav-
eled a lot. My longest relationship was six months. Her
name was Kathy." He steeples his fingers. "How about
you?"

Wow. What he's just said fits the life of a spy to a T,
only Kathy was probably Katya.

"I don't have much to brag about either," I say.
"I've been with about three and a half guys altogether.
My longest relationship was with Jay, but it was
doomed from the start. Our name as a couple was
'Blue Jay.'"

Max lifts his eyebrows. "Three and a half? Sounds
like that TV show, although I think it was two and a
half there."

I draw back. "I didn't date an underage boy."

He chuckles. "I figured."

"I call it half because one guy only got halfway to
the promised land the one and only time we had sex.
Probably TMI for you."

His jaw muscles bunch. "Like I said, I don't like to
share. A story like that makes me want to track down
the half and zero him out."

Gulp. Max probably has the license to track down
my hapless ex and take him out. But he wouldn't.
Would he? Just in case, I'd better get his mind off that
idea. Plus, I'm now calm enough for cyber nookie.

Yep. Femme fatale mode officially activated. I pitch
my voice huskily. "Are you somewhere private?"

He looks around. "Yeah. This is my childhood
bedroom."

I give him my best flirtatious smile. "Go close the door."

He disappears for a second, and I make sure my door is closed too.

"Have you ever gotten a girl naked over Signal Private Messenger in this room?" I ask when he's back.

His nostrils flare. "I haven't had the pleasure, no."

"Well then." Heart hammering, I unbutton the top of my blouse. "If you're a good boy, you might experience that pleasure tonight."

Without my prompting, he's shirtless in an eyeblink.

Yummy. Those pecs, those abs, that smooth, golden-tinted skin... "Take the rest off," I say breathlessly.

He does.

Damn. Maximus is ready for battle. So are my hormones.

"Your turn," Max murmurs, his green eyes darker than a Russian forest full of bears.

Calling on all of my femme fatale-ness, I strip, this time thankfully without a blush. Sergeant and Captain report for duty, turning diamond hard.

I cross my legs, hiding my sex from him... for now.

He drinks me in like a man who's just crossed a desert. "Radiant." His voice deepens. "A true sonechko."

I beam at him. "You're pretty luminous too. I want a close-up today." I gesture at Maximus.

The smirk on Max's lips sends a zing to my clit. "Ladies first?"

Evil. But then again, this is how you earn your

membership in the Femme Fatale Association of America.

I uncross my legs, fighting a blush that threatens to commit treason again. "Fine, but don't touch yourself until this lady is finished. Deal?"

Eyes glued to the screen, Max grunts something unintelligible—an acknowledgement, I presume. I place the phone between my legs, close enough to my aching pussy that it fogs up the screen.

"Touch it." His command is guttural, desperate.

It's a good thing he can't see my face. I've lost the battle with the blush. My Femme Fatale Association of America membership is revoked.

Still, I reach for my clit with one hand and use the other to push a finger into my opening. I know that's something he likes.

Max makes a sound that makes me think of a wounded bear. Is that what all super-turned-on Russians sound like?

An orgasm builds up quicker than last time. Stronger too. Panting, I glance at the screen.

Max is being good and not jerking off, as I asked him to, and Maximus is filled with so much blood it looks on the verge of turning into a werewolf.

Why is this so fucking sexy?

Must have something to do with the hunger in Max's eyes.

He picks up the phone and brings it to his face. His jaw is taut, his voice sandpaper rough. "Come for me."

If the idea was to make me feel like I'm coming as I sit on his face, mission accomplished. With that image firmly in my mind, I indeed come, and win the Femme Fatale Association of America Moan of the Year Award.

As I recover my senses, I notice beads of sweat on Max's forehead and wonder if I was too cruel by asking him to wait until I'm done.

Maybe. But it was hot.

"Your turn," I say.

He sets up the phone next to Maximus.

I grin wickedly. "Pull back. Some of him isn't in view."

He does as I say, and now I can see Maximus in all his glory, as well as Max's balls—still unnamed, though my own name is applicable to them right now.

"Go," I say magnanimously.

Grabbing his throbbing dick with his fist, Max moves his hand up and down with ruthless precision.

I should be making notes for blowjob reconnaissance, but I'm too turned on, so I touch myself again instead.

"Double standard much?" The question sounds pained.

I make my voice as husky as I can. "You want me to stop?"

"Fuck, no," Max growls.

I thought so.

Matching his speed stroke for jerk, I bring myself close to orgasm, then slow down, waiting to cross that boundary as I watch him.

"Tell me when," I gasp as the pressure builds inside me anyway.

Something unintelligible follows, and Max's hand

moves so fast it blurs. Just when I think I'll blow up if I edge any longer, he grunts something approximating, "Now!" and shoots his load.

My toes curl almost painfully, and every one of my nerve endings screams in joy as the orgasm explodes inside me.

I'm still shaking from the power of it when someone knocks on Max's door. "Everything okay in there?"

Huh. I suppose the timing could've been worse.

Max holds the camera farther out so I can see his blissed-out face. "Pick this up tomorrow?"

With a naughty smile, I wave at him and hang up.

Sleepy and spent, I crawl under the blankets. If cyber sex was this intense, I can't even imagine what the real deal with Max will be like.

I want it.

Badly.

Unprofessionally too.

I close my eyes.

Machete decides to commandeer half of my pillow, and when I hug him, he purrs.

Do not make Machete regret letting you live, pitiful human.

I start to drift off, and maybe it's my blissed-out brain going into wishful-thinking land, but as sleep claims me, I can't help but wonder:

What if Max *isn't* a Russian spy?

CHAPTER
Twenty~Two

OVER THE NEXT THREE DAYS, I fall into the most wonderful routine ever. I go to work, come home, and have videocalls with Max where we talk about everything and nothing before engaging in cybersex sessions that get more orgasmic and inventive each time.

When I come home on the fourth day, I find Gia there, questioning Olive about Beaky's ability to camouflage.

Huh. Is Gia planning to have an octopus in her show? Could she even handle an aquarium with her germaphobia? It would be only a matter of time before she asked herself where Beaky poops, and the answer would make her brain melt.

"I've come to cash in my favor," Gia says to me and darts a glance at Olive. "We might want privacy for this."

Crap. When Gia put me in touch with Clarice, I promised to write her some mischief-causing software in return. Oh, well. A deal is a deal.

I usher Gia into my room, where I get my computer out.

"So," I say. "You still want to mess with people's autocorrect?"

She nods excitedly. "I've come up with some mappings already. When they type *mustache*, your app will change it to *moist acne*. Any mention of *dimples* will become *nipples*. *Dear* will turn to *dead*. *Kiss* into *kill*. *Lol* into—"

"You don't need to define that yet," I say. "I never hard-code things like that into any of my software."

Gia grins. "I'll be able to decide my own mappings?"

I nod. "Targets too, within limit."

She rubs her hands together, like the evil vampire she resembles. "I'll start with Holly."

Holly, her twin, is also her best friend, which just goes to show that with friends/sisters like Gia, who needs enemies?

Not for the first time, I wonder why Holly and I aren't closer. We have plenty in common, not the least of which is our computer science background. I know she doesn't like the chaos of all our siblings together, but I bet we'd be good one on one. I'll have to reach out to her one of these days.

"—and then I want the transcript of the conversation emailed to me," Gia is saying when I tune back in.

"No," I say. "That's not what you asked for. I can give you the line before the autocorrect blunder, and the one after that. You're not snooping on everyone's conversations at all times."

She pouts. "What if I gave you your wallet back?"

I pat my pocket. Fucker. My wallet *is* missing.

When did she steal it? How?

The spy in me is crazy with jealousy, but I know that if I ask her to teach me this, she'll demand my firstborn in return—and Max might mind if I make such a deal without consulting him.

I narrow my eyes. "If I don't get my wallet back, the app will not happen." Gia doesn't look chastised, so I add, "I might also tack on extra zeros to all of your utility bills."

"Here." She hands me the wallet. "Also, I respect how much you pretend to care about privacy... Miss NSA."

I check that my money is still mine and pocket the wallet. "Just to clarify the design for the application: Alice types out a text to Bob. Before the text—"

"Who's Alice?" Gia asks. "Who's Bob?"

My sigh is theatrical. "They're fictional characters we use in discussions about cryptographic protocols. Would the names Olive and Mom work better for you?"

"Make that Oyl and Octomom, and you've got my attention."

I outline what I plan to do using Oyl and Octomom as the text sender and receiver, respectively. Eventually, Gia is satisfied, which is when I kick her out.

"I will have a show outside The Palace soon," she says on her way out. "You'll be there... right?"

"I will," I say earnestly. "Just let me know the time and the place."

"The place is a Russian restaurant called The Hut,

no relation to Jabba. The owners are Holly's boyfriend's parents. They hired me to be a part of the entertainment for their other son's birthday."

Hmm. A Russian restaurant. "Can I bring a plus one?"

"Sure," she says. "Who?"

I bring her up to speed as quickly as I can, finishing with, "So you see, it would be educational to witness how Max reacts to Russian food and people. Maybe he'd give himself away? Also, maybe Holly's boyfriend would be able to tell if Max is Russian? I've heard that Russians can almost always identify someone in their ethnic group."

"Isn't that true of any ethnic group?" Gia asks. "The reverse of the old 'such and such group all look the same.'"

I shrug.

"You hope he isn't Russian, right?" Olive chimes in, having joined us in the hallway.

"Yeah," I say with a sigh. "But I'm also being a realist. There are good reasons to think he is."

"Then go ahead, bring him," Gia says. "I'll talk to Holly to see if she can arrange an opportunity for her beau to speak with yours."

"When is the gig?"

When she tells me, I wince. Max is flying in that morning, and I had big plans, where the only magic would be the glory of Maximus in my vajayjay (codename classified).

Then again, if I manage to prove Max isn't a spy, I could sleep with him as a girlfriend, which sounds infinitely more appealing than doing so as a femme fatale spy.

Ugh. I suppose it's time to put my cards on the table.

Truth is, I've never been sure that I have it in me to sleep with someone as an assignment. I've been hoping and assuming that I do, but that has been partially due to picturing Max as the target. Even in his case, despite all the cyber warm-up, I'm not sure I could do it if I knew he was the enemy. As for the idea of seducing someone who isn't Max, just thinking about it feels as nauseating as coming face to face with a penguin.

Gia taps her foot. "So, will you be there? If all goes well, this might be my official opening at The Hut. It'll win you major brownie points if you show up and clap."

"Sorry, I spaced out for a second. I'll definitely be there and will clap even if the magic sucks." Grinning, I add, "I didn't catch everything you said about your opening, but I'm sure it was TMI."

With a slow head shake, Gia departs.

As soon as she's gone, Olive bursts out laughing, and Beaky changes colors a few times—at which Olive grins.

Hmm. I've been wondering if she imagines speaking with him the way I do with my cat. As kids, all of us sextuplets would do that with our favorite animals at the farm, so it's likely. Before I can ask her, my phone dings.

It's Max.

Excusing myself, I rush to my room and pick up. "Miss me already?"

He smirks. "What do you think?"

"I think you should get naked," I say.

The smirk morphs into a hungry expression. "We'd better be quick. I meant to tell you—the whole family is here for the anniversary and to celebrate the birthday that's just passed."

So, no usual talk? Oh well, the sight of him naked should make me feel better about it.

We strip and cybersex each other to orgasm. One for him and two for me. Who said life is supposed to be fair?

"Please congratulate the birthday boy and the happy couple," I say when my clothes are back on.

He looks like he wishes I'd stayed nude. "Do you want to tell them yourself?"

I blink and parrot dumbly, "Tell them myself?"

He's bluffing, surely. There's no way his actual family is there in Canada. They live in Russia. I figured the place he's in is a safehouse where he and his handler work while he's there, with the room decorated with animal posters as part of the cover.

"They would be thrilled if you did," he says. "I told them about you, and they're curious to meet you."

"Meet *me*?" This question doesn't come out much smarter than the last.

"Yeah." He grabs the phone, and my view goes topsy-turvy. "Come."

I'm going to meet his family? His parents?

As he walks to his destination, I catch glimpses of the house where Max allegedly grew up.

This has to be a trick, right? Like that scene in *The*

Americans when one of the husband-spy aliases (spoiler alert) married a secretary who worked in FBI counterintelligence. He also had a "family" in that show, but it consisted of his handler pretending to be his mother and his spy wife masquerading as his sister.

Side note: If any of Max's aliases were sleeping with *any* women the way the male spy did on that show, I wouldn't be as blasé as Keri Russell's character. Nope. I'd go on a murdering spree. And hey, maybe that could lead to a different CIA career, that of an assassin spy à la Jason Bourne. In that scenario, I'd even welcome that sweet amnesia.

Max stops walking and says something in what must be Ukrainian. He then holds the camera so I get a good view of a large dinner table filled with enough food to feed Kiev for two years.

As I scan the people sitting there, my mouth gapes open.

"Everyone, this is Blue." Max begins pointing at the people around the table. "Blue, this is Mama, Papa, and my siblings—Seman, Matviy, Andriy, and Zlata."

Finally shutting my mouth, I stupidly blink at the Stolyar clan.

If you were to take Max and use CGI to turn him into a silver fox, you'd get Papa. The three brothers look almost as identical to Max as my sisters do to me. Even Mama and his sister resemble him strongly. They have the same beautiful, thickly lashed eyes and shampoo-commercial hair.

"It's a pleasure to meet you all," I stammer.

My thoughts are racing. This is not a fake family.

Not without CGI or magic—and not the kind Gia does. But would the Russian government fly so many citizens to Canada just to fool me? Or has Max smuggled himself from Canada into Russia somehow? Unless they all live in Canada just to support Max's cover?

All those options sound like overkill, which begs the question that is like a ray of hope to my heart.

Maybe Max truly isn't a Russian spy?

CHAPTER
Twenty-Three

"NICE TO MEET YOU, BLUE," everyone says in unison, and I push away my unruly ruminations to focus on the situation at hand.

"Max has told us a lot about you," Andriy says.

No accent. Another clue they're either not in Russia, or he studied English in the same place as Max.

"What he didn't mention is how attractive you are," says the other brother—Seman, I think.

"He was probably worried you'd ogle her, and he was right," Matviy, the third brother, says.

"And then you wonder why he never introduces us to the women he dates," the sister—Zlata—chimes in.

Her voice is as pretty as the rest of her, and again, no hint of accent here either.

"No, that's because he doesn't date." Seman winks at Max. "Or didn't."

Max turns the camera to face himself. A smile is playing on his lips. "The wait was worth it."

"Children," Mama says. "Let the guest get a word in."

Okay. Definite Eastern European accent here, but that fits with Max's story of being second-generation Ukrainian.

"Before she tells her story, how about a toast?" Papa says, his accent thicker than his wife's.

Seman grabs a bottle of horilka. "The old man makes sense for a change."

Papa raises his shot glass. "*Za zustrich.*"

Everyone downs their shots. I'm glad I'm not there in person, as I'm not in the mood for the burn of horilka.

"We shouldn't keep Blue on the phone to watch us eat and drink," Max says when the glasses are back on the table.

"You're right," Mama says to him and looks at the camera. "Blue, I hope you come in person next year. This is your official invitation."

Wow. "Thank you," I say. "But I don't have to hang up. I don't mind watching you eat or drink, honestly."

In fact, I appreciate this chance to learn more about Max, but I don't add that.

"Nonsense," Papa says. "If you can't share our meal, I'll feel inhospitable."

Seman elbows his father. "Maybe that's because your hospitality rules predate technology?"

I sigh. "I don't want anyone to feel inhospitable. I just wanted to congratulate you all on the anniversary and the birthdays."

Mama looks at Papa and says something in rapid-fire Ukrainian. All I make out is the word *krasa*, which I've seen in a Russian fairytale in reference to a beautiful maiden.

"She said you're not just beautiful but polite too," Max whispers into the phone's speaker.

I grin and speak up for everyone. "I'll let you get back to your feast."

"See you next year," Mama says, and the others echo her words.

"I'll call you tomorrow." Max blows me an air kiss.

Since his family is watching, I touch my cheek instead of my butt after I catch it. Saying my congrats once again, I hang up.

Wow.

I feel prom-date giddy. Max and I might actually work. Like for real—which is only possible if he's not working for Russia. And maybe he's not? Is it possible he's been telling the truth from the start? That he's really just a second-generation Ukrainian and isn't spying for foreign interests?

There are problems with that theory, no matter how much I want it to be true. What about the shady stunt he was about to pull after the poker game? And what's with the investment bankers?

Damn it. Was this family encounter a carefully planned theater? If so, it almost worked.

Still, I'm hopeful now. I don't believe I'm important enough to stage something like that. He doesn't know that I saw him speak to the bankers or witnessed his attempt to hack into someone's phone. Why would he try so hard to convince me he's not a spy if he has no reason to think that I suspect him?

No answers arrive, but the trip to the Russian restaurant is coming up. Let's see what that reveals.

CHAPTER
Twenty~Four

AFTER I FINISH my first assignment at work the next day, I check into Max's siblings. I figure if his cover is sloppy, I won't find them, but if his cover is good—or if Max was honest with me—they *will* exist.

Yep. The brothers and the sister have a very solid online presence—more than Max himself, which is an odd detail if this is fake.

I can't help but be relieved. Sloppy cover would've meant kissing the Max-is-not-a-spy scenario goodbye.

Another work project lands in my inbox, and I work on it all through lunch. I manage to finish everything early, so I leave my building and head over to Fabio's place for my training.

———

"We've got a code red on our hands," Fabio says when I tell him about my upcoming date with Max.

"What do you mean?" I ask.

He looks me up and down, his upper lip curling at my plain gray slacks and work-appropriate white shirt. "I mean that you might well benefit more from grooming advice than any sexual techniques."

"What's that supposed to mean?"

He rolls his eyes. "Gay or straight, men are visual creatures, and you have to make sure we like what we see."

I pinch his bicep. "That was a rhetorical question. Why are you dissing my looks?"

He pulls his arm away as if I have a stinger, then grabs a tall mirror and places it in front of me. "Just look."

I take off my wig. "This is my new haircut. He said he liked it. The rest is my work attire. I'll obviously dress up for the date."

Fabio exhales an exaggeratingly relieved breath. "You'll wear different shoes too, right?"

I resist the urge to pinch him again. "Yes. I just wear sneakers to the office to be comfy."

He scratches the top of his head. "Okay. Can we go to your place, so you can show me what you plan to wear?"

"I can do one better." I take out my phone and show him a picture of me wearing the dress I plan to put on, then another with the shoes.

He wrinkles his nose. "You've worn this stuff before?"

"Just that once," I say.

"Fine. What's your hair situation down south?" He looks at my crotch.

Seriously? "I got waxed right before our first lesson." It was just in case Max happened to see me naked during that poker game, but I don't add that.

"Brazilian?"

I nod.

He purses his lips. "How's your butthole looking?"

Can I use a Krav Maga move on him right now? Not a kick to the balls—he needs those for work—but maybe a strike at the nipple area? "I just told you I got the Brazilian."

Another eyeroll. "What about bleaching?"

I blink at him. "There's not enough hair growth to bleach."

"Not the hair, dummy, the skin around the back door. It should be nice and pink."

"What color is it now?" I blurt.

"How the fuck would I know? And before you ask, I don't want to see it."

Seriously, just one punch at any of the soft places on his body. "I wasn't going to show it to you."

"Sure, sure." He smirks. "But you *are* going to the bathroom to check."

"Stupid cream manufacturers," I mutter. "Trying to make women feel ashamed in order to sell their snake oil. We should feel proud of our genitals as they are. I'm not sure I'm even going to show Max my asshole, but if I do, he should be so thrilled that I'm letting him see it that he doesn't care what hue it is."

Fabio's smile turns evil. "Preach it, sister. But you *are* going to the bathroom to check, right?"

With an annoyed grunt, I head over to his bathroom.

I can't believe I'm doing this. Then again, taking a look won't hurt.

But how?

I try bending myself into a pretzel to get a view, but it's a no go. I try to find a good angle to see it in the mirror. Another failure. Fine. I take out my phone, bend over, spread my legs, and take an anal selfie—or analfie, as I'll call it going forward.

If anyone at work hacks my phone and sees my analfie, I will murder their butthole.

Sighing, I take a look.

Fucking fuck. My butthole is brown. Did it take a trip to Hawaii and get itself a nice tan when I wasn't looking? Or has it always been like this? Why does my stupid intuition say that it should be skin-colored like the rest of the butt, or at least pink, like the insides of the vag? It's like that with the other orifices—ear holes being skin-toned and lips pink (mine anyway).

Is the date with Max important enough to get a treatment? A big part of me says no, but another part, the one in touch with my inner femme fatale, retorts with a resounding yes. In fact, the Femme Fatale Association of America guidebook would have three options for this situation: a) bleach the offending area, b) wear a bejeweled butt plug to cover it up, or c) tan naked with a butt plug until skin everywhere else matches that of the butthole. Since b) would make walking uncomfortable and c) might cause skin cancer, I guess a) it is.

Looks like I'm doing this. Damn Fabio and damn the skin cream industrial complex.

When I return to his living room, Fabio gives me a smug look. "So?"

"How do I bleach the stupid thing?"

He pulls out his phone. "You see my guy. You don't want to do this yourself. I've heard horror stories."

I exhale a breath. "A guy? As in male?"

"Gay. I checked"—he waggles his eyebrows—"if you know what I mean. He would probably rather look at rotting fruit than at your butthole."

"Great, I'm flattered."

He pulls out his phone and dials a number. "Hey, Ishmael, can I bring a friend to see you?"

Ishmael? Are we talking biblical or from *Moby Dick*? Knowing Fabio, I bet it's the latter. Probably a nickname alluding to a dick.

Even though the phone isn't on speaker mode, I can overhear Ishmael's deep yes, who, and why.

"Blue. My childhood friend," Fabio replies.

"The asshole?" Ishmael asks.

"Yep, needs to lighten up," Fabio says with a grin.

"I'm right here," I say loud enough for Ishmael to hear. "And I'll be the one tipping."

"Fine, we'll call it 'changing the ringtone there,'" Fabio says to me. "Better?"

I heave a sigh. "Do I have to do it right now?"

"Yes," both say in unison.

"You'll need some time to recover before you take a dick in there," Ishmael says.

"This is the first date," I say. "We're not jumping into anal."

Fabio gives me a pitying look. "Blue, you're still on my training time, and I value my reputation." He squares his shoulders. "No student of mine will go on a date with an unbleached butthole, and that's that."

CHAPTER
Twenty-Five

THE BUTTHOLE-BLEACHING SALON is in the West Village and looks extremely high-end.

"Nice and clean," I whisper to Fabio.

"Yeah," he says. "Bodes well for your anus."

Before I can reply, a muscular giant of a man lumbers toward us. He's got to be a professional body-builder—his biceps have triceps.

He doesn't seem gay to me, but this is coming from the girl who had no idea that Fabio played for the other team. If I'd known, I wouldn't have shown him my privates.

"Ishmael!" Fabio gives the guy a hug, or tries to. His arms wrap around approximately one pec.

Huh. Maybe the behemoth is called Ishmael because he's large enough to catch a whale with his bare hands... by the dick.

"Are you the client?" Ishmael looks down at me the way I might at a tiny bug.

I mutely bob my head. This man is so huge he activates the lizard part of my brain, the one in charge of preventing me from getting myself squished.

Is the intelligence community aware of the weird effect an oversized person can have on someone? Should the CIA put their interrogators on a cocktail of steroids and growth hormones?

Still looking at me, Ishmael gestures at the nearby door. "Come."

"Good luck," Fabio sing-songs.

I shoot him a hateful glare and follow the giant.

Ishmael ushers me into a small, clean room and waves his meaty hand at a table that looks like a night-stand next to him. "Drop your pants and get into the puppy pose."

If he weren't gay and I weren't faithful to Max, I'd ask him to buy me dinner first, but as is, I do as I'm told while cursing Fabio under my breath.

"Spread your butt cheeks," Ishmael booms.

"Wait, what are you going to do?"

"Laser it," he says curtly.

Oh. I thought it was going to be a cream. I guess Big Laser is in on this scam.

"Ready when you are," Ishmael growls.

Flushing like a particularly shy lobster, I spread my cheeks and cringe.

I'm ready for the laser to shine where the sun doesn't.

CHAPTER
Twenty-Six

THE PAIN IS SO sharp I can't help but yelp.

This is what a supervillain would feel if Superman decided to shoot his eye lasers into her ass. I wouldn't be surprised if there was smoke coming out of me, which would be a flattery-free twist on the expression "blow smoke up one's butt."

"Sorry," Ishmael says. "Some people are more sensitive to the laser than others."

I can't help but feel he means people of a certain gender, but maybe I'm just being overly sensitive.

"Is everything okay?" Fabio shouts from outside the room.

My tortured sphincter muscles clench as I yell back, "Fine! Don't open that door, or I'll kill you."

"I don't need to be traumatized anyway," Fabio retorts loudly.

"Do you want me to apply some numbing cream?" Ishmael asks.

Ugh. What's worse: letting Ishmael continue going

medieval on my ass, or the extra indignity of him applying the cream? Then again, who said it has to be him?

"Can I apply the cream myself?" I ask.

"If you prefer. Give me your hand."

I do, and he fits a glove onto my hand, explaining, "So your fingers don't get numb."

"Ah. Right. Look away."

"Done," he says.

Feeling my face redden further, I apply the cream. The cooling sensation is a pleasant change from the earlier burn.

Ishmael sighs impatiently. "Keep in mind, if you're doing that for more than five seconds, you're playing with it."

Great. A giant, ass-bleaching comedian.

I yank my hand away and push up to all fours. Then we wait, and as far as waiting positions go, this is my least favorite. Finally, my butt starts to feel numb—a weird sensation in and of itself. Reminds me of being at the dentist, except I have my pants on in there, thankfully.

"Ready?" he booms.

"Sure."

The horrible feeling comes back, slightly dulled, and I yelp in pain again.

"Still hurts?"

The fucker sounds surprised.

I clench my teeth. "Just keep going."

He does. I tell myself that this is training for the scenario where an enemy captures me and tries to make me betray my country. Bravely, I don't cave. I might not be able to withstand bird torture, but I can handle enhanced interrogation techniques that involve anal. Or at least a laser beam up the butt.

Fuck. Spoke too soon.

If I could spill some juicy secrets, I'd do so right about now. Instead, I tell Ishmael to stop.

The burning goes away. "I don't think it's a good idea to leave it like this. I'm halfway through."

"So?" I growl.

"You'll have a half moon on your anus," he says. "Or a smiley face if you look from the right angle."

I exhale a big sigh. The last thing I want is for Max to ask about a smiley face on my ass. "Fine. Let's finish this."

"Hold on. This might help." His heavy footsteps thud away and return.

Suddenly, my butthole freezes over.

"What the hell?"

He clears his throat. "The pain from laser is caused by heat, so I'm trying to cool the area with ice."

I give him a glare over my shoulder. "Shouldn't you ask me before putting ice cubes into my ass?"

Looking chagrined, he removes the ice. "I was trying to help."

"Just finish the fucking torture." I turn away and grit my teeth again.

He resumes, and it's actually more tolerable after the ice. Feeling surly, I don't tell him that.

"All done," Ishmael says after what feels like an hour.

I climb off the table, pull up my pants, and think of evil things I can do to Fabio.

Ishmael tells me how much I owe him, and I pay, adding in a big tip as a thanks for the ice at the end.

"How was it?" Fabio asks when we come out.

"You might want to avoid me for the next few weeks."

Something in my face must be very convincing. Fabio pales and backs out of the place, muttering something about having to go.

"You'll like the results," Ishmael says. "You'll see, you'll be back for touch-ups."

"Touch-ups?" The question comes out as a squeal. "That shit isn't permanent?" In my rage, my brain forgets just how big my aesthetician is, and I advance on him confrontationally.

He shakes his head and prudently steps back, apparently reasoning that a Yorkie with rabies could hurt a mastiff. "As you walk, you create friction, which creates pigmentation. The results might last about six months, but no more."

I hate everyone. "There's no way I'm doing this again."

"Fair." He hands me a cream. "That's for aftercare. Call your doctor if you develop a fever, have anal discharge, bleeding, blisters, or open sores."

I want to puke. "Your digital online presence had better pray I don't have to see a doctor."

Slamming the salon door loudly behind me, I take a cab home, my butthole smarting the entire way.

———

I feel miserable for the rest of the day, to the point where Olive accuses me of being crabby during dinner. Hey, for a marine biologist, "crabby" might mean something different than it does for normal people. It could be like her advice to keep my gills moist.

When I head to my room, I receive my usual post-dinner text from Max. As always, it's an image of an adorable creature—in this case, a fennec fox.

The surge of joy makes me forget the literal pain in my ass.

A fox that looks like a baby bunny? I write back. *No doubt it tricks the fluffy creatures into thinking it's one of them, then murders the whole family in cold blood.*

Well, that got dark quickly.

I locate a picture of a star-nosed mole and send it to Max, with a caption of: *This is what cute really looks like.*

He replies right away:

A mole again? And this time with nose tentacles? I never thought I'd type this, but those are the grossest of all types of tentacles.

I grin. *Videocall?*

He says he needs twenty minutes, and I use that time to refresh my makeup and put on my nicer home T-shirt.

When we get on the phone, he tells me about his day, but I don't reciprocate. Operation Laser into Butt is need-to-know, and unless he's here and I'm desperately craving some anal, he doesn't need to know. Instead, I tell him about the Russian restaurant outing to see if he'll want to avoid it.

"I'd love to go with you," he says, and I wish I could kiss him through the internet.

He's either not aware that other Russians can spot their own or is especially brave/cocky.

"You won't be too tired?" I ask. "It's the day you fly in."

"Nope, it's fine. I'll even have time to pick you up."

"You sure? The restaurant is in Brooklyn, which is on the way from the airport. Picking me up would be a major detour."

He flashes me a dimpled grin. "I insist. On our first date, I'm picking you up even if that means going to Brooklyn three times. Maybe four."

"Fine, but come up when you get here. As a reward, I'll let you see my cat and my sister's octopus."

His grin widens. "Your pussy cat and an octo-pus?"

Heat covers my face and other regions. "Seeing *that* might have to wait until after the event."

His voice turns growly. "I can't wait."

Here we go. Activating femme fatale mode. I lick my lips seductively, just the way he likes.

He looks insta-hungry. "Strip."

I do as he says, and he joins me.

Will my butt get in the way of masturbating?

Nope. The cybersex that follows is the best thus far. If anything, once my brain is bathing in the post-orgasmic endorphins, the pain in my ass is but a distant memory.

CHAPTER
Twenty-Seven

OUR WORK-THEN-CYBERSEX ROUTINE continues gloriously as my butt heals, all the way until the day Max is due back.

Working on that day is difficult. Instead of concentrating on **classified**, I think about Maximus in all of my holes, even butt—though I know I should give it more time to heal.

Speaking of the butt, when I get home from work, I take an analfie to check it out.

Nice and pink. Not sure if the pain was worth it, but hey, it's done now, and I feel a little more femme fatale-ish this way. Max had better appreciate it—assuming I show it to him, which is on my agenda.

Speaking of Max, he texts me when he lands.

Shit. I have to get ready for the restaurant.

It takes me over an hour to perfect all the grooming, makeup application, and dress-up. The final touch is some double-sided tape between my boobs and on the bodice of the dress. I don't want Sergeant and Captain to make a premature appearance tonight.

When I'm happy with how I look, I take a selfie and shoot it over to Fabio.

Amazeballs, he replies.

Is he still trying to appease me after Operation Laser into Butt?

Just in case, I prance over to the living room and ask Olive what she thinks.

"Wow, sis," she exclaims. "The spy won't know what hit him."

Even Machete must like it, or at least that's how I interpret his rubbing against my leg.

Don't feel too flattered, feeble human. Machete has marked you so the cats outside his castle are aware that eating your face is Machete's prerogative.

"Hey," I say to Olive. "Do you need to get any groceries or anything like that?"

She grins knowingly. "Max is going to come up?"

I nod.

"I'll get some sunblock," she says and uses up a whole tube on her face and arms despite the late hour.

Hey, whatever it takes to get some privacy.

Ten minutes after Olive leaves, Max texts me to let me know he's outside.

Come up, I reply.

As I wait, butterflies waterboard each other in my stomach. I haven't seen him for a week. True, we've seen each other on our screens, but that's not the same thing. What if—

The doorbell chimes.

As I pull open the door, I can smell his maple-lavender scent—and then Max is in front of me in all his delicious glory.

"Hi." His voice is dripping with sex, his honey-flecked green eyes scanning me from head to toe and turning darker in the process.

Meanwhile, I'm scanning him right back. He's wearing a perfectly tailored navy suit that emphasizes the impressive breadth of his shoulders and the lean-ness of his waist. It makes me want to rip it off him—along with his crisp white shirt and whatever boxers or briefs are attempting to contain the growing bulge in his pants. Unless he's commando?

Oh, crap. Just the thought of that makes me feel like I'm about to combust. How violently would Gia kill me if I skipped her show to fuck his brains out?

"Hello," I breathe.

His nostrils flare, and with no further preamble, he clasps my upper arms, pulls me to him, and crushes his lips against mine.

CHAPTER
Twenty-Eight

THE KISS IS HOT. Hotter than all of our cybersexing combined. As his tongue strokes sensually over my lips and dips into my mouth, I feel like every tastebud on my tongue has turned into a clit. Gasping, I rise up on tiptoes and press against his hard body, my arms winding around his strong neck as I return the kiss with growing fervor.

After a couple of dizzying minutes, he reluctantly pulls away. His voice is rough with frustration, his jaw taut. "We need to go soon."

I blink up at him dazedly. I'm pretty sure the scorching heat between us has fried at least a few of my brain cells. "Yeah. I—we should."

He steps back and gives me another hungry once-over. "You look stunning."

I lick my throbbing lips. "Thanks. And you should always wear a suit, or better yet, nothing at all."

A sexy smirk curves his mouth. "Noted. Now, where are the animals you promised?"

Animals. Right. Trying not to think about my over-stimulated libido, I grip his hand and lead him into the living room, where I gesture at the giant aquarium. "That's Beaky."

Max studies the octopus with a mixture of awe and unease. "Wow. He's just like that picture you sent me. Definitely something horror-movie-esque about him."

Beaky must not like his statement. That or it's a coincidence that he changes his color at this very moment.

"Come, let's find the cat." I grab his hand again and try not to melt into a puddle of need as his strong fingers squeeze gently around mine.

As we look for Machete, I realize it's for the best that I haven't ravished Max yet. What if the damned cat attacks Maximus the way he did Bill's dildo and kiwis?

"There he is," Max says, pointing at a corner in the kitchen. A warm smile illuminates his face as he approaches the cat. "He's beautiful."

Things happen too fast for me to react.

Max bends and extends his hand—a kamikaze maneuver.

Machete rushes at the hand.

I cringe, fully expecting sharp claws to rake Max's flesh.

Instead, in a nanosecond, Max is holding the cat against his chest, and the evil creature is actually purring.

What the fuck?

Is Max a cat whisperer?

This must be something they teach at the Russian

spy school. They start with how to seduce a human, but by lesson sixty-nine, it's all about how to seduce a cat.

After all, a spy needs to be a master of all kinds of pussy.

I narrow my eyes at Machete. "Traitor."

The cat couldn't care less what I say.

Machete approves of this human. His symmetrical face makes Machete want to curl up on it and take a long nap.

No way. The only pussy on that face will be mine.

"You're going to get fur on your suit," I say, recovering my wits.

"Right." Max gently puts Machete down.

The cat darts me—or maybe the world—a death glare.

Machete's fur is a decoration. A badge of honor not worthy of impudent gnats.

———

We make it out of my apartment with all digits and limbs intact, and Max ushers me into a cab. As we battle the usual traffic, he tells me about his flight home, which apparently included a chatty old lady who sat next to him on the plane.

As I listen to him describe her antics, I can't help but think that she was hitting on him. What straight woman wouldn't? I know I'd be up for Maximus even if I were pushing a hundred.

Finally, the cab turns onto Brighton Beach, and we pass by storefronts that have signs written in Russian.

The people who enter the stores wouldn't look out of place on the streets of Moscow circa twenty years go.

I watch Max's face for any signs of nostalgia.

Nope. He's either not a spy, is schooling his features, or isn't the sentimental type.

Our cab stops.

My heart sinks as I take in the restaurant that is our destination. I point at the horrific objects in front of us. "Am I hallucinating that?"

Max follows my gaze and frowns. "If you're talking about the giant chicken legs that serve as columns for the restaurant, I see them too."

I *am* talking about the giant bird legs. If he were to say they belong to some fiendish chicken, I'd believe it —not that this makes the horrifying sight any better.

I grip my head in my palms. "Why? Why would someone do this? Is this some Russian version of Halloween?"

Even then, something this terrifying would be the equivalent of using real cadavers to scare trick-or-treaters.

Max grimaces and pats my shoulder. "I'm pretty sure those legs allude to the fairy tales featuring Baba Yaga. If the Russian version is anything like the Ukrainian one, Baba Yaga is an evil witch who eats children, and she lives in a hut in the woods that stands on giant chicken legs."

"I guess that tracks. Nothing says pure evil like anything with bird body parts. They could've just as easily given this restaurant the legs of Freddy Krueger while they were at it."

"Are you going to be able to go inside?" he asks, eyeing me with concern.

I suppress a shudder. "I think so. They're not real. Do you think this means they serve a lot of chicken?"

He takes out his phone and swipes across the screen for a few seconds. "No more than normal. Which makes sense. If I'm right about the theme, the meat of children would be a bigger concern, but fortunately, that's not on the menu either."

"Fine, let's go." I grasp his hand as tightly as I can, and let him lead me toward the horrific legs.

This must be what the entrance to hell looks like. When we're next to them, I close my eyes and let Max guide me like a Seeing Eye dog.

Why does Gia need to perform in venues that have bird-related impediments? Does it have anything to do with the Zombie Tit Massacre? She was there too. Maybe this is her way of processing that trauma?

I hear a door open and close, followed by the hum of voices and the faint din of cutlery on china. Delicious, savory smells waft into my nostrils. Gingerly, I crack open my eyes and release my death grip on Max's hand.

"Are you okay?" he asks with a soft smile.

I nod, scanning our surroundings in fascination.

We're inside the restaurant. The place is teeming with marble and crystal, and there's a stage in the middle of the large space. That must be where Gia is going to perform her show. For now, though, the stage is occupied by a pudgy bearded dude wearing an outfit that looks like an explosion at the glitter factory. Oh, and he's singing—or more like butchering—"Wrecking Ball" with a thick Russian accent.

"I pray he doesn't take his clothes off or lick power tools, à la Miley Cyrus in the video," I whisper at Max.

He grins. "Do we have an assigned table?"

Great question. I text it to Gia.

As I wait for a reply, I notice how nicely dressed all the patrons are. It reminds me of those black-tie infiltration scenes that feature in every spy movie and show.

Maybe Max and I should team up and steal the borscht recipe from the kitchen?

Instead of replying via text, Gia runs up to us.

Wow. She's usually even paler than Olive, but her makeup today would make Dracula's geisha look tan in comparison.

"Thank you for coming," she says. "The show will start in a few. For now, why don't you join us?" She points to a large table with the best view of the stage.

"Sure," I say. "Let's go."

Gia looks at Max. "Won't you introduce us first?"

Ah. Right. "Max, this is Gia, my sister and tonight's entertainment. She's a magician, so mind your possessions."

Oops. Why did I warn him about that last part? I could learn something about him if Gia stole his wallet.

"Nice to meet you," Max says, pointedly covering his inner jacket pocket.

Gia grins. "Thanks for showing me where you keep something worth stealing."

"No flirting with my date," I whisper loudly.

She rolls her eyes. "I have my own."

And boy, does she. When we reach the table, a guy *almost* as hot as Max gives her an adoring look. This is codename Tigger. His real name is Anatolio Cezaroff.

Gia starts introducing everyone clockwise around the table. As she does, I evaluate them as a spy might.

The dark and broody birthday boy is Vlad Chortsky. Next to him is his girlfriend, Fanny—a round-faced beauty who's blushing for some unknown reason. Alex Chortsky is Vlad's more cheerful-looking brother who's my sister Holly's boyfriend. Good for her—the Chortskys clearly have great genes.

Speaking of good genes, the Cezaroffs are hot too. At least Tigger's brother Dragomir is. Apparently, he's dating the Chortsky sister, Bella—a woman who pulls off the femme fatale look much better than I do. I make a mental note to befriend her and ask for tips.

Last but not least are the matriarch and patriarch of the Chortsky clan, who are the owners of this restaurant. They're named Boris and Natasha, and they look and sound exactly like those characters from *Rocky and Bullwinkle*. Natasha is wearing more makeup than all of Fabio's drag queen friends combined, while Boris boasts a unibrow that a caterpillar might want to have a passionate affair with.

"Happy birthday, Vlad." Max shakes the broody man's hand and puts an envelope in it.

A bribe to make sure he doesn't recognize him as a fellow Russian? It's either that or a birthday gift—a great idea that I should've thought of.

"You're late, so you have to do penalty shots," says Boris.

Natasha narrows her eyes at her husband. "Why do you care? You're not drinking vodka, remember?"

Interesting. Boris is holding the biggest beer mug I've ever seen with some dark ale in it. He's the only one, too. Everyone else has vodka shot glasses in front of them.

Boris looks at the vodka bottle longingly, the way I'd look at Maximus if Max whipped it out for me. "Traditions are traditions, regardless of my sobriety."

Drinking beer is sobriety?

"How about we toast to the health of the birthday boy," Max says and grabs the vodka bottle.

He then pours shots for everyone except Boris.

When Max is by Natasha, she gives him a carnal once-over and thanks him in a voice so husky Max could use it as a sled dog back in Canada. As Max is filling Gia's glass, Natasha winks at her. "You and your sisters have a gift for finding the most attractive men."

Bella rolls her eyes. "Mom! Those men include your son. Is it too much to ask that you behave like a married woman for one evening?"

Natasha looks like she's about to say something cutting to her daughter, but Dragomir jumps to his feet and says, "I wanted to add my warm wishes to Max's."

Everyone joins in with the same sentiments, and Fanny kisses the birthday boy on the cheek before blushing like she's just been caught giving him a hand job under the table.

We down the shots.

The only nice thing I can say about vodka is that it's not horilka.

By the time I catch my breath, Max has already piled a bunch of Russian food on my plate. Some of it looks like the things we ate at Salo, but some are different. It's all delicious, though, and I focus solely on the meal for a few minutes.

When the edge of my hunger has been blunted, I check out my sisters' plates.

Gia has a spread similar to mine, but Holly only has one thing on hers—the dumplings called *pelmeni*. Specifically, she's got seven of them, which means she still likes her prime numbers.

I catch her gaze. "Hey, sis, what's the largest known prime number?"

Holly smiles shyly. "It's a Mersenne prime, which means—"

"That it's an even number minus one," I say, mostly as a way to remind her that I deal with prime numbers as part of cryptography.

Holly's smile turns radiant. "That's not exactly wrong, but the precise definition is 'a power of two minus one.' Three and seven would be examples, but thirteen wouldn't." She looks around the table, and her smile wanes. "Anyway, the largest known prime as of right now is two to the power of 82,589,933 minus one."

Everyone looks ready for another shot to block out our conversation, but I'm hoping I've planted the seed needed for a get-together with Holly outside of family events.

Holly looks around the table again. "On a related note… Is anyone else joining us?"

Ah. Right. There are twelve of us at the table, and she'd prefer the prime thirteen.

"My friend Clarice is coming," Gia says to her twin reassuringly.

Natasha pouts. "Then there will be thirteen of us. That's unlucky."

"Bollocks," Holly retorts, and everyone stares at her. "Sorry," she says and takes in a deep breath. In a calmer tone, she explains, "Thirteen isn't unlucky in China, and they're seventeen percent of Earth's population."

Alex strokes Holly's back. "It's also not unlucky in India. Another seventeen percent of humanity."

Natasha opens her mouth but forgets what she was about to say when Clarice turns up.

I can't blame Natasha. It's not every day someone comes into a restaurant dressed like a pirate. Or into any place that's not hosting a Halloween party.

Like a broken record, Boris says something about penalty shots, and his wife reminds him he's a beer drinker now. Before anyone can save her from paying the penalty, Clarice pours herself a healthy shot of vodka and downs it like a professional Russian.

"Wow," Boris says. "She'll make some man very lucky someday."

Bella rolls her eyes again. "If she does, it won't be with her drinking."

This time, it's Boris who seems to be about to say something mean to his daughter, but Dragomir jumps to his feet once again. "It's time for Vovochka jokes."

Everyone looks pleased at this, and I recall that

Vovochka is the fictional butt of many Russian jokes, a bit like little Johnny.

"I've got one," Vlad says, much to my surprise. Out of everyone, I didn't expect the gloomy one to crack a joke, especially considering that Vovochka is a diminutive of Vladimir—the full version of Vlad's name.

"Young Vovochka walks up to little Fannychka and says, 'Can I make use of you… as a woman?' She frowns at him. 'You have such dirty thoughts.' He looks at her, confused. 'My tennis ball rolled into the girl's bathroom.'"

Fanny nearly chokes on her food, and everyone else chuckles.

"I've got one," Alex says. "The teacher comes to class wearing a pendant in the shape of a plane on her bosom. Throughout the lesson, Vovochka stares unblinkingly at the pendant. Finally, the teacher can't take it anymore and asks, 'What? You like the plane?' Vovochka shakes his head. 'I like the airport.'"

More chuckles, and then Gia pipes up. "I've got one, but the credit for it belongs to Tigger."

"I can't take the credit." Tigger lovingly touches her hand. "A Russian diplomat told it to me."

"Well, in any case," Gia says. "Vovochka is sitting on a tree with binoculars, watching his teacher change. She spots him and yells, 'Shame on you! Don't bother coming to school without your father.' Vovochka turns his head. 'Dad, you heard her, right?'"

Most people chuckle, but Tigger, Clarice, my sisters, and I laugh uproariously in support.

"I have one," Natasha says and darts a glance at

Bella. "Daughter asks her mother, 'What do you like more, doggies or butterflies?' The mother frowns. 'No tattoos.' The disobedient daughter frowns too. 'But Mom, please. I'll put it in the least noticeable place.' This is when Vovochka turns to his sister and asks, 'On your brain?'"

Only Boris chuckles this time. We've all caught some mother-daughter tension between the lines of that joke.

"Do they have to be Vovochka jokes?" Dragomir asks.

"Traditionally." Boris gives the word volumes of meaning.

"Well, I'd love to hear something different," Bella says pointedly.

"Okay," Dragomir says. "Anyone who's a stickler for tradition can replace Vika with Vovochka in the next one." He clears his throat. "Little Vika asks her mom, 'Where do you insert a tampon?' Her mom nearly chokes on an apple. When she recovers, she says, 'Well… into the same place babies come from.' Vika gapes at her mom. 'Into a stork?'"

The chuckles are more enthusiastic this time, but before anyone else can tell another joke, the pudgy performer speaks loudly on the stage. "Ladies and gentlemen, please join me on the dance floor."

Vlad and Fanny jump to their feet, followed by Holly and Alex, and the other couples hurry after them.

Max stands up and extends his hand to me. "Care for a dance?"

Does a bear shit on Moscow streets?

As I clasp his big hand, a zing shoots up my body,

and I feel like I'm floating as we make our way to the dance floor.

An unfamiliar slow song starts playing, with Russian lyrics I can barely make out. Max clasps my hand in a ballroom dance position, sending another zing to my feminine organs. Then he puts his other hand on my lower back, tripling the zings.

We begin to sway as the mustachioed singer belts out something in Russian about love, windows, and millions of scarlet roses.

My heart pounds faster. This reminds me of every scene where James Bond or some tux-clad spy copycat would dance with the femme fatale right before the heist portion of the black-tie infiltration. Or maybe this is more like a classic duel of seduction, one that I'm not sure who's winning. Maximus is at full mast against my belly, and on my end, if it were socially acceptable, I'd have my way with Max here and now. As is, I'm extremely tempted to flake out on Gia's show and find some private place to ravish my date.

But no. I have to support my sister.

Someone get me a medal.

Speaking of rewards, can I at least kiss him? Is that okay to do in Russian restaurants? More importantly, can I stop myself from becoming an exhibitionist if we do kiss?

Max must have the same idea. He leans down, and our lips are just about to lock when someone clears her stupid throat right behind me.

"What?" The edge in my voice could cut a bitch.

Letting go of Max, I turn and channel my sexual frustration into a glare.

I've met the woman in front of me before. Her name is Harry, and she's one of Gia's million roommate friends. She's into rope tricks—the magic kind, not bondage. Maybe bondage too. Who knows?

"Sorry," Harry says sheepishly. "We were just looking for Gia." She nods at a gaggle of other girls, and I realize these are the above-mentioned roommates.

"She's either here on the dance floor or at our table." I point in the direction of Clarice's pirate hat.

"Thanks," Harry says and backs away.

I turn back to Max to go through with the kissing, but the music stops.

"Now something to get your blood pumping," says the singer. "Gangnam Style."

And just like that, the joyful music of the K-pop sensation starts, and the mustachioed guy gets everyone into position—legs spread, but not in the way I want.

Wait, are his lyrics in Russian?

Yep. Something about horses, which I guess makes sense, given the "hold the reins" dance everyone is doing.

Is it weird that Max looks hot doing this? When he executes the lasso move, I want to be the thing he catches. When he bobs the reins, I want to be the one he's riding. Maybe I'll want some pony play later?

Speaking of "later," when is Gia's show going to start? I want this outing over so I can have some privacy with Max. Also, what's with the ever-growing crowd of people pouring into the restaurant? Are they here for the magic show?

Seems likely. Since there's no more room to sit at the tables, they aren't here to eat.

Halfway into "Gangnam Style" in the Russian style, nature calls, so I tell Max I'll be back and head over to the bathroom.

There's an attendant here. Fancy.

Leaving my stall, I come face to face with Bella, Holly's new BFF and the Chortsky sister.

She grins. "You look so much like Holly and Gia it's uncanny."

I smile back. "You should see the other five sisters I've got. We're literally identical."

"I've heard." She starts washing her hands. "I have to admit, I'm jealous. With two brothers, I've always wanted a sister."

"The grass is always greener." I turn on the faucet, and the attendant spurts soap into my outstretched hands. I nod in thanks before saying to Bella, "I think I speak for my parents and all my sisters when I say that we'd sacrifice at least two of us for one brother."

Bella dries her hands. "Well, if Holly marries Alex, you'll have one of mine. I'd give him a ten out of ten as far as bros go. Vlad too."

Huh. So Bella and I might end up related. That's cool.

Rubbing a towel over my hands, I ask something I've been dying to know. "Does my date seem like a Russian to you?"

She looks thoughtful. "Gia asked us that too. In my opinion, he doesn't. My brothers didn't think so either."

Is my glee visible on my face?

"What about your parents?" I ask.

"We didn't include them in this because they don't know the definition of the word *discreet*."

"Makes sense," I say. "And thank you."

"No problem." She glances at the bathroom attendant and says something in Russian. I think it's along the lines of, "Can you give us a moment?"

Supporting my translation, the attendant nods and leaves the room.

Weird. What's this about?

"I wanted to ask you for a favor," Bella says. "And I'm willing to pay for your trouble, of course."

Doesn't she own a company that makes sex toys? How can I help with that? If she wants my permission to make a replica of Maximus, that will be a "no." A very hard, mouthwatering "no."

"What's the favor?" I ask cautiously.

She takes out her phone. "I have a new line of toys that work over the internet. My paranoid brother wrote the app for it, and Holly took a look and deemed it secure, but I still worry some perv will hack it to take videos of unsuspecting users, so I figured I'd talk to you."

Oh. That sounds right up my alley. "Sure," I say. "Let's exchange info, and I'll tell you what I need to take a look."

She extends her carefully manicured hand. "Thank you so much."

I give it a business-like shake. "What's the name of the app?"

She tells me, and I search for it in the app store. When I lift my gaze from my phone, she's holding a giant blue dildo in her hands.

I blink and look her over. Where did she pull that out of? Is she like the movie femme fatales? They hide guns in tight outfits like hers, but the basic skill is the same.

I take a step back. "I'd rather get paid with bitcoin if you don't mind. Cash is fine too. A check even."

She waggles the dildo. "This isn't payment. It's a sample device the app controls. I figured you'd—"

"Can you mail it to my house?" I ask. "I don't have a place to stash something that size right now."

Maybe she'll tell me where *she* had it hidden?

She hands me her phone instead. "Can you add yourself to my contacts?"

I do as she asks, and when I look up, the dildo is gone—and I have no clue where she put it, only perverted guesses.

"We should go back," I say. "If the show starts and I miss it, Gia will make me disappear."

Bella grins. "Let's go."

It's a good thing we get moving when we do. As we emerge from the restroom, the singer announces that the show is about to start.

Finally.

The sooner the magic is over at The Hut, the sooner it can start in Max's bedroom.

CHAPTER
Twenty~Nine

I RUSH TO MY SEAT, only to do a double take.

Gia is still at the table.

How is she going to perform for the show if—

The lights dim, and a spotlight falls on the stage.

A woman dressed in Amish-looking clothing is standing there, a bow in her hands.

"Is that part of one of your tricks?" I whisper to Gia.

"No, this is a different show," she responds. "Mine is after."

A melancholy music begins playing, and a bunch of dancers appear on the stage. One woman with a garish outfit and heavy makeup performs a strange ballet number. Another one dances to a sad song, and then the lady with the bow dances to a heroic-sounding tune.

Why is this vaguely familiar?

I watch, fascinated, until I notice that the heroine has a bird pin on her new outfit.

Yuck. Bird.

Wait a second.

Is this an unauthorized ballet version of *The Hunger Games*?

This is a restaurant, and if I'm right, the subliminal messaging might well make folks buy more pelmeni than they should.

Yep. The theme music is from the movie, and now that I've made the connection, the next set of dances fits the theory perfectly.

I guess Russians aren't too keen on such trivialities as copyright laws. Or maybe The Hut actually licensed the rights?

On my end, I wish *The Hunger Games*—including this interpretation—wasn't so reliant on bird imagery. The fictional mockingjay that Katniss wears on her pin is a creature of nightmares, as it can imitate sounds better than a parrot. Not that the real bird that it's derived from—the mockingbird—is any better. All birds are mocking bastards. That's the main reason they produce sounds.

As if sensing my unease, Max scoots his chair closer to mine and drapes an arm over my shoulders.

I love it, though it makes me want to leave all the more.

In the periphery of my vision, I spot Gia and Tigger sneaking out.

Aha. I hope that means her show is starting soon.

The arena part of the ballet begins. It reminds me of the dance of the four little swans from *Swan Lake*, only with more dancers.

I shudder. *Swan Lake* is a horror ballet glamorizing creatures that can hold a grudge forever. What makes them extra blood-chilling is that they can fly at sixty miles per hour and break bones with a hit of their wings.

As the surreal ballet continues, I can't help but reflect on what Bella said about Max. If Max is truly not Russian, and therefore not a spy, our plans later tonight take on a new wonderfulness. Instead of seducing an enemy, which is cool, I'll be finally hooking up with my boyfriend, which is mind-boggling, since it means I won't have to guard my heart.

Unfortunately, I'm still not one-hundred-percent sure he's *not* a spy.

Returning my attention to the show, I realize that Katniss must be dancing her victory—though it looks like the "black swan" dance from the horror ballet, also made famous by the movie of the same name, where the worst possible fate befalls Natalie Portman. Spoiler alert: she turns into a bird.

The dancers leave, and Gia's show is announced.

Whew.

I clap, and my sisters and Gia's friends join in. Some even whistle.

Gia comes out with Tigger, which explains why they left together. She's wearing her most vampire-like outfit and makeup yet, while Tigger is dressed in an extremely low-cut, skin-tight leotard that exposes the entirety of his muscular chest.

Or is it called a tigertard when *he* wears it?

"Thank you all for coming to my show," Gia says, and the crowd goes wild again.

If I had any doubts that the extra people in the

restaurant have come to see her, they're gone. Their enthusiasm indicates that this is the main event they've been dying to see.

"I'll start with a classic," Gia says, nodding at Tigger.

He grabs two chairs and brings them to the middle of the stage. Gia makes some mysterious gestures, and it looks like Tigger goes into a hypnotic trance. He doesn't really, of course. According to a classified CIA file, hypnosis is not real, at least insofar as something that can be weaponized.

Moving like a zombie, Tigger walks over to the chairs and lies down so his head is on one chair, while his feet are on the other.

Is Gia showing off her boyfriend's strong core?

Nope. Gia pulls the first chair away, and Tigger is left balancing on his neck only. Before anyone can react, Gia pulls away the other chair, and Tigger hovers in the air.

Everyone in the crowd gasps, except maybe Gia's magic pals.

Gia waves her hands.

Tigger levitates higher.

The gasps grow louder.

Gia stops her voodoo for a moment. "Can I get a volunteer?"

A million arms shoot up.

She chooses a tall guy and asks him to check Tigger for any wires.

When the guy doesn't locate any, she thanks him and tells him to return to his seat.

With another wave of Gia's hand, Tigger's feet start to dip to the ground. Slowly, he levitates down before waking up and taking a courtly bow.

Gia bows too, and we all applaud, creating a noise proportional to the miracle we've just witnessed.

"Now for something lighter," Gia says. "I need another volunteer."

This time, she chooses the pudgy singer.

"What's your name, sir?" she asks.

He twirls his mustache. "Boris."

Wait, isn't that also the name of the patriarch of the Chortsky family? Now that I think about it, the two Borises kind of look alike.

"Can you check Tigger's nipples?" Gia says.

Boris isn't as confused by the command as I'd be. Grinning lecherously, he pinches Tigger's right nipple, then his left.

Wow. I'm glad Gia went for a gender reversal with her assistant.

Gia's eyebrows furrow regardless. "Did I say you could pinch my boyfriend's nipples?"

Boris pales. "I'm sorry."

She smirks. "Oh, it's okay. I just wanted to establish who's in charge here."

The audience chuckles.

"Now." Gia points at Tigger's right nipple. "Watch closely."

She walks over and covers the nipple with her gloved palm for one second. When she pulls her hand away, the nipple is gone.

I—and the whole audience—gape at the smooth skin on Tigger's right peck.

How?

Why?

"You can touch it," Gia says to Boris imperiously.

Boris gets handsy with Tigger's pec one more time, looking more and more puzzled as he continues fondling it.

"Is it there?" Gia asks.

Boris shakes his head and backs away. "No. And please don't make any of *my* parts disappear."

With a grin, Gia repeats the trick with the left nipple —which is when her magic friends finally join everyone else in a gasp.

Growing up with Gia, I learned that magicians don't repeat their tricks, since that can give away how they're done. Gia has just broken that rule and yet still hasn't been caught doing anything sneaky.

Boris checks the second missing nipple area.

Nothing.

Looking rightfully smug, Gia covers both nipple-less areas with her palms for a moment, then lets us see that Tigger's muscular chest has returned to its natural state.

The applause is thunderous this time.

Gia and Tigger bow.

For the next classic trick, Gia stands in a metal frame with her arms spread apart. Dramatic music starts to play, and Tigger passes through Gia's midsection, like in the movie *Alien*.

We all clap, but I'm probably not the only one thinking: did Tigger just sort of penetrate Gia in front of us?

The next trick could also be interpreted as a weird glimpse into my sister's sex life. Tigger binds her with chains and locks, then deposits her into a large chest, like his personal slave girl. He then stands on top of the chest, holding a cloth. With a flash of pyrotechnics, Gia ends up on top of the chest, and Tigger is found inside, now bound for Gia's pleasure.

"I'm beginning to think he's lost a bet to her," I whisper to Max after the insane applause dies down.

As if to confirm my theory, Gia cuts Tigger in half for her next trick, then puts him in a water torture cell.

Hey, he's lucky she didn't perform the cups-and-balls trick using his balls. Or maybe that's on the agenda.

Nope. His balls are safe. Gia seats him on a chair, covers him with a cloth, and makes him vanish.

"Now I'll have to work doubly hard without the misdirection provided by my scrumptious assistant," she says, and the women in the audience give her knowing nods.

The next few tricks are mentalism effects—which suit Gia well. She tells a number of people what they're thinking of, guesses someone's bank account number, and then disappears with a puff of smoke, like Batman, as her goodbye.

I leap to my feet and clap until my palms are sore, as does everyone else.

After a few minutes of this, Tigger and Gia walk out dressed in their restaurant attire and take a bow.

The clapping goes nuts again, and it takes Boris starting another song to get everyone to calm down.

"You were unbelievable," I tell Gia when she joins us at the table.

She grins. "That's high praise, coming from family."

It's true. We got tired of magic after years of her learning and using us as practice guinea pigs.

For the next few minutes, she quizzes me on which tricks I liked the most, and I tell her my honest opinion.

"Thanks," she says at the end. "I'm still working on my repertoire."

"No problem." I sneak a glance at Max, who happens to be talking to Vlad. "If you're not performing again tonight, I think we might head home."

She gives me a knowing look. "Good luck. Let me know what happens."

I jump to my feet and clear my throat to get everyone's attention.

Twelve pairs of eyes zero in on me.

"Max had a long flight today, so we're turning in early tonight," I say as calmly as I can.

Max winks at me, and the rest of the group look like they aren't buying what I'm selling.

Maybe it says "I want to fuck Max" on my forehead?

"It was lovely to meet you all," I say as I clutch Max's elbow. "And happy birthday again, Vlad."

Max covers my hand with his as he says his good-byes, and we hurry to the door. As we're passing through the entrance, I close my eyes again to avoid the feeling that I'm stepping out of a chicken's cloaca.

Max hails a cab.

"Your place?" I whisper seductively into his ear when the cab pulls up to the curb.

"Fuck, yes," he growls and opens the door for me.

Fuck yes, indeed. Fucking him is what I've desperately needed for many days, and it's finally happening.

As soon as he joins me in the car, I activate turbocharged femme fatale mode and channel my excitement into a panty-melting kiss that makes me tip the driver extra generously to compensate for the cleanup of the puddle I might've left behind on the seat.

———

Max's building is swanky, which is a point against him being a spy, I think, as they prefer to seem average. Well, whatever he really does for a living must pay well.

We make out in the elevator, and when we enter his apartment, I expect us to leave a trail of clothes on the way to his bedroom, like crumbs by Hansel and Gretel. Wait, no. They did it with candy, plus they were brother and sister. How about I expect us to rip each other's clothes off like something out of a James Bond film?

Yeah. That's better.

Except Max doesn't initiate either one of those options, instead saying, "Do you want a tour of my apartment?"

If I were a card-carrying femme fatale, I'd tell him, "Fuck, no, I want you inside me." But being the seductress wimp that I am, I nod and tell myself that this is just reconnaissance before I pounce.

Max leads me down a corridor featuring animal posters that remind me of those in his childhood bedroom. He shows me a cozy living room and then a study with bookshelves decorated from top to bottom with animal figurines, sorted by species. There are also stuffed animals, including the panda he bought on our first date. It's sitting among other bears.

This is when I spot it.

A horrific shelf teeming with birds.

Yikes. I never realized how creepy toy birds can be. They stare at me with their beady little eyes. Those horror movie dolls that come to life have nothing on these tiny atrocities.

Swallowing hard, I take a step back.

"Oh, crap, sorry," Max says when he notices where I'm staring. "I didn't think this through."

"It's fine," I lie.

"No." He turns me toward him and frames my face with his large palms. His voice is deep and soft, his eyes gleaming like polished jade. "I'll get rid of them, I promise."

Them? As in the birds? For some reason, I can't remember any birds.

I dampen my lips. "You can just keep them in a box. Or in a closet that I'll avoid."

"Come." He lets me go without a kiss.

What the hell?

I follow him into a modern-looking kitchen.

"Would you like some coffee to help you sober up?" he asks.

"Sober up?" My spine stiffens. "Who says I'm drunk?"

He pinches the bridge of his nose. "I'm sorry. You drank vodka, so I assumed that..."

Is this why he hasn't ravished me yet? Is he afraid to take advantage of me?

It's sweet and patronizing at the same time.

"With that assumption, you've made an ass of you and me," I say with a huff. "I'm ready to operate heavy machinery." I sneak a glance at Maximus. "But hey, you can go ahead and have a cup to get *your* brain into gear."

He smiles sheepishly. "I think I'm fine."

"Great." I tap my foot pointedly. "Is there another room you want to show me?"

"Yes." His eyes gleam hungrily. "The bedroom."

"Now *that* I can't wait to see," I say in a come-hither tone that would redeem me in the eyes of the Femme Fatale Association of America.

"You sure you're ready to see it?" The question comes out gruff, making me want to see "it" all the more.

"Are you free of STDs?" I ask.

He nods. "You?"

I take a step toward him. "I'm clean and on the pill."

"Good." He slowly advances. "Anything else you want to know before the end of the tour?"

This is my chance. I'm the closest I've been to having him by the balls—until it happens literally, hopefully soon. "Are you sure you're Ukrainian?"

He stops his advance. "What else would I be?"

"Russian, maybe?"

A hint of a frown mars his forehead. "No, I'm

Ukrainian, like I said. And just so you know, some Ukrainians would be offended by that question."

Now I feel like an idiot who doesn't know her geopolitics. Which I do. Like all would-be spies must. "I'm sorry."

"It's fine," he says with a shrug. "I'm not one of those easily offended. Being second generation, I don't harbor my parents' animosity toward Russia."

"Still, I *am* sorry. I didn't mean to imply there's no difference between Russia and Ukraine." I take in a deep breath. "That question was my roundabout way of asking something else."

He arches an eyebrow. "What?"

"It relates to my job." I drag in another deep breath, and as I let it out, I blurt, "Are you a foreign intelligence agent?"

There. Subtle as a rhino on ice, but at least the cards are now on the table. If he can convince me that he's not a spy, I'll enjoy what's about to happen that much more, so I watch him closely as he responds.

To my chagrin, he's got a poker face on. "I'm *not* a foreign intelligence agent."

Crap. Are his stony expression and expressionless tone attempts to hide the truth, or hurt at being accused of such a thing?

I'm leaning toward the latter, and therefore, I'm about ninety-nine-percent convinced he's not a spy.

Good enough. I grab his hand. "Show me the bedroom."

Some of the stoniness leaves his face, and the honey flecks in his eyes darken with rekindled hunger.

Squeezing my fingers in his big, warm hand, he leads me into a luxurious bedroom where someone has laid out flower petals and candles in a scene that is more Hallmark movie than spy flick.

My heartbeat picks up pace. He *has* been planning to bring me here. I was beginning to wonder.

"One second." He releases my hand and lights the candles.

Ugh. Tease much?

When he's done, I almost give him a military salute. I'm clearly under the influence of Sergeant and Captain, which are standing at attention.

"So?" I say and then bite my suddenly dry lower lip. All of my body's moisture is obviously somewhere else.

Finally channeling movie spies, Max swoops down on me and claims my lips.

Yes!

Devouring me, he begins peeling my clothes off.

Double yes.

He rips off his shirt and suit pants along with his underwear, exposing Maximus at full mast.

"Finally," I gasp.

His response sounds like a bear growl as he picks me up and lays me down on the bed.

Here we go.

CHAPTER
Thirty

WE KISS AGAIN, our tongues tangling fiercely as he greedily runs his hands down my body, sending waves of heat to my core. His maple-lavender scent teases my nostrils and my skin prickles with a pleasurable chill as he turns me onto my stomach and starts kissing the back of my neck.

Fuck. This is so good.

He slides his tongue down my spine before stopping to lap at the dimples in my lower back.

I'm panting now, my heart racing a mile a minute. Why is this so hot? Also, can he see my bleached butthole?

Maybe. He growls, "You're so fucking gorgeous," and it's feasible he's talking to my butt.

Recalling my femme fatale mode, I mutter, "I want you. Now."

He shows off his outstanding manhandling skills as he turns me over. Despite the romantic décor, something animalistic dances in his eyes as he takes me in. Something beastly that I love.

Maybe he's one of those deep cover agents who don't know what they are until they hear a trigger phrase that "activates" them. For the Winter Soldier, that trigger happened to be "longing, rusted, seventeen, daybreak, furnace, nine, benign, homecoming, one, freight car" said in Russian. But for Max, the trigger could be my bleached asshole.

Maximus twitches as Max gives Sergeant a hard nibble.

Can nipple attention make you come?

No clue, but I'm on the verge of *something* when Max switches his attention to Captain, skillfully sucking it in.

A moan escapes my lips. From nipple play. Maybe he did attend that seduction school after all?

When I moan again, he meets my eyes and lavishes my belly with hard kisses, moving ever lower until I feel his breath cooling my overheated sex.

He gives my clit a slow lick and growls, either to create vibrations or because he's officially gone into beast mode.

My next moan is more desperate, and it encourages his next lick to be even more devastating.

My eyes roll back and my breathing rate skyrockets.

I'm on the verge of coming, and it seems that his clever tongue is keeping me there, just beyond the edge.

Evil. I want to pass that threshold so badly I'd reveal what my clit's classified codename is, along with anything else he wants to know.

No wonder they teach seduction techniques at those schools.

He cups my right breast, his thumb expertly kneading Captain. His voice is rough velvet. "Come for me."

And just like that, the command and the vibrations it sends to my clit push me over the edge. My toes curl, every muscle in my body tightens, and I feel like I'm falling through the bed as fireworks explode in my nerve endings and I come with the loudest moan to date.

He regards me with purely male satisfaction. "Good job, sonechko."

Breathing raggedly, I force my limp muscles to function and sit up. Because that's what a femme fatale would do. "Your turn to be good."

He arches an eyebrow.

"Stand on the bed." My husky command is straight from the Femme Fatale Association of America rulebook.

Muttering "fuck yeah," he stands up.

I get on my knees. How fortuitous—our heights are just right for me to be eye level with Maximus.

Max's eyes are wild as he gazes down at me.

Maintaining our eye contact, I give Maximus a lollipop lick.

Max grunts.

Maximus twitches.

Feeling encouraged, I channel my inner cat as I lap Maximus up and down.

Another grunt. Another twitch.

It's time for escalation. I take Maximus's head into my mouth.

Damn. It's like silk stretched over bulletproof glass.

I swallow him deeper.

Max's pupils widen.

With a smirk, I cup his balls (codename Kiwis) with my left hand.

Max groans. "What are you doing to me?"

Oh, I haven't done nothing yet. Teasing the underside of Maximus's head with my tongue, I gently pull on Kiwis.

A tormented plea-curse is my reward.

I speed up, doing my best to match the rhythm of Max's jerking off—something I've studied thoroughly over our week of cybersex.

Kiwis feel tighter in my hand.

"I'm close." Max sounds like he's in pain as he squeezes those words out.

I pull Maximus out to reply, "That's okay. I want you to come right in my mouth." With that, I return to my ministrations, swallowing deep as I watch Max's eyes widen almost to the size of kiwis—the fruit.

I lied, though. As hot as having him come in my mouth would be, I want him inside me that much more, and if he comes, the penetration will have to wait however long it takes Maximus to recover.

With that thought, I slow down. He kept me on the edge earlier, so this is a case of an eye for an eye.

Speaking of eyes, I close mine so I can focus on the rhythm. This seems to help. I can feel the most minute reactions from Maximus and Kiwis this way, and I slow my pace accordingly. When I feel some of the tension leave Max's body, I go faster again.

On the third such cycle, Max growls like a hungry bear whose honey was stolen.

I pull away and smirk up at him. "You don't like it when I tease you, huh?"

His jaw flexes. "I don't like it. I love it."

Wowzah. He's got to be careful with the "L" word when I have Kiwis in such a vulnerable position. It takes all of my training not to accidentally squeeze too hard.

"You deserve a special treat." I pointedly lick my finger, making sure to cover it with the drool I generated when he was down my throat.

His eyes look the wildest yet.

Smiling deviously, I get Maximus back into my mouth and squeeze Kiwis with my right hand as I direct my newly lubricated finger toward Max's butt.

This is his chance to stop me.

I position my finger in such a way that my destination is crystal clear.

He grunts in pleasure. I guess he's rolling with it. I'm glad. This is advanced class material at the Femme Fatale Association of America.

Very gently, I begin searching for codename Walnut.

Max seems to freeze in place. Hopefully, that's a good thing.

There. Soft and smooth and interesting to the touch —must be Walnut. I gently massage it as I speed up my rhythm with Maximus.

"Fuuuck!" Max shouts.

Have I hurt him? I pull my finger away from Walnut but keep sucking Maximus, figuring that will produce enough endorphins to cancel out any pain.

Ah. No. That wasn't pain in any case.

Max grunts as Maximus becomes diamond hard, then erupts right into my throat.

Oops. I'm too skilled for my own good. Coitus will have to wait now. But hey, I've never felt sexier than I do as I catch Max's gaze and demonstratively swallow.

He growls something in Ukrainian that reminds me of the Russian word for "unbelievable."

Yeah, believe it.

He kneels on the bed. "It's your turn again."

I swallow audibly. "My turn?"

He looks me over like a predator. "Get on all fours."

I obey, gladly. This is a cornerstone femme fatale pose. Plus, he'll surely notice my bleach job this way if he didn't before.

He squeezes my buttocks.

That's interesting.

Suddenly, there's a tongue entering my sex from behind.

My turn indeed. This development isn't merely interesting. It's riveting.

Max's finger makes contact with my clit.

The surprises never cease.

His oh-so-clever tongue swipes over my folds.

If he's being competitive and trying to prove that his seduction school is superior, it's an arms race that I can get behind.

The finger and tongue synchronize.

A juicy orgasm coils in my core as my breathing picks up pace.

If he's going to tease me again, will I be able to take it?

He speeds up.

I clench the sheets with my hands.

He goes faster still.

How long is his tongue? I could swear I feel it igniting nerve endings on my cervix.

"I'm close," I say breathlessly, figuring it's only polite to warn him the way he did me.

He grunts something in a satisfied tone, and the vibration from that sound catapults me right into orgasm land.

Every muscle in my body tenses and releases as I cry out, the hot streaks of pleasure zinging through my nerve endings. When it's over, I nearly collapse.

"No, stay like this," he murmurs.

"Oh?" I look dazedly over my shoulder.

He demonstratively licks the finger that was just on my clit. "I'm not done with you."

With that, he puts the finger where his tongue was a second earlier.

I turn back and close my eyes.

The finger unerringly locates my G-spot, or I assume that's what it is. I feel a tingly burst of plea-sure that ignites the beginnings of another freaking orgasm—which, if it happens, would be a record for me.

"You're gorgeous," he says roughly.

Is he talking to my butt again? As if to confuse the

issue, I feel his breath smack in the middle of the bleached area.

Just how closely is he looking at—

Wait a second.

His tongue connects with the area in question.

My brain short-circuits.

This feels good but also weird. Hot and dirty, and a little tickly.

This is what the final exams must be like at the Femme Fatale Association of America. Except maybe I should be doing it to him? Oh, whatever. I can't think straight.

Also, I'd give anything to replace that finger inside me with Maximus. Still, even the finger is getting me closer to release—but before I tip over, both the tongue and the finger are tortuously removed.

"You ready?" Max murmurs hoarsely.

I look back over my shoulder, beyond frustrated. "Ready for what?"

And then I gape at the gloriously erect Maximus. It looks as if the earlier orgasm happened to some other dick.

That's some seriously quick recovery time. Can they teach *that* at the seduction school?

Realizing I'm wasting precious moments during which I could be getting properly fucked, I gasp out, "Ready." To give him extra encouragement, I arch my back and slightly lift my butt.

His face taut, Max teases my opening with Maximus.

As I envelop him, a moan escapes my lips.

He goes deeper, sliding in and out.

My moans rise in volume.

He thrusts slowly, once, twice, thrice.

"More," I gasp.

He squeezes my tush roughly, and his thrusts deepen. Only it's still not enough, and I find myself begging for faster and harder. I'm beginning to think Max likes animals so much because he is one—in bed. In response to my pleas, he pistons into me with bestial ferocity, and the mother of all orgasms appears on my horizon.

He speeds up more.

Did I just howl? This is doggy style so—

He reaches over and squeezes Sergeant, hard.

Ladies and gentlemen, we're about to experience some turbulence. Please fasten your seatbelts.

My tsunami of an orgasm makes landfall.

As I scream and moan, my inner muscles contract over Maximus, milking him with violent desperation.

With a growl, Max comes inside me, causing a small aftershock orgasm to follow the crazy one that I still haven't recovered from.

"Well, then," I say hoarsely. "I'm done."

I collapse onto the bed, my muscles like the gelatinous *holodets*.

I hear Max leave. A few moments later, he comes back with a damp towel and turns me over to clean me up, but I'm too worn out to even open my eyes as he gently runs the towel through my folds.

"You know." I can hear his smile, and it makes me

feel like a fleece blanket has been wrapped around me. "It's usually the guy who goes all comatose after."

Instead of responding, I roll over onto my side, grab his pillow, and pretend-snore.

With a chuckle, he hugs me, turning me into his little spoon. His warm breath bathes my shoulder, his body big and strong around me, and I can't help but be awash with contentment.

Only one thought mars the perfection of the moment as I float gently into sleep.

That was good. Maybe too good. Did he attend that Russian seduction school, after all?

CHAPTER
Thirty-One

I wake up as the first ray of dawn peeks through Max's bedroom window.

Did I dream that epic session last night?

Nope. A slight soreness inside is proof that what we did was delightfully real.

I grin goofily at Max, but he's sleeping like a hibernating bear. A gorgeous, powerfully muscled bear with hair that deserves its own Instagram account and lashes that make me wonder if he secretly uses Latisse.

Moving softly so as not to wake him, I get up, pick up my clothes, and locate a bathroom down the hall.

How thoughtful. He prepared a sealed toothbrush for me.

As I brush my teeth and start dressing, a nagging thought intrudes into my bliss.

Was Max thoughtful or calculating last night?

If all is as it seems, then it's the former, and he gets an A+ as my boyfriend. However, if he's a spy, it could be the latter, and he also gets an A+, but this time for wrapping me around his finger. Speaking of fingers, is the sexy hair on his knuckles a part of his seduction ploy?

Once my mind goes in this unfortunate direction, a bunch of data points resurface, ones I managed to ignore when I was buzzed on vodka and lust. For example, what was the deal with that attempt to bug someone's phone at the Hot Poker Club? Why was he talking to those bankers under such cloak-and-dagger conditions? Why was his phone protected like Fort Knox?

I stare at myself in the mirror as my euphoric mood fades. How have things gotten to this point? How have I let myself develop feelings for Max without resolving all of my doubts?

Because that's the uncomfortable truth: I left my heart unguarded, and now the idea that he might be a spy is as terrifying as an angry ostrich.

I fight the urge to wake him and start an interrogation. If he's a spy, he'll prevaricate, and if he's my boyfriend, he'll cease to be one.

What would a proper femme fatale spy do in this situation?

The answer is obvious, and it sends tendrils of excited fear through my body.

What if I snoop around his house while he's sleeping and find evidence to support one of the two theories?

I can almost picture a devil on my shoulder (who kind of looks like Gia) urging me to go for it. After all, what I'm contemplating is the bread-and-butter of someone who works in my field, because if Max *is* a spy, the security of our nation might be at stake. If there were an angel on the other shoulder, she would look like Olive, and her arguments would boil down to defining the concept of invasion of privacy.

Forgetting right and wrong for a second, if I do this, how can I make sure I don't get busted?

I can't. The best I can do is to have an excuse ready for why I'm where I shouldn't be.

A scheme presents itself right away. Not as devious as something Gia might cook up in her magic-twisted brain, but it should work in a pinch.

I take out my phone. As I thought, I have about a twenty-percent charge left. I turn on "battery saver" mode, and just like that, at a glance, it looks like my phone is almost out of juice.

There. I can walk around Max's house with my phone in my hand, and if he catches me snooping, I'll tell him I'm looking for a phone charger.

I guess the devil wins. If I don't find any kompromat, I'll tell Max my biggest secrets to appease my conscience. Or I'll come clean... ten years into our marriage.

Before I can lose my courage, I tiptoe into the living room and scan the coffee table.

There's a book about African safaris. Great. Now I know what we could do as a cool birthday present for Max on our diamond anniversary, right before I come clean about today.

There's no phone charger in sight, which is good. I'm totally justified to keep looking.

I'm all stealth as I enter his home office. No smoking gun here, and no phone charger either, which is actually odd.

I sigh. I've been leaving this room for last, but there's no helping it. I walk into the study and cringe under the gazes of evil bird dolls.

They're just toys. They can't hurt anyone.

I turn my back on the birds to give myself a second to catch my breath—and come face to face with the wall safe.

Bingo. A classic place to keep one's secrets. Speaking of classics, the lock is of the dial kind, which is smart of Max. These have a low failure rate and don't require electricity to work. And this is lucky for me, as this is precisely the type of safe Gia taught me to crack.

I dart a furtive glance at the door. If I start doing this and Max walks in, I won't be able to talk my way out of it. He won't believe I'm stupid enough to look for a phone charger in a locked safe.

Despite the risk, I can't help myself. I press my ear to the safe door and rotate the dial until I hear two clicks near each other. From there, I use my phone to record the data I need to proceed, and after what feels like an hour, I'm able to finally unlock the safe.

I gape at the contents inside, my stomach filling with liquid nitrogen.

Fuck.

Fuck.

Fuck.

He's a spy after all.

The smoking gun is right here, and it's literally a gun. Also, a pile of currencies and an assortment of passports.

This must be his getaway stash, a spy classic for a reason. Dazedly, I open the French passport at random. Felix Stone. Is this a fake name, or is Maxim Stolyar fake? The passport expired last year, which is sloppy, but its mere existence is damning.

I check the German one. Yet another name, also expired. Why have this if you're not a spy?

The implications hit me like an elbow to the gut.

I slept with the enemy thinking he could be my boyfriend.

I feel used. Dirty, and not in a good way. Even though I met Max because I thought he was a Russian spy, I feel beyond betrayed. Somehow, he convinced me that he wasn't what I thought he was—or I managed to convince myself.

I can't believe how surprised and hurt I am. Can't believe how deeply I'm mourning the loss of a relationship that never really existed in the first place.

My hackles rise, and I don't even know what hackles are. Max is evil incarnate. How dare he send me all those cute animal pictures? How dare he give me all those orgasms? How dare he fake being such a great catch?

The worst part is how helpless I feel. I have no clue what to do now. This isn't just a case of a broken heart. I have to decide if I should report him. I probably *should* report him. But even now, hurting from his betrayal,

I'm worried about what will happen to him if I do that. Also, what will happen to me? Am I going to lose my job if my agency learns that I slept with a foreign agent? Will they think me a security risk?

For a treacherous moment, I wonder how bad it would be if I didn't report him. Will I be able to live with myself? Will my country suffer?

Also, for a moment, I wonder if I should take things in the direction of the *Homeland* series finale.

But no. I'm not nearly as good of an actress as Claire Danes. Hell, she has more acting ability in her chin than I do in my whole body.

Also—and maybe I'm crazy—but the thing that upsets me the most is not that he means my country harm, but that he lied last night when I asked him if he was a spy. He knew I was asking it as a prerequisite of allowing myself to sleep with him, and yet he lied—which is like lying that you're single when you're not.

Maybe worse.

Oh, shit. Does he have a wife in Russia? Where do the lies end?

Wait a second. I forgot the most important point of them all. Given that he's a spy, if he catches me here, my life will be in danger. He's hurt me emotionally, so it's all too easy to imagine him hurting me physically too.

Well, not if I grab this gun.

I take it, but I find it's not loaded. No bullets in sight either. That's kind of useless.

Okay, I'll get some proof and close the safe so I can gracefully escape. I pull out my phone and snap a photo of a couple of the passports. Later, I can find out if they're government-issued or fake.

My heartbeat spikes. If he's not interested in me as a girlfriend, what does he really want? Did he lock the front door? Will he let me leave? I need to set up something like a dead woman's switch—schedule an email to someone at work to let them know about this, and delete it later if I make it out alive.

Hands shaking, I pull up an app that gives me emergency access to my work email. Regular use of this is frowned upon, but that's immaterial right now.

I'm about to send my message when I see an email in my inbox. The subject is "Re: Personal Favor," and it's from the Canada expert.

Apologies about the delay. I finally got a chance to look at Maxim Stolyar for you. No wonder you had trouble. I had to liaise with the folks at the CSIS about this, and they said he was one of theirs. They—

I stop reading, stunned.

The paradigm shift almost takes my breath away.

I should feel relieved. Thrilled even. Max isn't Russian. He's Canadian, just like he said he was. CSIS stands for Canadian Security Intelligence Service. They have an annual budget of half a billion and are a formidable ally.

Yet for some reason, my anger hasn't abated. Anyone who is "one of theirs" can't claim *not* to be a foreign intelligence agent.

Max still lied to my face last night. And he had less reason to do so.

Fucking fucker. Why couldn't he have said, "I can't

answer your question" or "It's classified?" But just to lie, when I told him that I was part of the N—

Someone angrily clears his throat.

Fuck.

I spin around and glare at the source of the noise.

It's Max. Like in a twisted mirror, his expression shows the fury raging inside me.

"What the fuck is this?" he asks in a hard voice.

I jam my phone into my pocket and match his tone. "You tell me."

Max takes a heavy step into the room. "I asked if you were looking into me for your job. You said no."

He sounds hurt. The nerve of this guy.

I clench my teeth. "This isn't for my job. More like personal research."

His forest-green eyes turn uncharacteristically cold. "How socially acceptable."

My arm muscles quiver as I fight the urge to slap him. "Last night, I asked you if you were a foreign intelligence agent. You denied it, but last I checked, Canada wasn't part of the US."

Aha. He looks guilty now. At least for a moment. Then his lips flatten, and his eyes shoot fresh icicles. "I told you the truth. I'm not in the CSIS. Not anymore."

"Bullshit!" I shout over the pulse pounding in my ears. "I've seen you conduct clandestine operations."

Fuck. Maybe I shouldn't have admitted that.

He looks like I *have* slapped him. "You what?"

"Forget it," I growl. "What's the point of this conversation? Clearly, whatever this was, it was a mistake, one that's now over."

Correction. *Now* he looks like I've slapped him. Maybe even kneed him in the groin. "Fine."

"Fine?" I turn on my heel. "Fine."

Eyes burning, I rush out of the apartment and sprint for the elevator as if chased by a rabid falcon.

CHAPTER
Thirty-Two

I FIGHT the urge to cry the whole cab ride home. When Olive greets me, it's all I can do to shoo away her concern and get to my bedroom. There, I finally let my emotions get the best of me, and for the next I don't know how long, I sob and wallow in self-pity.

At some point, a furry creature cuddles up to me. I hug him to my chest, feeling a modicum better when he begins to purr.

Machete doesn't like anyone besides himself upsetting his insignificant human. Just point Machete's claws in the right direction, then look away before the sight of the ensuing massacre scars you for life.

I start to hiccup. As much as this whole situation sucks, I don't want Machete to harm Max. Not to mention, there's a good chance that the feline traitor might just rub himself against the source of my angst. After all, theirs seemed to be a bromance at first sight.

My alarm blares.

Shit. I forgot about work.

My trip to my building happens in a daze. Scenes of my time with Max play out in my mind's eye: the video sessions, the dates, the amazing sex…

For some reason, I always thought that breaking up with someone would be like ripping off a Band-Aid—hurts at first, but you feel better soon after making the right decision. Bullshit. This feels like the reverse of that. Like ripping off the Band-Aid but getting that famous "death by a thousand cuts" as a result.

I eat breakfast at my desk, and it's tasteless. The work on the project my boss gives me happens on autopilot. My lunch tastes like cardboard, and there may even be a crying session in the bathroom.

I've got to hand it to my coworkers. Not a single one makes the "Do you have the blues?" joke. I guess they have a good sense of self-preservation.

The rest of my workday is even more robotic.

As I head home, I get a text from Olive.

Sorry for the last-minute notice, but my first interview went so well they want me to come to Florida for the follow-up. I scored really cheapo tickets for a flight tonight. Can you please feed Beaky?

This is followed by detailed instructions on the care and feeding of octopuses.

Great. Now even my sister has abandoned me. What's next? A tiny cloud directly over my head, like in an antidepressant commercial?

———

When I get home, it's empty and lonely, and my dinner is more tasteless than breakfast and lunch combined. After another brief cry, I feed Beaky and text Olive that I've done it.

Her phone dings nearby.

Poor thing. She forgot it in her rush to get to Florida. Hopefully, our grandparents will let her borrow one of theirs.

Feeling drained, I grab Machete and stroke his fur. As he purrs, the angry fog in my brain finally starts to lift, and I begin to think semi-coherently.

So Max is a spy. Or was. Hurray for my instincts. The key thing is that he's not a spy now, or claims not to be. Also, even when he was, he wasn't an enemy agent, but one of our allies'.

If you look at it from a certain angle—something that was hard to do until now—I might have *slightly* overreacted when I broke up with him. That is, if it's really true that he's not with the CSIS anymore. If that's the case, he didn't actually lie. He's not *currently* a foreign intelligence agent. In fact, that would explain the expired passports.

But if he's not with the CSIS, what was he doing acting like a spy? Why try to bug someone's phone at the Hot Poker Club? Why use tradecraft during his meetings with the investment bankers?

I pull up my work email and come back to the message from the Canada expert in case it can shed some light.

Fuck.

I'm such an idiot.

If I'd just finished reading the email this morning, the conversation at Max's house could've gone very differently.

Maybe. Or maybe not. He still would've been pissed at my snooping.

In any case, I reread everything once more, from beginning to the very end.

Apologies about the delay. I finally got a chance to look at Maxim Stolyar for you. No wonder you had trouble. I had to liaise with the folks at the CSIS about this, and they said he was one of theirs. They didn't say what he did for them, but him being second-generation Ukrainian is our clue. They say he retired a few years ago and now consults for corporations, though reading between the lines, I get the feeling he didn't completely leave the field. Even though his private-sector work is hush-hush, it sounds like corporate espionage, of the legal kind.

Anyway, I hope this helps—and that we're even now.

I read it twice more.

Max is retired.

Retired.

That means he didn't lie to me. He's *not* a foreign intelligence agent.

Not currently.

But... he does do corporate espionage, which could easily explain whatever he was doing with the bankers and that phone. It could also be why he looked thrown by my "Are you a spy?" question. Do you call someone who does corporate espionage a spy?

I think so. Especially a former spy. Once a spy,

always a spy. Still, I said "foreign intelligence agent," and he isn't that.

This could also be why he was cagey when he told me he was a "corporate consultant."

But why? Had he told me that he engaged in corporate espionage, I would've thought it super cool. Maybe I would've even asked him for a job. I've been so preoccupied with my dreams of the CIA that I never considered this direction, but it's a much more realistic option for someone like me.

I leap to my feet and begin pacing, my earlier funk dissipating.

It was a mistake to break up with Max. I see it clearly now. But I did break up with him, and I can't change that. The important question is: how can I fix it?

No idea, but a big gesture is probably required. And maybe groveling. After all, I wasn't entirely truthful with him either.

If I do make a gesture, what should it be?

I pace back and forth, getting dirty looks from both Beaky and Machete.

Finally, it hits me.

I can help Max with his current assignment. Yeah, that's it. With the new context of corporate espionage, I finally see the connection between the Hot Poker Club and the investment bankers. At least I think I do.

It's Sloppy Stack. That's whose phone Max was trying to bug.

Sloppy Stack has to be the key, or more specifically, the software company he works for—the one that makes trading platforms.

Yay. I love this feeling of things clicking.

I jump on my laptop, and my fingers dance over the keyboard.

As I theorized, the two banks are clients of Sloppy Stack's company, and if my theory is right, they are Max's clients as well.

I go into analyst mode and read everything I can get my hands on until I come across two articles featuring the investment banks in question. Apparently, both banks lost a bunch of money when some hedge funds anticipated a large move they'd just made in the market. Both banks said some foul play was involved. Neither had proof.

Great. I now have enough confirmation of my theory to justify doing the slightly less legal portion of my research.

First things first. I launch a set of tools that aren't classified, but which I'd rather not disclose in any detail.

The first one is the least harmful. In fact, it's something my dad uses for his perfectly legit job as a penetration tester, which—as my dad says—"isn't as dirty as it sounds."

What I'm doing is testing the security at Sloppy Stack's software company. That's not an evil thing. In fact, if I told them my results, it would be a public service.

The security is not terrible overall, but lousy for a bunch of computer science types. I could get in and not risk getting caught, for sure.

This next part my dad hopefully never does. I get

into Sloppy Stack's company's intranet, and then I locate the code repository where the trading platform files live, focusing on the parts Sloppy Stack is responsible for.

Yuck. Sloppy Stack isn't just sloppy with poker chips; he is sloppy with his code too. I still find what I'm looking for eventually, though.

A back door.

As I suspected, sneaky Sloppy Stack coded himself a way of learning what his company's clients do with the trading platforms they buy—like, say, pumping a lot of money into a specific stock, which would result in that stock's price dramatically going up.

I'd bet all of my bitcoin Sloppy Stack is selling this illegally gained information to the highest bidder—which would explain how he had the money for the Hot Poker Club buy-in.

Emboldened, I dress and rush back to work.

The office is empty, which is good.

I fire up **classified** and do what Max tried but failed to do: get inside Sloppy Stack's smartphone.

Wow. Sloppy Stack has a gambling problem. A major one if his emails and texts are anything to go by.

According to some of these, he owes money to shady people. In fact, the dummy is at the Hot Poker Club right this second, probably losing his illegally gained funds yet again.

Wait.

If he's at the game, could Max be there too? After all, he never finished his phone-bugging operation on the day we first met, and I can see that Sloppy Stack took a break from the Hot Poker Club until today.

My heartbeat speeds up. I picture Max getting caught with the bug and then getting hurt by Bogdan, the dangerous owner of the Hot Poker Club.

Fucker. What are the chances that Max has already bugged Sloppy Stack's phone outside of the game? Low. He was in Canada until yesterday. Today is likely the first time he's had a chance to repeat that attempt. That's what I'd do.

Shit. I should warn Max. Must warn him.

But how? I can't exactly call him. They make you turn off and put away your phone.

My legs begin moving before my brain even catches up.

The answer is simple. I have to head over to the Palace and talk to him face to face.

Yeah. That's it. That's what I'll do.

In record time, I make my way to my Aston Martin, and as soon as the motor roars to life, I floor the gas pedal.

Time for a James Bond-esque car race.

CHAPTER
Thirty-Three

ACCORDING TO THE GPS, this trip should take twenty-five minutes. My goal: make it there in ten.

Everything goes smoothly at first. Then, when I round the third corner, my tires screech and the car skids, but I'm on the next street and alive, though I might want to be a little more careful on the turns from here on.

The speed limit is twenty-five miles per hour. What a joke. When I can, I go four times that.

A yellow cab stops at a stop sign—the nerve of the guy. I swerve sharply, switching lanes in an eyeblink, then fly past him like the sign doesn't exist. I do the same with a red light at the next intersection.

Two blocks later, I have to slow down in order to spare the lives of a couple of drunken pedestrians, and five blocks after that, I see a police car, so I slow down again. Even if I could charm my way out of a ticket, the stop would be a delay I can't afford.

In nine minutes and thirty seconds, I pull up to the Palace.

I nearly trip as I exit my car and toss the keys at a valet guy.

"Can you keep it here near the entrance?" I stick a hundred-dollar bill into his hand as an incentive.

He nods, wide-eyed, and I rush for the entrance.

Which is when I remember a problem I've completely blocked from my mind.

A huge nightmare of a problem.

Birds.

Lots of birds.

CHAPTER
Thirty-Four

FOR A SECOND, I hope that maybe someone acquired common sense and decontaminated the lobby. When I step in, however, that hope is squashed, like a blueberry under the cruel beak of a peacock.

The birds are still here.

Peacocks with their abominable tails, and parrots that look even more like evil clowns thanks to the adrenaline coursing through my veins.

I back the fuck out of the lobby and grab the valet I've just tipped. "I need to use the back entrance to the hotel. I know there is one. I used it the other day."

As in someone took me through it blindfolded, but hey, that's still me "using it."

He shakes his head vehemently. "No one is allowed back there. Security precautions."

Fuck. I don't have time to argue or seek this back entrance. I guess today is the day I force myself to walk through a bird-infested lobby. I only wish I had one of those bomb-fighting suits, like they wore in *The Hurt Locker*.

Taking a deep breath, I enter the lobby again.

It's going to be okay. The parrots are in cages. What are the chances they escape today of all days?

That helps. A little.

I take another step in.

I can do this. I'm a spy, damn it.

My next step is surer.

But then, as if he was waiting for this very moment, a peacock rushes me.

With an undignified shriek, I run away from the beast—and it takes all my willpower to dash in the direction of the elevator instead of back outside.

Another peacock must smell blood in the water. It tries to block my way.

I zigzag to the right, making a wide circle around the evil creature. My throat is raw from my uninterrupted shriek, and it feels like something is tearing in my leg muscles as I sprint for the elevator with everything I've got.

"You okay?" the concierge yells after me.

I don't have the energy to tell him that, of course, nothing is okay. Okay has been dipped in tar, covered in feathers, and is chasing me as we speak.

Closing the remaining distance to the elevator, I stab the button and prepare to fend off any attacking peacocks with bone-crushing Krav Maga kicks.

The peacocks must realize they've cornered a wild animal and that the fight might not be worth it. After all, presumably someone at this hotel feeds them—and they don't know how good I might taste.

The elevator finally arrives. I leap inside and jab at the basement button like my life depends on it—because it probably does. The doors slide closed, shutting out the horrors outside. Doing my best to catch my breath, I strategize my next moves.

I'm about to go where I shouldn't. Crash a private game. How do I get away with it?

I dismiss a bunch of ideas off the bat. Pretending to be room service won't work, as fun as it might be to do the spy movie classic where I mug or bribe a maid for her outfit. Maybe I should go into the air vents? Nope. Again, as much as I'd like to cable-drop somewhere, *Mission Impossible* style, I don't think there's an air vent inside the sauna where the Hot Poker game is, though there may be one in the locker room.

No. I'm going to use the good old KISS principle, popular among software developers: Keep It Simple, Stupid.

If challenged, I'm looking for the bathroom. That's it.

I can act out that cover easily. All I have to do is remember how I nearly peed my pants during the peacock attack in the lobby.

The elevator doors open. I exit and dash for the nearest corridor.

No staff here at this hour. That's good.

I sniff the air. A faint chlorine-and-lemon scent is detectable, so the Hot Poker Club can't be far.

I run on carpeted floors, making turns using my

nose and intuition. One of those things is reliable because on the next turn, the carpet under my feet becomes tile—which I recall from my earlier visit.

Great.

The smell I was following is extra strong on the next turn, and then I spot a door in the distance.

I bet that's the locker room.

The problem is, two burly guys are standing in front of it.

As I get closer, I recognize one. He's the brave soul who scared away a pigeon for me.

Crap. Now I'll feel bad fighting my way in—which also may not be the best idea, considering that these guys could be armed.

I stick to my simple plan and use all my acting ability to run like a woman with a bladder about to burst.

"What the fuck?" the unfamiliar guard says as I whoosh toward them.

"I need the bathroom." I dance from foot to foot like a gushing fountain is about to spew from my urethra.

The guy I recognized seems to recognize me back. He frowns. "Are you playing today? I didn't realize you're a regular now."

"I just need the bathroom," I repeat, and without waiting for them to stop me, I rush into the locker room.

"Wait!" someone shouts.

I do not. Instead, I sprint for the steam room as if all the peacocks and parrots of the world were on my tail.

As I burst into the room, the steam blocks the players at first.

Blinking, I make out the owner, Bogdan, with his chips in a sculpture arrangement again. Sloppy Stack is also here, his stack of poker chips predictably sloppy.

The two bouncers barge in after me. They reach out to grab me, but Bogdan stops them with barely a glance.

Sweating bullets, and not just from the heat, I scan my surroundings once more—and realize that two things don't make sense.

One: Max isn't here.

Two: Clarice is, though I don't recognize her at first without her pirate outfit.

The lack of Max is mysterious. Have I already missed him? Seems doubtful as there's no empty chair.

The presence of Clarice makes sense when I think about it. She *was* going to come play here. I gave her the buy-in funds myself.

I guess her game day is today.

Hmm. Has her hair always looked this nice under that bicorn, or whatever her hat is called? Also, why is she staring so lustfully at Bogdan? Haven't I told her he's dangerous?

Speaking of danger, Bogdan narrows his eyes at me. "What are you doing here?"

Clarice turns from him to me, her eyes widening. "Blue?"

Shit. Time for an exit strategy. My hand dives into my purse as if it's got a mind of its own.

Gia would be proud of my next stratagem.

My hand comes out with a tampon. I rush over to

Clarice and thrust it into her hands with the seriousness of a relay race athlete handing over a baton.

Predictably, the men act as if the tampon were a leper, all of them drawing back as one.

Being a magician, Clarice is as adept at deception as Gia. She snatches the tampon as Gollum would his precious ring. "Thanks, Blue. You're a life saver."

I make eye contact with Bogdan. "Sorry about the interruption." I prepare to tell him that I'm a government agent, and that killing me would be really bad for his business and health.

"How did you find this place?" he asks, his expression stony. "Didn't they blindfold you on the way in the last time?" He levels a glare at the bouncers.

"Oh, they blindfolded me very well," I say quickly. "Especially this gentleman." I point at the guy who rescued me from the pigeon. "I just happen to have a very good sense of direction, and my boyfriend told me which hotel the game was held at. He's a regular."

Bogdan arches an eyebrow. "Maxim Stolyar?"

"How did you know?" I blurt.

He smirks. "I always watch what happens at the table."

Right. He picked up on our body language and extrapolated. A dangerous man in more ways than one.

"Speaking of Max, I actually lost track of him today," I say. "He didn't come here, did he?"

Clarice shakes her head.

"Cool, cool." I wish I really *could* use the bathroom at this point. "I guess I'll be leaving?"

Damn it. A tough-as-nails spy wouldn't make that last bit sound so much like a question.

"Escort her," Bogdan says to the bouncers imperiously.

I back away. "Thank you." I wave at Clarice. "Good luck."

After we leave the steam room, I ask, "Can I use the bathroom?"

Did the bouncers practice eyerolling in sync like that, à la teenage girls?

The pigeon slayer points at the nearby stalls. "Go."

I use the facilities and then meekly let the dudes lead me through the corridors. When I see us heading for the regular elevator, I halt. "Any chance you could take me through the back entrance?"

"Why?" the pigeon slayer asks.

I study the carpet under my feet. "There are birds in the lobby."

More eyerolling is followed by a grudging, "This way."

Yay. They lead me out of a door in the back, then show me the way to the front of the hotel.

The valet I tipped gets my car posthaste.

As soon as I climb inside, I floor the gas, screeching away from the place before anyone changes their mind about letting me leave.

Once I'm far enough away, I ponder my destination.

Should I go visit Max at home?

It's late, so it might be a bit weird. Then again, if I don't, I'll be awake all night, wishing I'd gone there.

Thus decided, I drive straight there or, more precisely, race.

———

Seven minutes later, I ring Max's doorbell. He doesn't open. His peephole doesn't darken either, so it's likely he's not home. Or maybe he's that good. He knows it's me, and he's not even approaching the door.

I fight the urge to pick the lock. If he's home, I wouldn't be helping my case, and if he isn't, what's the point of breaking and entering?

Sighing, I return to my car and drive home slowly, as in double the speed limit.

———

After I park my car in my basement lot, I take the elevator up and debate if I should call Max, given that I failed to arrange a face to face.

Before I come to any decision, the elevator stops in the lobby, and a familiar man enters.

Where do I know him from? And how does he know me? Because he must. His nostrils are flaring and his jaw is tight as he glares at me, which isn't something you do with strangers.

Usually. Unless you're a psycho.

"You cut your fucking hair?" he grits out, his breath smelling like a distillery.

Ah. I remember now. I saw his face in a picture at Olive's place.

This is Brett, her asshole ex. He thinks I'm her. But what's he doing here?

"How did you find me?" I ask, figuring I'll play along.

He curls his upper lip. "Stupid bitch. I can always find you."

My eyes turn into slits. "What did you just say to me?"

In a flash, I realize he must think Olive is here because of some app he put on her phone—the phone she forgot at my place.

Is it hypocritical of me to think him a much bigger asshole over that, considering that I put a tracker on *his* phone myself? Though I totally forgot to set up an alert to warn me if he comes close to Olive. I'll have to correct that mistake—and make the range a hundred feet.

Also, thank goodness he's come across me instead of Olive.

"I said 'stupid fucking bitch,'" Brett barks, savoring every word.

I get into a Krav Maga stance. "You're making a huge mistake. You've got one chance to leave and never think of me again. One chance only."

He sneers. "That haircut makes you look like a fag."

I clench and unclench my fists. "Fine. One *more* chance. Don't make me hurt you."

The elevator stops.

"Leave," I say icily, stepping out of the elevator. "While you can."

With a scoff, Brett lunges at me.

I think he means to grab my elbow, but that's not going to happen. I pivot on the balls of my feet, and he finds air where the elbow just was. Before he can recover, I smash a fist into his midsection.

Air leaves his lungs with an audible whoosh, but it sounds like "Bitch," so I backslap him in the face.

To his credit, he recovers quickly and tries to punch me.

I duck, but before I can finish this fight with a signature Krav Maga ball-busting kick, there's a blur of movement behind me.

I turn and watch in stunned fascination as a strong fist connects with Brett's jaw, knocking the asshole out.

I blink uncomprehendingly at Max—the owner of the fist. "What are you doing here?"

"Who is this?" Max kicks Brett's unconscious body with the tip of his shoe.

"Brett. Olive's ex. Seriously, I was just looking for you."

"One sec." Max pulls out his phone and dials a number.

"911, what's your emergency?" a chipper voice says on the other line.

"A man just attacked my girlfriend," Max says. "Can you please send someone over?" He gives her the address.

He called me his girlfriend! Does it mean he's forgiven me, or was it just the easiest way to explain the situation to the phone operator?

When Max hangs up, I'm about to ask him what he's

doing at my place when he says, "Do you have handcuffs?"

Right. Brett might come to his senses.

"Give me a second." I run into my apartment and nearly trip over Machete.

Don't bother with the police. Leave Brett alone with Machete. He'll never bother anyone again.

I locate a pair of handcuffs covered in leopard fur—something I hoped to use on Max at some point.

When I return and hand them to Max, he attaches Brett to the staircase before studying me with an unreadable expression.

"You were looking for me?" he asks.

I nod vigorously. "Why are you here?"

He sighs. "I was looking for you. Obviously."

"Why?" I ask.

Brett begins to curse and struggle against his bonds.

I nod at my door. "Want to talk inside?"

Max agrees.

We step into my apartment and I close the door, cutting out the annoying noises coming out of Brett's mouth.

Machete greets Max by rubbing against his pant leg.

Machete doesn't know what's so likeable about this insignificant human, but Machete goes with the flow and does whatever Machete wants.

Beaky changes color, and Machete skedaddles.

I plop on the couch and tap the cushion next to me.

Max sits down where I suggested. "I wanted to apologize."

I almost jump back to my feet. "Me too!"

A smile touches his eyes. "Me first."

I mock pout. "That's not very gentlemanly of you, but go ahead."

His face is serious once again. "When you asked me if I was a foreign agent, I should've told you about my CSIS past."

I nod. "And about the corporate espionage too."

His eyes widen. "I was just about... How do you know about that?"

Smiling deviously, I tell him that I not only know about his work in general, but that I figured out his current investigation specifically, and that I solved it for him.

"I have no words," he says. "Okay, maybe three: you are dangerous."

I scoot closer to him. "Dangerous in an awesome way, right?"

His dark-forest gaze heats up. "The most awesome way."

I put my hand on his knee. "If you'd like, I can make it so that Sloppy Stack's misdeeds are reported to the SEC, and you can tell your clients that it was you."

He covers my hand with his. "I repeat, I have no words."

"Good," I say. "Now it's my turn. I'm sorry I invaded your privacy the way I did, and I'm especially sorry that I said we were over."

He leans toward me. "No. I'm sorry I didn't try to convince you to stay and talk things out. And that it took me all day to realize I must get you back. You're—"

I shut him up with my lips, and he kisses me back with the most wonderful ferocity.

As his hands roam my body over my clothes, I want to strip, badly.

Why is this so hot? Are we about to have makeup sex?

I reach to unzip his pants when my stupid doorbell rings.

Max pulls away. "Must be the police."

Oh. Right. I forgot about Brett, and the rest of the human race for that matter.

I stand up and readjust my outfit. "You know, I didn't need you to protect me from that asshole."

Max laughs. "Oh, I know that. I think I was actually protecting that asshole's balls. It's a male solidarity thing."

Chuckling, I open the door for the police officers and offer them coffee. Drinks in hands, we sit in my kitchen and talk. I tell them that I work for the government, which wins them over right away. I then explain how Brett was horrible to my identical-looking sister, and that he mistook me for her today, and that I'm going to press charges. They reassure me that Brett is going into lockup to sleep off the alcohol in his system, and they recommend that my sister get a restraining order.

"So, where were we?" I ask Max when the officers leave.

He waggles his eyebrows. "I think you were going to give me a tour of your apartment."

I clutch at my nonexistent pearls. "There's only one room you haven't seen at this point: my bedroom."

He eyes me hungrily. "Show me everything."

I do, gladly. The second we're in the bedroom, we attack each other.

The sex is more urgent than last night. Sweatier and more desperate.

As we lie there in the afterglow, Max props himself up on an elbow and meets my gaze. "Apologizing was just one of the reasons I wanted to talk to you face to face," he says, his voice low and serious.

I bite my lip. "Oh?"

"I also wanted to tell you something."

My heartbeat skyrockets. "Me too!"

His eyes crinkle in the corners. "Me first."

I feel like I might burst from excitement. "Yet again not very gentlemanly of you, but go ahead."

His eyes gleam. "You're a pair to my three of a kind. A bamboo to my panda. A—"

"A shaken, not stirred, martini to your James Bond," I blurt. "Salo to your bread. A—"

He cups my cheek with his hand. "What I'm trying to say is that I love you, sonechko. With everything I've got."

"And that's what I was trying to say too! I mean, I love you too."

The smile he gives me lights up my entire world, and as our lips meet again, I know that wherever we go from here, I'll always remember this moment. And hopefully many such moments to come.

Epilogue

MAX

"WHAT IS THAT?" I point at one of two tiny creatures that look like antelopes. They're my current frontrunner for the cutest animal I've ever seen.

Blue smiles radiantly, something she's been doing a lot on this trip to her parents' farm. "The horny one is Buzz," she says. "The one without horns is Bean."

I shake my head. "You know I was asking what kind of a creature Bean and Buzz happen to be. Not their names."

I've been stumped more times than I care to admit here at the farm—and only partly by the species of the furry residents. More often than that, I've been bewildered by the behavior of Blue's adorable hippie parents, like the time her mom gave us a set of very specific bedroom tips. Or the time she lectured us on the importance of lubrication. Or when her dad rubbed my feet after Blue and I came back from a long hike and I made the mistake of mentioning that my feet felt tired. Or the time her dad gave me a shoulder rub—this was after I asked his blessing to do what I'm about to do—because he thought that I was too tense. Or the time her dad massaged my head for no reason at all. Or—

"That's a dik-dik," Blue says, breaking my train of thought.

I stare at the tiny antelope-like creature. "A what?"

"You heard me right. That's a dik-dik." She grins. "They're indigenous to the southern regions of Africa."

I don't bother checking her dubious statement on my phone this time, like I did the other day with Salty —who turned out to be exactly what Blue claimed: a pink fairy armadillo endemic to central Argentina.

I toss Bean and Buzz some blueberries. "I can't believe I'm going to say this, but dik-diks are cute."

She snorts. "I think you mean to say"—she makes her voice deeper—"'I like dik-dik.'"

I resist making the obvious joke about her likes and my dick—which she thought important enough to codename Maximus. "The dik-dik are cuter than pink fairy armadillos."

She gasps theatrically. "You're nuts. Salty is the most adorable creature here at the farm. How many other animals do you know that are pink?"

I know better than to mention birds like the roseate spoonbill and the flamingo, especially on this special day. "Do you mean here on the farm? Pigs. If you mean in general, there's the nudibranch and other sea creatures."

She bites her lip. "I'd like to ride your nudie branch."

Fuck. Blood leaves my brain and rushes down to Maximus.

Maybe I can postpone my plan and drag her back to our room?

"Mom is cleaning the house," Blue says, clearly reading my mind. "Dad is shoveling horse manure, so even a roll in the hay is out." She leans in, licks my ear, and says huskily, "How about we go on a hike and stop by that meadow again?"

Fuck, yeah. That's the very meadow I was going to take her to anyway, but now, we'll kill two birds with one stone—an expression I only use mentally nowadays.

We head out and argue about animal cuteness on the way, particularly when any creatures cross our path. When I spot birds, I shoot them with a Nerf gun. The little orange darts wouldn't hurt the feathered critters even if I hit them, but I aim for the branch they sit on, and I'm a good marksman.

We also talk about the next mission we're going to go on. I was able to convince Blue to work for me instead of the CIA. She claims that all it took was watching *Duplicity*, a corporate espionage flick featuring Clive Owen and Julia Roberts.

"What's this?" Blue asks when we reach the meadow.

I grin.

At my request, her mother asked her to have a "girl talk" earlier today, so I had a chance to sneak out and scatter rose petals all over the ground, enhancing the romanticism of this already-beautiful place.

I turn to face her. "I want to tell you something."

Her eyes widen. "Me too."

"Me first." I tuck a strand of strawberry-blond hair behind her ear. She's grown it out in the six months we've been together, and it now matches the wig she'd worn the day we met. The day she barged into that poker game almost naked.

The day I decided to make her mine.

She cocks her head. "Still not a gentleman, but go."

I fish out the ring box and enjoy the look of astonished joy on her face as I drop to one knee. My voice roughens. "Blue, sonechko... I can't picture my life without your 'very particular set of skills.' You bring honor to the Femme Fatale Association of America, and now, I would like the honor of making you my wife."

Taking a deep breath, I open the box.

"Yes," she gasps and jams her finger into the ring before I even take it out of the box. "Now get up. It's my turn."

As I stand up, I experience that now-familiar feeling of being stumped. "You still want to tell me something?"

"Well, yeah." She stares at her ring with fascination, turning her finger this way and that.

Looks like I owe her friend Fabio a huge favor. He was spot on when he claimed she would "go gaga" for this ring.

Finally, she lifts her gaze to my face. "What I have to say circles back to cute creatures. In this case, I think we'll have a consensus too." She pulls out a stick-like object from her pocket and thrusts it into my hands.

"You might not want to lick that," she adds. "I peed on it."

I stare at the plastic stick. There are two lines in the little window in it.

A pregnancy test.

Two lines, and on the side is an explanation.

Two lines means pregnant.

Pregnant.

Shock and joy radiate warmth throughout my body, like a shot of boiling horilka.

How? When? Actually, who the fuck cares? We're talking about a little creature that's part Blue. It'll surely be cuter than a panda. Maybe even cuter than a dik-dik.

Blue sounds uncharacteristically uncertain as she says, "We should've used a condom when I took that antibiotic, I guess. I know it's—"

I silence her with a kiss. Lifting her off the ground, I spin her around, the way I might do with codename Little Creature.

"Did you forget I know Krav Maga?" she says through giggles.

I set her down with a grin. "Now that you've gotten what you needed from me, you're busting out the ball-busting kicks?"

"Nope." She unbuttons the top of her shirt, exposing smooth, lickable skin and the swells of her deliciously round breasts. "I still have a need for your kiwis." The shirt falls on the grass. "Urgent need."

The beast inside me awakens. My clothes feel as tight on my body as if I were about to turn into a were-bear, cock first. She reaches for the clasp of her bra, and I lunge at her, stripping on the way.

Giggling, she breaks into a run, and I chase her to the middle of the meadow, where I preemptively laid out a blanket. Catching her there, I take her down like a dik-dik, but carefully.

Because she's a pregnant dik-dik.

Pinning her arms over her head, I smile down at her flushed face. "I love you," I tell her in Ukrainian.

She grins back. "I love you too. By the way, who's seducing whom right now?"

I bite her earlobe just the way she likes and inhale her sweet feminine scent. "Me, you?"

"Not fair," she breathes.

I nibble on her delicate neck. "That's the thing about spies. We never play fair."

She moans. "That's true. So fucking true."

We interlace our fingers, and I commence with my seduction. Or maybe she commences with hers—it's hard to tell.

Rock hard.

As we cuddle together afterward, with her curvy butt nestled against now-satisfied Maximus, I look at the blue sky and picture our future together, as well as what codename Little Creature might look like.

A big grin stretches my face. This future of ours will be full of adventure, love, and joy. And butt play.

I'd never say this out loud, but I'm not in danger of getting the blues with Blue by my side.

Sneak Peeks

Thank you for participating in Blue and Max's journey!

Looking for more laugh-out-loud romcoms? If you haven't already, you've *got* to meet the Chortsky family from the *Hard Stuff* series! Read Vlad's story in *Hard Code*, Bella's story in *Hard Ware,* and Alex's story in *Hard Byte.* And be sure to check out *Royally Tricked,* a royal romance starring daredevil Tigger (from *Hard Ware)* and Blue's older sister Gia!

Also, you'll definitely want to pick up *Of Octopuses and Men,* an enemies-to-lovers romcom featuring Olive, one of Blue's sextuplet sisters, and her sizzling hot (and infuriating) new boss.

We love receiving feedback from our readers, and we are always interested to know what you'd like to see in books to come. Want your favorite side character to have their own book? Mention it in a review! We take all suggestions into consideration, and if you sign up for our newsletter at www.mishabell.com, you'll be the first to know who will be featured next!

Misha Bell is a collaboration between husband-and-wife writing team, Dima Zales and Anna Zaires. When they're not making you bust a gut as Misha, Dima writes sci-fi and fantasy, and Anna writes dark and contemporary romance. Check out *Wall Street Titan* by Anna Zaires for more steamy billionaire hotness!

Turn the page to read previews from *Of Octopuses and Men* and *Royally Tricked*!

Excerpt from Of Octopuses and Men

BY MISHA BELL

My grandparents' grumpy neighbor is as hot as the lethal Florida sun. And like the sun, he's bad for me. My taste in men is the worst—just ask my ex and his restraining order.

What am I doing in Florida with my grandparents, you wonder? Well, my best friend is an octopus, and he needs a bigger tank, so I took a job at an aquarium in the Sunshine State.

I didn't expect that sexy, long-haired grump to try to buy my octopus for some nefarious purpose. Nor did I expect to make out with him during a late-night swim at the beach.

And the last thing I expected was to run into him on my first day at my new job… where he's my boss.

———

The quivering purple tentacle slithers in between the girl's legs.

I dart a wary glance at my grandmother.

Figures. While most grandmothers might have a heart attack seeing something like this, mine is watching with fascination, like a rookie gynecologist.

A second tentacle joins the fun.

Grandma's fascination heightens, now matching that of a rookie proctologist.

I swivel my head from the TV to her and then back. Finally, I cautiously ask, "Grandma... why are we watching tentacle porn?"

With a slight frown, she presses the pause button. "It's called *hentai*. They draw these cartoons in Japan."

Seriously, Japan? Eating raw octopus isn't enough? Now you have to corrupt my already uncomfortably sex-obsessed grandmother?

I sigh. "Why are we watching hentai?"

She waggles her perfectly groomed eyebrows. "This is something your grandfather and I enjoy. Figured it would be up your alley."

Cthulhu help me, if TMI could turn into a person, it would be my grandma. She's even worse than her daughter—my mom. "Why would you think tentacle porn is 'up my alley?'"

She glances at the large aquarium by the window, the one housing Beaky, my BFF who just happens to be a giant Pacific octopus. "You really love that thing, and you've been going through a dry spell, so I—"

I clear my throat loudly and pointedly. "Are you suggesting I get into bestiality?"

I do love everything to do with octopuses. Since I'm a marine biologist and one of eight sisters, it's only logical. But that doesn't mean I want to have sexual relations with them.

She shrugs. "Like I said to my scatophiliac friend at bingo the other day, I don't kink-shame."

I pinch the bridge of my nose. "I don't have a 'sex with octopuses' kink. I'm not even sure there *is* such a thing."

She grins. "It's called Rule 34. If you can conceive of it, there's a porn of it."

I purse my lips. "If someone has sex with any living being without their consent, I reserve the right to shame them. And I don't care if they molest an octopus, a goat, or a cockroach."

Grandma nods to Beaky. "You keep saying how smart he is. Maybe he could do sign language with his tentacles?"

She's just as difficult to argue with as my sister Gia. Which is fitting, considering Gia was named after her. I try anyway. "Beaky and I are just friends."

"You can be friends with benefits."

Ugh. "We're strictly platonic."

"Well... I was cleaning your room and stumbled upon your tentacle dildo." To my shock, she looks bashful as she says this—a definite first.

I flush the shade of red Beaky turns when he's trying to look menacing. Then I recall that Florida is famous for sinkholes.

Can one swallow me right now?

"I got that on a lark, Grandma. Besides, octopuses

don't have tentacles. You're thinking of squid and cuttlefish."

"Oh?" She studies the tank in confusion. "So what do you call those eight appendages?"

I walk over to the tank and grab its remote control. "Arms."

She blinks at me. "What's the difference?"

I know I'm going into my marine biologist mode in front of the wrong audience, but I can't help myself. "If the suckers are all over—"

"Suckers?" She waggles her eyebrows.

"Ugh, Grandma, stop. Like I was saying, if the suckers are all over, it's an arm. If they're only at the tip, it's a tentacle. Arms also have finer control, while tentacles are elongated and—"

"Okay, okay, I'm sorry," she says.

I narrow my eyes. "Sorry that you suggested I have relations with my octopus? Or sorry you snooped in my private drawer?"

Her grin is as mischievous as a naughty kid's. "Sorry I asked."

With a huff, I activate the motor under the aquarium, and the whole thing begins to roll. "In case it's not clear, Beaky and I are going for a walk."

Waving goodbye, my grandmother resumes her porn, looking just as fascinated as before.

Hey, I'm not judging. I watch and re-watch *Aquaman* whenever I feel frisky.

The anime girl moans in the squeaky, high-pitched voice that's characteristic of the genre. Do Japanese men find childish voices sexy?

Fine. Maybe I'm judging a little.

Having outstayed my welcome, I guide Beaky's motorized tank into the dining area, where I find my grandfather sitting at the table, lovingly reassembling a sniper rifle. Like my grandmother, he's in great shape, especially for an octogenarian. With his thick hair and muscular arms, he could donate testosterone to younger men.

He looks up from his gun, a smile twisting his weathered lips. "Ah, Caper. What are you up to?"

I grin. My name is Olive (my parents are evil in their hippie-dippie-ness), and when Grandpa calls me Caper, he means "little olive," which makes me feel like a little girl again. Obviously, I'll never tell him that his nickname for me is botanically incorrect: capers are the flowers of a shrub, while olives are a tree fruit from an altogether different species.

"Taking Beaky out for a walk," I reply, nodding at the tank.

Grandpa squints at the glass, and Beaky chooses that exact moment to make himself look like a rock—as he does every time Grandpa tries to look at him.

Grandpa rubs his eyes. "Is there really an octopus in there? I feel like you and your grandmother are trying to make me think I'm going senile."

"No. It's Beaky who's messing with you."

I can't blame my grandfather for not spotting my eight-armed friend. When it comes to camouflage, octopuses blow chameleons out of the water. Also, if a chameleon was literally in the water, no amount of camouflage would save it from becoming an octopus's lunch.

Grandpa shakes his head. "Why?"

I shrug. "He's a creature with nine brains, one in his head and one in each arm. Trying to puzzle out his thinking would give anyone a headache."

Grandpa squints at the tank again, but Beaky stays in his rock guise. "Why do you walk him, anyway?"

"To keep him from being bored. What he really needs is a bigger tank, but for now, he'll have to make do with a change of scenery."

"Bored?"

"Oh, yeah. A bored octopus is worse than a seven-year-old boy hopped up on caffeine and birthday cake. In Germany, an octopus named Otto repeatedly shorted out the Sea Star Aquarium's entire electrical system by squirting water at the 2,000-watt overhead spotlight. Because he was bored."

Grandpa lifts his bushy eyebrows. "But don't you make puzzles for him? Let him watch TV?"

I nod. Making puzzles for octopuses is actually what I'm famous for, and how I got my new job. "Toys and TV help," I say, "but I still get the sense he's feeling cooped up."

Grunting, Grandpa delves into his pocket and pulls out a handgun the size of my arm. "Take this with you." He thrusts it at me.

I blink at the instrument of death. "Why?"

"Protection."

"From what? We're in a gated community."

He thrusts the weapon at me with greater urgency. "It's better to have a gun and not need it."

I don't take the offering. "The crime rate in Palm Islet is ten times lower than in New York."

Grandpa takes the clip out of the gun, checks it, shoves in an extra bullet, and snaps it back in. "It would give me peace of mind if you took it."

"By Cthulhu," I mutter under my breath.

"Bless you," Grandpa says.

"That wasn't a sneeze. I said, 'Cthulhu.'" At Grandpa's blank stare, I heave a sigh. "He's a fictional cosmic entity created by H. P. Lovecraft. Depicted with octopus features."

"Oh. Is that him in your grandmother's sexy cartoons?"

"Absolutely not." I shudder at the thought. "Cthulhu is hundreds of meters tall. He's one of the Great Old Ones, so his attentions would rip a woman apart as quickly as they would drive her mad."

"Fair enough." Grandpa attempts to shove the gun into my hands again. "Take it and go."

I hide my hands behind my back. "I don't have any kind of license."

"You're kidding." He regards me incredulously. "Tomorrow, I'll take you to a concealed carry class."

I fight a Cthulhu-sized eye roll. "I'm kind of busy tomorrow, starting a new job and all."

With a frown, he hides the gun somewhere. "How about this weekend?"

"We'll see," I say as noncommittally as I can before grabbing my handbag from the back of a nearby chair and pressing the remote button again to roll the tank into the garage.

My grandparents, like other Floridians, prefer to leave their houses this way, instead of, say, through the front door.

As soon as my grandfather is out of sight, Beaky stops being a rock, spreads his arms akimbo, and turns an excited shade of red.

"You should be ashamed of yourself," I tell him sternly.

We are the God Emperor of the Tank, ordained by Cthulhu. We shall not bestow the glory of our visage upon the undeserving. Hurry up, our faithful priestess-subject. We want to taste the sunshine on our suckers.

Yup. Ellen DeGeneres talked to a fictional sentient octopus in *Finding Dory*, while my real one speaks to me in my head. And I'm not alone in having these imaginary conversations. Ever since my sisters and I were kids, we've given animals voices. In my mind, Beaky sounds like nine people speaking in unison (the main brain and the eight in his arms), and his tone is imperious (octopuses have blue blood, after all). Oh, and his words come out with that faint gargle-like sound effect used in *Aquaman* when the Atlanteans spoke underwater.

I open the garage door.

It's super bright outside, despite the ancient oaks that provide plenty of shade.

With a sigh, I take a big tube of my favorite mineral-based sunblock from my bag and cover myself with a thick layer from head to foot. The UV index is 10, so I wait a few minutes, and then I cover myself with a second layer. I do this furtively in the garage to avoid my grandparents teasing me about taking a job in the Sunshine State while being paranoid about sun exposure.

And no, I'm not a vampire—though my sister Gia looks suspiciously like she might be, with her goth makeup and all. Avoiding the sun makes legitimate scientific sense given the harmful effects of UV rays, both A and B, as well as blue light, infrared light, and visible light. They all cause DNA damage. This issue got on my radar a couple of years back when Sushi, my pet clownfish, developed skin cancer, probably due to her aquarium being by a window. I've been careful ever since, even going as far as gluing a triple layer of UV-protective coating over Beaky's tank.

Now, do I realize that I worry about the sun a tad more than anyone who isn't a paranoid dermatologist? Sure. But can I stop? Nope. I think some level of neurosis is programed into my DNA, at least if my identical sextuplet sisters are anything to go by. But hey, when I'm in my eighties and look younger than all my sisters, we'll see who has the last laugh.

Sunblocking finished, I throw on a lightweight zip-up jacket that's coated in UV-protective chemicals, a wide-brim hat, and giant sunglasses.

There. If I were really taking this too far, I'd be wearing one of those Darth Vader visors, wouldn't I?

My heartbeat picks up as I follow Beaky's tank out into full sun, but I calm down by reminding myself that the sunblock will do its job. When the tank rolls down the driveway and onto a shady sidewalk by the lake, my breathing evens out further.

So far so good. Now I just hope I don't get too many annoying questions from nosy neighbors.

A pair of herons take flight nearby as we stroll along the lake shore. Beaky stares at them intently and changes his shape a few times.

We wish to taste those things. Be a good priestess-subject and deliver them to the tank.

I pat the top of the tank. "I'll give you a shrimp when we get back."

We both spot a raccoon digging in the grass by the lake, likely looking for turtle or gator eggs.

We wish to taste that too.

"I'll give you a shrimp without the puzzle," I tell him.

Usually, I put his treats into one of my creations, making the meal extra fun for him, but if he's worked up an appetite by watching all the land animals, I don't want to delay his gratification.

A five-foot alligator slowly crawls out of the lake.

Yup, we're definitely in Florida.

Spotting it, Beaky picks up two coconut shells from the bottom of his tank and closes them over his body, appearing to the world—and to the gator—like an innocent coconut.

"That thing can't get you in the tank," I say soothingly. "Not to mention, it's scared of me. Hopefully."

The statistics on alligator attacks are in our favor. In a state with headlines like "Florida man beats up alligator" and "Florida man tosses alligator into Wendy's drive-through window," the gators have learned to stay far, far away from the insane humans.

Because Beaky doesn't read the news or check online statistics, his eye looks skeptical as it peeks out from the coconut shells.

I return my attention to the sidewalk—and spot him.

A man.

And what a man.

He could've starred in *Aquaman* instead of Jason Momoa. If I were casting the leading man for my wet dreams, this guy would definitely get the role.

The thought sends tendrils of heat to my nether regions, specifically the part I privately think of as my wunderpus—in honor of *wunderpus photogenicus*, an amazing octopus species discovered in the eighties.

By the way, I once took a picture of my wunderpus, and it's also *photogenicus*.

But back to the stranger. Strong, masculine features framed by an impeccably trimmed beard, cyan eyes as deep as the ocean, a tanned, muscular body clad in low-riding jeans and a sleeveless top that shows off powerful arms, thick, blond-streaked hair that streams down to his broad shoulders—he'd look like a surfer if it weren't for the broody expression on his face.

Beaky must've forgotten about the gator because he's out of his coconut and looking at the stranger with fascination.

Figures. Aquaman has the power to talk to octopuses, along with other sea creatures.

I realize I'm also gaping at him and tense as he gets closer. Unlike back in New York, where it's customary to pass a stranger without acknowledging their existence, here in Florida, everyone at the very least greets their neighbors.

What do I say if he speaks to me? Do I even dare open my mouth? What if I accidentally ask him to have his way with me?

Wait a second. I think I've got it. He's also walking a pet, in his case a dog of the Dachshund breed, a.k.a. a hotdog dog, the most phallic member of the canine species. All I have to do is say something about his wiener—the one wagging its tail, not his Aquamanhood.

When the man is a dozen feet away, he seems to notice me for the first time. Actually, his gaze zeroes in on Beaky's tank, and his broody expression turns downright hostile—jaw clenched, mouth downturned, eyes flinty. The insane thing is, he looks no less hot now. Maybe more so.

What is wrong with me? No wonder I end up dating assholes like—

His deep, sexy voice is the kind of cold that can create a wind chill even in this humid sauna. "How much for the octopus?"

I blink, then narrow my eyes at the stranger, my hackles rising like spikes on a pufferfish. He wants to buy Beaky? Why? Does he want to eat him?

This *is* the state where people eat gators, turtles (even the protected species), bullfrogs, Burmese pythons, and key lime pie.

Gritting my teeth, I point to the tail-wagging dog at his side. "How much for the bratwurst?"

A sneer twists his full lips. "Let me guess... a New Yorker?"

Aquaman? More like Aqua-ass. "Let *me* guess. Florida man?" I can picture the rest of the headline: "... steals octopus in tank and tries to have sex with it."

Given what my grandmother said about Rule 34 and where I am, it's not that far-fetched. I once read an article about a Florida man who tried to sell a live shark in a mall parking lot. What's sex with an octopus in comparison?

His thick brown eyebrows snap together. "The stories you're alluding to are about transplants. They're never about actual Floridians."

"Oh, I've read what you're talking about," I say with a snort. "'Florida man receives first-ever penis transplant from a horse.' I'm pretty sure the article said that the brave pioneer was born and raised in Melbourne— that's two hours away from here."

Oops. Have I gone too far? Everyone does seem to carry a gun here. And since I found him attractive earlier, with my dating track record, he might well turn out to be dangerous.

Instead of pulling out a weapon, the stranger rubs the bridge of his nose. "Serves me right for trying to argue with a New Yorker. Forget the news. That tank is too small for that octopus. How would you like to live your life inside a Mini Cooper?"

I suck in a breath, my stomach tightening. "How would *you* like to be walked on a leash?" I jerk my chin toward his wiener, whose tail is no longer wagging. "Or to be forced to ignore your screaming bladder and bowels until your master deigns to take you for a walk? Or to have your reproductive organs messed with?"

He glowers at me. "Tofu isn't neutered. In fact, he—"

"Tofu?" My jaw drops. "As in, a tofu hot dog? Talk about animal cruelty."

The veins popping out in his neck look distractingly sexy. "What's wrong with the name Tofu?"

Before I can reply, Tofu whines pitifully.

"Great job," the stranger says. "Now you've upset him."

"I'm pretty sure you did that." *By naming the poor dog Tofu.*

"This conversation is over." He turns his back to me and tugs on the leash. "Come, Tofu."

Tofu gives me a sad look that seems to say, *I don't like it when my daddy and my new mommy argue.*

With a huff, I roll Beaky's tank in the opposite direction.

———

Go to www.mishabell.com to order your copy of *Of Octopuses and Men* today!

Excerpt from Royally Tricked

BY MISHA BELL

A daredevil prince wants to pay me mega-bucks to train him to hold his breath underwater for ten minutes? Sign me up.

Except I'm a magician, not a stunt consultant. My record-beating dive without air was a trick. Of course, I can't tell that to my client, the royally hot Anatolio Cezaroff, a.k.a. Tigger. Not if I want to be able to pay my rent.

Also, I'm not exactly comfortable around germs. All germs, including those lurking on uber-attractive men. So falling for my gorgeous client is out of the question, and I fully intend to keep my distance.

That is, until he offers to train *me* in bed.

———

"Holly?" an unfamiliar male voice says from the street.

I glance at the newcomer, and suddenly, it's my turn to gape.

I didn't realize this kind of masculine perfection existed outside of Hollywood.

Chiseled features. A Roman nose. Vaguely feline hazel eyes that zero in on my face predatorily, making me feel like an about-to-be-devoured gazelle.

I swallow the overabundance of saliva in my mouth with a loud gulp.

The stranger's broad-shouldered, muscular torso is clad in a tight white t-shirt, and despite the raggedy jeans riding low on his narrow hips, there's something regal about him—an impression supported by the strange design on his belt buckle. It resembles a crest that a medieval knight might put on his shield.

I've been told I compare people to celebrities too much, but it's hard to do with this guy. Maybe if the love between Jake Gyllenhaal and Heath Ledger in *Brokeback Mountain* had borne fruit?

Nah, he's even better-looking than that.

Realizing that I'm staring at his face too intently for it to be considered polite, I drop my gaze lower and notice that he's holding two leather straps in his fists. Leashes, presumably.

Half expecting to see willing sex slaves on the other end of those leashes, I instead find two weird dogs.

At least I think the creatures are dogs.

One sports black-and-white spots that make it look like a panda. Actually, given the creature's ginormous size, I can't rule out the possibility that it *is* a bear. And, if looking like an endangered ursine species wasn't odd enough, the beast is wearing goggles.

Is it because of bad vision, or is the panda about to go snowboarding?

The second creature is eyewear-free and reminds me of a koala, just much bigger and with a lolling canine tongue.

I force my gaze back to their ridiculously handsome owner. "Hey," is all I can manage. My overactive hormones seem to have robbed me of the ability to speak.

The stranger narrows those hazel eyes. "You *are* Holly, right?"

This is your chance, my inner magician pipes up. *Trick the hot stranger. Fool his pants off.*

Banishing lust with a heroic effort of will, I inwardly rub my hands together, à la evil villain. Until I adopted my current pale-skinned, raven-haired stage persona, I was mistaken for my identical twin on a regular basis, even by people closest to us. Our oval-shaped faces are exactly the same, right down to sharp cheekbones and a strong nose. I was literally born for this particular deception.

Adding the slightest touch of poshness to my voice, I say, "Who else would I bloody be?"

There. If he knows that Holly has a twin named Gia (as in, me), he'll voice that guess now and I'll stand down.

Maybe.

I bet I can bluff him out even if he does know I exist.

He stares at me intently. "You've changed your hair."

"*Addams Family* cosplay," I say in my best Morticia Addams voice. It's not my most convincing lie, but the guy looks like he's about to buy it anyway. Then I see a problem. Waldo, who's blinking in confusion, is about to speak. I kick his leg under the table and cheerfully ask the stranger, "Have you met Waldo?"

I'm hoping the hottie will extend his hand and introduce himself, thus letting me learn his name.

My evil ploy is thwarted by the panda. It pulls on the hottie's pant leg with its teeth. Seeing this, the koala does the same on the other side, except its movements are clumsy, puppy-like, leaving a hole in the pants.

If this is how the dogs get his attention, no wonder he wears something so raggedy. Also, yuck. I hope he washes that dog saliva off his pants ASAP.

"One second, guys," the stranger says to his furry friends in a warm, paternal tone that tugs at something in my chest. "Can't you see I'm talking to Holly?"

Score! He believes I'm Holly.

Looking up from the dogs, the stranger gives Waldo a once-over. Does he also think my friend looks like Willem Dafoe, only when he played Aquaman's mentor, not the Green Goblin from *Spider-Man*?

Before I can ask, the stranger's gaze returns to me. "That's not your boyfriend."

I blink. He knows Holly's boyfriend? Where does my sister find all these hunks? This one is even hotter than her Alex.

"Indeed," I say, channeling her again. "This bloke is just a *friend* friend."

The stranger's wicked smirk is like a flick on my clit. "I don't think men and women can be just friends."

They so can. My sisters and I have been friends with one particular guy forever, and he's never made a move on any one of us. Granted, he's gay, but still.

Waldo stands up, all wounded dignity. "Look, chum, I'm allergic to dogs, so if you don't mind…"

"Chum?" The stranger's feline eyes are mocking as they capture mine. "See? He doesn't like me horning in on his territory."

The heat that flashes through my body is no longer lust. The nerve on this guy. "I'm nobody's territory." And certainly not Waldo's. He's never made a move on me either, not in the entire eighteen months we've known each other.

Waldo's face reddens, and he tightens his grip on the knife that he never gave back.

Seriously? Can testosterone make you *that* stupid?

"She's right, chum," Waldo says in his most menacing voice, which, if we're honest, sounds a bit like he's doing a Cookie Monster impersonation. "You'd better skedaddle."

The stranger curls his upper lip at him. If he's aware of that knife, he doesn't show it. Another testosterone-poisoning victim, no doubt.

"Skedaddle?" He looks back at me. "Where did you find this Waldo?"

Okay, that's it. I'm the only one allowed to make "Where's Waldo?" jokes at my friend's expense.

The hot stranger has just crossed a line.

I push my chair back and rise to my full five-foot-five height. "How about 'get the fuck out of here?' Is that a better choice of words for you?"

This is when the panda growls at Waldo—a threatening sound one wouldn't expect to come out of such a cute, if overlarge, dog. It reminds me of this news report about a man who tried to hug a panda at the zoo, only to end up in the hospital after the frightened bear mauled him.

Paling, Waldo sets the knife on the table. There are clearly at least ten brain cells inside that thick skull of his.

The stranger pats the bespectacled beast's head and murmurs something soothing in a language that sounds Eastern European.

Huh. He didn't have any accent when he spoke to me, but English must be his second language. Otherwise, he wouldn't address his dogs in that foreign tongue.

Crap. With our luck, the hottie is some Russian mobster.

"Sit down," I hiss at Waldo, and to my relief, he does as I say.

Make that twenty brain cells.

The stranger's beautiful eyes roam over my face before narrowing again. "You're not Holly. She's nice." A touch of that wicked smirk returns to his lips, and his voice deepens. "Whereas *you* are naughty."

That does it. No more Mrs. Nice Magician.

I slowly saunter over to him.

Although… maybe this isn't such a good idea.

Now that I'm closer, I realize just how tall he is. And wide-shouldered. The giant dogs threw off my perspective, creating a visual illusion that their owner was normal-sized. He's not. Worse yet, he smells divine, like ocean surf and something ineffably male.

A trick under these conditions will test all of my abilities.

Hold on. Will the dogs get mad that I'm so close?

As if reading my mind, the stranger gives them a stern command, and they sheepishly fall behind him.

Was that command intended to make *me* want to behave like a good, obedient bitch? Because I kind of want to.

No, screw that. I'm sticking with my plan, which requires me to get within pickpocketing distance.

"Do you want to see just how naughty I can be?" I ask in the sultriest voice I can muster.

Is it normal for human eyes to go all slitty like that, as if he were a lion?

"How naughty is that, *myodik*?" the stranger murmurs.

Did he just say "me dick?" Nah. It was something in whatever language he used with the dogs. Still, his dick is now firmly on my mind, which doesn't help the hormonal overload situation.

Forcing away the X-rated images, I purposefully lick my lips. "I'll steal your wallet. Or your watch. Your choice."

The supposed choice is misdirection, obviously. My

real target is neither of those things, but he doesn't need to know that.

His nostrils flare as his gaze drops to my lips. "Is it stealing if you warn me?"

If it were possible for me to forget my concerns about germs and consider placing my lips on someone else's, I'd do that now. It's the strongest such urge I've ever felt.

"What's the matter?" I say breathlessly. "Chicken?"

He pats the right pocket of his jeans. "How about you steal my wallet?"

I take in a steadying breath. "Thanks for showing me where it is."

Before he can reply, I delve into that pocket. I need major misdirection for what I'm really trying to steal.

By Houdini's eyebrows, is that what I think it is?

Yup. There's no mistaking it. As I brush my gloved fingers over the wallet, I feel something else behind the fabric of the pants.

Something big and very hard.

Well. Someone is overly happy to be pickpocketed.

Maybe he *was* saying "me dick" before?

I do my best to hold his gaze and not clear my suddenly dry throat. "Can you feel me stealing it?"

As I speak, I work on unclasping the fancy buckle—his belt being my real target.

His lids lower to half-mast, and his voice deepens further. "Your nimble fingers are exactly where I want them."

Crap. Between my gloves and his ridiculous sex appeal, I'm having trouble with the clasp.

But no. I can't get caught. That would be like revealing a magic secret—the biggest taboo I can think of.

"These fingers?" I ask huskily and gently stroke his hardness through the layers of fabric, using the misdirection this slutty move creates to pull harder on the clasp with my other hand, finally opening it.

I'd like to see David Blaine do *that*.

The stranger's low, guttural groan is animalistic and makes my nipples so hard they feel on the verge of turning inside out. He now looks like a lion about to pounce.

Gulping, I yank my hand out of his pocket and try to give him a sneaky smile. It comes out faltering instead. "I changed my mind. I'll steal your watch."

I grab his wrist and give it a tight squeeze while pulling out the belt with my other hand.

Yes! Got it. Hiding the belt behind my back, I pout at the watch. "On second thought, I think I'll let you keep your possessions."

He looks triumphant, probably convinced that his sex appeal has defeated my pickpocketing skills. Since it almost did, I can't really fault him for thinking it.

I carefully back away. "Oh, by the way, did you lose this?"

I show him my prize.

Eyes wide, he shifts his gaze back and forth between my hand and his pants.

"How?" he asks.

The question is music to my ears.

"Extremely well," I say, but I can't manage my usual bluster.

He extends his hand to get the belt back. "You're a dangerous woman."

Two things happen simultaneously as I step toward him to return the belt.

The panda tries to get his attention again by pulling on his left pant leg. Not wanting to be outdone, the koala does the same thing on the right side—only this time, there's no belt holding the pants up, and they slide down.

All the way down.

Fuck. Me.

The biggest erection in the history of phalluses juts out and—though this could be my imagination—winks at me.

He's been commando all this time?

Me dick indeed.

I gape at the ginormousness. Even though I touched it and felt its size when I was rummaging in his pocket, I never would've imagined it like this.

Smooth. Straight. Delectably veiny. It just begs to be touched, or sucked, or licked—but I can't for reasons that are difficult to recall right now.

A concealed carry license should be required to pack that kind of heat. And also whatever license you need to operate heavy machinery. And a hunting license. Maybe even a 007-style license to kill—

Behind me, I hear Waldo gasp. Poor thing. I bet even *he* is ready to get on his knees for a taste, and to the best of my knowledge, he's straight.

I can't tear my gaze away.

If that cock were a magic wand, it would be one of the Deathly Hallows—the one Voldemort wielded at the end. And if it were a banana, it would be just the right-sized snack for King Kong.

The stranger should be turning red with embarrassment and scrambling to cover himself, but instead, a cocky smirk lifts the corners of his lips. "Like what you see?"

I do. So much so I want to pull out my phone and take a selfie with it.

To my huge—and I do mean *huge*—disappointment, he pulls up his pants. His voice is husky. "Like I said. Naughty. Very naughty."

Snatching the belt from my nerveless fingers, he loops it back into his pants and saunters away with his dogs, leaving me standing there, mouth agape.

"Can you believe that guy?" Waldo asks somewhere in the distance, his tone outraged.

No. I can't.

I can't believe what just happened, period.

All I know is this wasn't what I had in mind when I set out to fool that guy's pants off.

———

Go to www.mishabell.com to order your copy of *Royally Tricked* today!

About the Author

We love writing humor (often the inappropriate kind), happy endings (both kinds), and characters quirky enough to be called oddballs (because... balls). If you love your romance heavy on the comedy and feel-good vibes, visit www.mishabell.com and sign up for our newsletter.

Made in the USA
Coppell, TX
14 May 2022